French Exchange with Rubies

By STEPHANIE McCARTHY

Published by Kindle Direct Publishing, 2020.

Contents

Author's note

This book is a story inspired by real-life events. It is a combination of facts about my life and certain embellishments. Names, dates, places, events, details and characteristics of all people mentioned in this book have been changed to protect their privacy, and any dialogue has been recreated based on my memories. The reader should not consider this book as anything other than a work of literature.

I have taken some liberties with language. When we first met, neither Elodie nor I spoke each other's language with any degree of useful fluency, leading me to exaggerate her abilities in English in order to recreate conversations which were in reality conducted with gestures, drawings and endless consultations of our dictionaries. With regards to secondary characters, I have endowed them with an ability to speak English which they did not possess. I hope this does not distract from your enjoyment of the book.

About the author

I would dearly love to make this page similar to the round robins we receive at Christmas from those many people we haven't seen for donkey's years. People who let you know how many Nobel prizes they have won this year, or how they spent January navigating single-handedly around the world on a small raft, or how eight-year-old Susie has just finished her thesis on Political Tensions in the Middle East. Yes, that would be great. Unfortunately it would all be lies. So, here's the truth. I am simply ordinary. I went to an ordinary girls' grammar school in the days when all the teachers were single because they had to choose between teaching and marriage, whereas nowadays everyone *knows* how easy it is to combine a high-flying career with five children and still have time to climb the Three Peaks. I am married with a brilliant husband, two daughters of whom I am quite incredibly, ridiculously proud and three of the most wonderful grandchildren on the planet. And that's about it, really. Oh, and I live in Harrogate, in the UK.

Acknowledgements

Thank you to my wonderful family for your support, and to Jim Bruce of ebooklover.co.uk for his invaluable help with my manuscript

Chapter 1
Marseille 1969

The class of sixteen-year-olds gazed at Mrs Thomas with the kind of blank incomprehension she had no doubt come to expect of us.

'You will visit Marseille for three weeks,' she explained briskly, 'and you will each stay with the girl you have been writing to for the last year.' She beamed round at us from the staff desk; tall and self-assured, with a prominent nose and wispy fair hair pulled into a tight chignon at her neck.

'I expect it to improve your French enormously,' she continued. 'You will get the chance to attend a French *Lycée*....Yes Susan? A *Lycée is* the equivalent of our grammar school here. I have a very dear friend who teaches there and we have arranged this visit between us. It will take place during your Easter holidays and there will be....'

'The holidays, Mrs Thomas?' came the plaintive cry from the back of the room.

'Yes Katie, during your Easter holidays,' came the sharp reply. 'And please don't forget that it's our holidays too! Madame Bernois is every bit as willing as I am to give up our free time to make sure that you can have this great opportunity. And *if* you'd allowed me to finish'– she glared at the hapless Katie, who opened her desk lid to cover her confusion, 'I was going to add that there will be a programme of excursions arranged for you all, with your French partners. Now,' she said briskly, forestalling any more outcries and picking up a packet of long white envelopes, 'I want you to take this letter home to your parents – Alright, Naomi, your *father* then. You can put your hand down now. Charlotte dear, come here and give these out, will you..?'

Charlotte Maddox was often chosen for these jobs, being extremely competent in everything she did, and almost always towards the top in all her subjects. A pillar of the school, in fact, which made her rather less than popular with many of the girls, however lauded she might be by the staff. Her friend Lydia Holmes was altogether different. It was generally thought that she had befriended Charlotte in the vain hopes that some of the glamour might be magically transferred over to herself by some process of osmosis. She was often in trouble and always able to wriggle out of it with smooth, plausible excuses. She was never in the forefront of any drama, but somehow she was always implicated.

'Lydia loads all the bullets,' Mrs Thomas had once said darkly, 'and she leaves others to fire them. Then she sits back well out of range and waits for the explosion.'

'I agree, totally,' Mrs Stephens, chemistry, joined in crisply. 'Whenever there's trouble, if you dig deep enough, there she'll be. Are you sure you want to cope with her in Marseille, Daphne?'

'Don't worry. She'll be staying with Madame Bernois' family. She can't get into too much trouble with them. She'll be fine. Don't worry.' Mrs Stevens looked slightly doubtful. She sighed deeply as she flicked open a chemistry exercise book, took up a green pen and began to write. In the event, it turned out that Lydia Holmes was the least of Mrs Thomas's problems.

They began when she found the Marseille trip more difficult to organize than she had anticipated. There were not enough pupils to fill the coach. Mostly because it involved paying a hefty subscription, and most of the group came from the kind of families where a trip to Blackpool was the height of decadence. Going abroad, as it was coined, was out of most people's reach, and those who braved the uncertainty of air travel, unfamiliar currency and the foreign food mostly stuck to relatively benign places such as the Costa del Sol, where there was sure to be at least one venue run by a British couple serving a full English breakfast.

Mrs Thomas was undeterred, and to fill up the remaining places, she opened up the trip to anyone in the school who had reached the age of sixteen, regardless of whether they took French or not. The only criteria became the parents' ability to pay the necessary funds.

I took the letter home to my parents without any real enthusiasm, but to my huge surprise, they were both delighted, especially my mother Nesta, who was forever on the lookout for anything to enhance her social status. She liked to think of herself as a leading light in the community. She had derived enormous pleasure from introducing a bridge club, and would clean and polish the house for the whole day before hosting a card party. Tiny as she was, as chairwoman of the board of governors at my school, she chivvied the other members of the board, her slim figure with carefully set brown curls dashing about and delegating duties to the most appropriate people, all of which culminated in well organised fairs and other fund raising events throughout the year.

Dad too was quietly pleased, although he very rarely became excited about anything. As the manager of our local bank, he was used to weighing up the advantages and disadvantages of any situation before deciding on a course of action. His salary alone, although adequate, would not have been sufficient to satisfy all my mother's shopping needs, and it was fortunate for all of us that she had inherited a considerable sum of money from her parents, which had been carefully invested and provided us with the additional income for the small luxuries she loved. On the whole we had always been a contented family, and at that time, I believe that my mother was the only one who had some inkling that this state of affairs might not last as long as she wished.

As an adult, I can appreciate that her busy social life meant brief periods of respite from what must have been a tense period for her, although from my perspective as a self-obsessed sixteen-year-old, I was unable to empathise with her. Not being a particularly perceptive person, I realised afterwards that I had completely failed to pick up on any of the low-voiced conversations between my parents, and thought nothing at all of the hasty changes of subject that I could sense had occurred when I entered a room.

One of them happened as I went into the dining room for lunch. I was desperate to go to Susie Greene's barbecue. Popularity was an unknown concept to me, being one of those people who took hours poring over set homework which was supposed to take forty minutes. I suspect there were others who took far longer than the allotted time, but unlike naive little me, they conveniently forgot to mention it. Working hard and revising simply wasn't cool, and my reputation suffered accordingly. To put it bluntly, I was known as a swot, but I knew no effective way of dissembling. Attending Susie's barbecue might gain me a few steps on the precarious path towards coolness.

I was about to go into the dining room door when the words from inside stopped me. I froze, and inclined my head towards the door, listening intently. I hadn't consciously meant to eavesdrop – it never occurred to me to even think about what I was doing; my whole being was caught up in the words. They were muted by the distance but I heard:

'She'll find out sometime...' This was my mother, her voice sounding subdued. 'Isn't it better now – give her a bit of time?'

'And if it turns out alright in the end? All that worry for her, for nothing – ?'

I opened the door to find both of them staring at me. Were they wondering how much I might have heard? And what had been said before I heard them?

'What will I find out?' I asked. A tiny part of my mind was interested in the answer, but most of it was taken up with the barbecue. This was going to be the one social event where I shone. I would chat easily to everyone, I would be amusing, entertaining. My voice wouldn't tail off as it usually did when I detected the tiny signs of boredom in my audience's uneasy body language.

'Do you remember how funny Steph was that night?' people would say. 'I couldn't stop laughing...' And that would be the starting point. From then on I would be as popular as Charlotte.

Dad's reply was so swift and decisive that I took it at face value. 'We were a bit worried that you'd find out that I might be promoted, that's all,' he stated blandly. 'And if it turns out that I don't get the job, you'd have had all that worry for nothing.'

He immediately went to the cutlery drawer and busied himself setting out the knives and forks. Mum was taking the casserole to the table. The words I had heard and Dad's glib reply really ought to have roused real suspicions, but I am almost ashamed to write this: they didn't.

'It's on Saturday, it doesn't start till six o'clock,' I told them as Mum was dishing up a beef stew which she had actually made herself. 'I expect it will finish about nine-ish...'

She paused, a ladle full of watery stew hovering above the dish as she glanced anxiously towards my father; a look that barely registered with me.

'What, this Saturday?' Dad asked. 'I'm sorry, love, but I won't be able to take you. Can't you ask one of your friends to take you?'

I was frankly annoyed, besides being intensely irritated by the mention of friends I didn't possess.

'*Why* can't you take me? It's not far – she only lives at....'

'It's not that,' Mum cut in, depositing the stew on his plate, 'but it will clash with your dad's hospital appointment. You really will have to miss it if you can't get a lift with one of the others. Dad would take you if he could, but he does have to get to his appointment.'

She sounded as if she meant it and so I capitulated, but sulkily. I looked mutinously at Dad.

'Why do you need to go to hospital anyway? You're not poorly.'

He didn't look ill, and he hadn't taken any time off work. To me he looked as he always had – tall, with neatly brushed back brown hair, a somewhat angular frame and a calm, kindly manner that very little ever disturbed.

'It's just a routine check up,' he said hastily. 'It's nothing for you to be worried about.' After glancing at Mum with a tight smile, he sat down and spooned up his stew with every appearance of enjoyment.

My own view of his appointment, and naturally my own perspective was the only one that counted, was unequivocal irritation, leading me to sulk for most of the evening as I knew that I would have to ask for a lift from someone, and I hated asking for favours. It didn't even occur to me to wonder why he would need a routine check up from the hospital. In the end, Janet Matthews' parents took me and brought me home again when they collected their daughter.

The barbecue itself barely warranted all the arrangements, as I worked my way around the outside edges of the highly animated groups with a paper plate of sausages and crisps in my hand, making as if I was one of them, which I patently was not. A cable from the house was connected to speakers which blared out the distinctive voice of Lulu singing ''Boom-Bang-a-Bang,'' and several people were jigging along to its beat whilst simultaneously balancing plates and eating.

Lydia was in the centre of a group which included the only boy, a cousin of Susie's named Marcus. I watched as she drew away from the group to fill a plate with food from the griddle and then return, sidling up to him. She was rewarded by a friendly smile as he took it from her. They chatted animatedly for a few minutes, and I watched, fascinated, as she flicked her hair over her shoulder and tilted her head to one side with interested smiles, until the two of them moved away and disappeared around the corner of the house. So that was how it was done. In my head I was practising the saucy flip of hair and the sideways provocative glace when I noticed Janet and a couple of nearby girls looking at me oddly, and realised that I was actually miming what I had just seen. I wasn't sorry when the barbecue ended, and I tried to put the whole dismal event out of my mind and concentrate on the next group event; the visit to Marseille.

Mum thought that a trip to France would be just the thing for me. I would return home fluent in the language, and with that particular polish that only a spell in a foreign country can hope to achieve. I could already imagine her talking to her friends at the weekly bridge meetings...

'Stephanie is in France,' she would say with a light smile as she expertly shuffled the deck of cards. 'The South of France, of course. She's gone with a group of her school friends.....'

She would make it sound as if I'd organized the whole trip on my own, just for a bit of giggly, school-girly fun. Not only that, but I believe she was confusing a three week trip to France with several years at an expensive Swiss finishing school.

Marseille in the late nineteen sixties was a different place. For a start, it was not on the tourists' destinations map in the same way that towns such as Nice, Cannes and Juan-les- Pins were. Since the time of the Greeks and the Romans it has been a vital European trading port, with very little need of tourists to bolster its economy.

There were far fewer cars than there are today, and the metro had not yet been built. The *'Vieux Port,'* famed for films such as 'The Godfather' and 'French Connection' was just that; an old port with gently bobbing fishing smacks and corpulent housewives in flapping slippers and cotton overalls, with wicker baskets over one arm, eager for the freshest fish to make *bouillabaisse*, and chefs' minions from local restaurants sent out at dawn to haggle with the fishermen for the best bargains.

Had my parents known exactly *where* in Marseille we were heading, they might have been just a little less enthusiastic, for my French pen friend was a girl named Elodie who lived in the thirteenth *arrondissment*, or suburb, of Malpassé. A few kilometres northwest would bring you to the notorious fourteenth *arrondissement* of La Busserine, which is known to this day as one of the centres of poverty, violence and Islamic fundamentalism in

France, despite the valiant efforts of successive governments to defuse the tension. Unsurprisingly they face an uphill struggle against the wars of retaliation which show no signs of abating, mainly because if one of your loved ones has been beaten up or murdered over a drug dispute, no one is going to start playing the Happy Families game any time soon. Revenge and grief are close associates.

Not that I ever had any trouble in that direction. No-one approached me asking me to deliver a little parcel to the local *patisserie*, promising to reward me with more money than I had ever handled. Being a former badge toting girl guide, I would probably have counted it as my good deed for the day and refused any recompense with a deprecating shake of the head and a polite smile. No one had ever warned me about suspicious packages.

Both of my parents had always been very vocal about not getting into strangers' cars. Exactly *why* I should avoid this was never totally explained to me, but I came to my own conclusions. If it was a lift home, I reasoned, a stranger might not know his way to my house and leave me in an unknown location from where I would have to find my own way back home. That made perfect sense to me and on that basis I always avoided strangers' cars.

Undoubtedly there must have been streets near Malpassé that were best avoided if you were not desperate for your daily heroin fix, but as schoolgirls who were visiting the town purely for educational purposes, we happily explored the town completely oblivious of its dubious reputation.

I expect French exchange trips have evolved enormously in the last fifty years. I don't know if any checks were made on the host families. Today it would take whole reams of form filling, inspections, suitability of location, health and safety checks and dietary requirements, with complicated arrangements where certain people had mobile numbers and instructions to call a pre-designated group of others in the event of emergencies. In those days the teachers got together and arranged everything between them. Life used to be so much simpler, if a touch more risky.

With her customary thoroughness, Mum went through my wardrobe, very anxious that I should make a suitable impression on my arrival in France.

'No, there's not much here that will really do,' she had said thoughtfully as she flicked through the hangers in my wardrobe, making tutting noises as she threw one or two dresses onto my bed. 'French people are known worldwide for being smart, especially the women. You'll be an acting ambassador for Leeds. We must show your French friend that you know how to dress and behave.'

Eventually she found a dress that passed muster. 'This one might do,' she said a little dubiously, picking up the green print and holding it up against me. 'It might be a bit short, though, by the time you go, don't you think?'

I knew that she didn't require an answer, and I felt that my taking on the role of the city's designated ambassador was straining the bounds of credibility, but I knew the impossibility of dissuading her from any opinion, once formed, so I stayed silent.

'We're not sending you off looking like a child from the slums,' she continued. 'We'll have to make sure that you have a fresh set of good quality clothes...Yes, you'd better take this one, but there's nothing else here quite suitable. You're growing out of everything all at once. We need to go shopping and get you decently kitted out. And luggage too,' she added. 'First impressions are so important. You know my motto...'

I *had* heard it – many, many times. 'Yes, I know – *Only the best and nothing but the best*,' I quoted dismally. 'But I *have* clothes. I've got a wardrobe full – most of them still fit me.'

She sat on my bed, fingering the green dress as if doubting its suitability after all. 'But nothing new,' she stated firmly. 'When you're going on a trip like this, you need a new outfit. We'll have a look around Marshall & Snelgrove and see what they have.'

I sighed. A few days after the consent form was returned to school with the deposit, I was whisked off to town with her, getting off the bus in City Square, passing The Majestic which was *still* showing 'The Sound of Music,' (Mum had seen it five times now, although Dad had flatly refused to go with her after his first viewing), and along Park Row to eventually reach Marshall and Snelgrove. Here, Mum chose several smart cotton dresses with the right designer labels on them. I was not heavily involved in this process other than standing around in my bra and knickers while the dresses were handed to me to be tried on. From early childhood I had heard about the importance of dressing and speaking correctly. She had even sent me to have elocution lessons for a while and always corrected my speech if I ever lapsed into poor habits such as dropping an 'h' or using bad grammar. As a result my accent was more home counties than west Yorkshire, putting me at even further odds than I already was with several of my schoolfellows.

On the appointed day I joined the group of pupils at school whose families wanted them to have this great treat. I was faintly embarrassed, as all the other girls were clutching canvas bags or had haversacks, or small suitcases whereas I was toting matching brown leather cases, one for clothes and one a toiletries case, both with shiny brass corners and my initials stamped in gold. I hated them.

Ignoring the few stifled sniggers from people I didn't like much anyway, I clambered onto the coach with the others, sitting with Janet Matthews who appeared to be as friendless as myself. It took us as far as Dover where we boarded the ferry, and from Calais, a train for Gare St. Charles, the main station in Marseille. It was early evening and we had *'couchettes'* reserved for our party, which were essentially travelling bunk beds with each compartment sleeping six girls.

At some point in the night I woke up and stared out of the window in great excitement. The train had slowed down, and the station of Amiens was sliding by. The blackness of the night was relieved by the distant town itself, lit up as it was with innumerable clustered pinpricks of yellow lights. I was actually in France. This was a different country! I had never been out of England in my life and I was almost too keyed up to go back to sleep, although I must have done, as when I woke up we were pulling into Gare St. Charles.

From there, a second coach took us on to the *Lycée,* where a small group of excited chattering French people were waiting outside to claim the 'English girl' who would be their guest for the next three weeks.

We clambered down the coach steps into the glaring heat, scrambling to retrieve our luggage before we surged forward in a throng, looking for our hitherto unknown penfriends. Each girl was holding up a large card with her name on it, and I soon spotted the name Elodie, written in large, uneven capitals. She was slightly smaller than I, and far chubbier, with reddish hair cut in a neat frame around a pointed face dusted with freckles. Unlike the rest of the group who were mostly in sleeveless tops and battered shorts, she wore a knee-length pleated skirt in pale blue, a trim white tee shirt, a gold-coloured necklace set with large red stones, and brown leather sandals with white ankle socks.

As others were doing, I went up to her and she surprised me by kissing me on both cheeks. I found this a bit embarrassing to be honest. We didn't go around randomly kissing our friends in Leeds. But I said a tentative '*bonjour*' as we had all been told, and hoped she didn't take this as some kind of indication that I was fluent in her language.

There were two adults accompanying Elodie. One was a tall, wiry and sparse man with a receding hairline. He looked uncomfortably ill at ease in his brown suit which had evidently been chosen for smartness with little regard to comfort. The other was a short, stout barrel of a lady who looked very old and far too wrinkly to be Elodie's mother. She came forward with a massive grin and gave me two resounding smacking kisses on my cheeks before she enveloped me in a great bear hug. She too had the dark red hair, which was arranged in tight curls all over her head. It later transpired that they were her grandparents and that her parents lived in a place called Bormes-les-Mimosas further along the Riviera coast.

They all led me to their waiting car, the old lady pouring out a torrent of French in my direction whilst Elodie maintained a reserved silence, only glancing my way occasionally with the polite smiles aimed at making a stranger feel at ease. We set off amidst blazing sunshine and a deep blue sky through a bewildering series of narrow streets which were lined with tall apartment blocks, all with shutters, most of which were half closed as protection against the glaring heat.

In the many suburbs we passed our French textbook leapt into vibrant life, and shops with names such as '*Boulangerie, Pharmacie, Pièces Détachées, Meubles, Parfumerie, Mairie, La Poste*' (Bakery, Chemist, Spare Parts, Furniture, Perfume Shop, Town Hall, Post Office), all suddenly became much more than lists of vocabulary to be learned. So, it hadn't all been a dastardly plot to waste our time. These places were actually real and I was astounded. I saw no large department stores such as we had at home, like Schofields or Lewis's or Marshall and Snelgrove where a smartly dressed doorman would help ladies from their taxis. This prestigious establishment stocked my school uniform and my mother would occasionally dress in her best clothes, making sure that she wore a hat and matching gloves, and even have her hair freshly permed, simply to shop there. I can remember how the store operated, with money being placed in a metal canister that was whisked upwards in a pipe, before any change due arrived by the same method.

Here in Marseille each shop had its own speciality. Small shoe shops flashed past; little boutiques selling only leather items, greengrocers and *patisseries* with windows full of the most tempting pastries.

In place of the neat streets of brick terraced or semi-detached houses I was used to were houses clad in white, grey, blue and pink *crépie*, a kind of render, many of them with peeling facades exposing jagged parts of the foundation blocks beneath. Instead of drab grey slate, these buildings were roofed in red tiles. This was amazing! I had learned all the words they threw at us, I had studied and been tested on the irregular verbs to the nth degree, I had drawn maps of the place, I had learned names of departments, and written essays about the culture and yet no-one had ever thought to tell me that French buildings had red roofs. This omission, I felt, was betrayal of a high order. To be fair, when I grew up I realized that in northern France roofs are made from grey slate like ours, but at that time I thought red roofs were *'de rigeur'* (I had even learnt some of the clichés) in the whole of France.

We finally arrived at a neat detached house with a garage and small garden planted up with rows of lettuces, their leaves already yellowing and wilting in the searing midday heat. On the porch outside the front door was a long trestle table covered with brightly patterned oilcloth decorated with fading images of rows of lavender, bordered by yellow and blue diagonal stripes. There were several battered looking chairs around it. Overhead was an old vine with twisted, gnarled stems and clusters of tiny grapes. Up until now, grapes had been presents that you took on a hospital visit, and I thought it all most exotic to see them growing in a garden. Inside, the house had no staircase, which made me think the house must be a flat, as I had seen an upper floor reached via an outdoor stone staircase, but Elodie explained that the house had been built like that on purpose; the ground floor was for herself and her grandparents and the first floor for her parents whenever they visited.

'But,' she added sadly, 'my parents have not come for a very long time so the first floor, he is nearly always empty.'

As the visit progressed I grew accustomed to her odd use of pronouns. I told her repeatedly that it was easier to simply use the word 'it,' when describing objects, but she couldn't seem to get it, and continued to call things 'he' or 'she,' as the French noun dictated.

Her grandmother insisted on my calling her Mamy, as Elodie did, and she was obsessed with food. The following morning she flung on a capacious apron that all but submerged her and began a frenzied flurry of chopping, scraping, weighing out ingredients, grinding spices and beating hunks of meat. In the midst of the tumult she turned to me with hands dusted white with flour and demanded to know what I liked to eat. I was slow to process this question and it would have taken me at least half an hour to formulate any kind of meaningful answer, so I smiled vaguely, hoping that she wouldn't ask again. It was a futile hope.

'*Qu'est-ce que tu aimes manger?*' she repeated, a little louder. *What do you like to eat?* And when no reply was forthcoming, she leaned towards me, her face inches from mine and repeated the words slowly and clearly, as if to a particularly backward five year old. I backed off a little as the knife she was holding had a particularly nasty point to it.

'*Manger! Quel est ton repas préféré?*' *What is your favourite meal?* It took me some moments to translate her words in my head, but this time I thought I understood.

Did I have a favourite food? Not really. I was accustomed to eating whatever my mother saw fit to dish up. If there was anything, I supposed it would have to be fish and chips which were a staple in our house every Friday, but I was almost sure that fish and chips shops were pretty thin on the ground in Marseille. What else was there? After much casting around in my mind for long-forgotten vocabulary, I finally pitched on the one thing that I believed was the same name in English and in French.

'Paella,' I said, nodding vigorously to emphasise that this was, absolutely, my favourite food.

'*Ah, paella! Ça c'est bon!*' she beamed approvingly, before turning away to make vigorous use of her sharp knife on a couple of lettuces. She said a lot more than that but since I didn't understand a single word, I remained silent. The paella I was referring to was a classic sixties dish. It came in a handy packet from Vesta and was made up by adding water to various yellow powders and bits of fish and tiny morsels of chicken. Once reconstituted, it was adequately filling, if not gourmet food.

I might equally have pitched on chicken supreme from the same company which we ate regularly, or lemon meringue pie, also made from ingredients taken out of a box. This came complete with a special yellow capsule of intense lemon flavouring that you added at the last minute to the custard before it solidified into a lemony gunge which was topped with authentic meringue that you prepared yourself.

But as I had no idea how to translate either of these, I had plumped for paella and Mamy was determined to produce an unforgettable classic example. Which she did. She set off for the fishmonger and the local market and before we were ready for school she was back, her wicker basket loaded with a couple of chickens with their drooping heads still attached, an impossible variety of unidentifiable fish, some of which were still gasping in their last squirming throes of life, and packets of rice. There wasn't a box in sight.

She shooed us off to school and set to work.

The kitchen, when we arrived home for lunch, was even hotter than outside; the sink was overflowing with dirty pans, but the table with its garish oilcloth was pristine, with shining cutlery set for the two of us. I was completely unprepared for the massive heaped casserole of food which she proudly set down in front of us. Lunch was available at school but Mamy had no faith in either the quantity or the quality of the cuisine and so Elodie was required to come home each day for her midday meal. The paella would have fed most of the street with some leftovers; there was a steaming mountain of it; fluffy golden rice studded with chunks of fish, prawns and bite sized pieces of chicken. The aroma was absolutely delicious, and it bore no more resemblance to a Vesta paella than it did to fish and chips.

Mamy's serving spoons were twice the size of any I had ever seen. She carefully piled a huge spoonful on my plate and followed it up with three more before I could protest. I did not have a huge appetite to begin with, and coupled with the anxiety brought on by the strangeness of the situation, I soon languished in front of all this food. Mamy became visibly distressed. She begged me to try some more, and indicated the still half full paella pan, clearly with the intention that I should finish the lot. Elodie, meanwhile, smiled at me and almost imperceptibly shook her head.

'*C'est pas grave,*' she whispered.

Grave? Grave? Seeing my confusion, she said in careful English, 'not matter.'

Her English turned out to be marginally better than my French, but I could see we would not be having any in depth conversations about the state of the world any time soon.

I made a pantomime of patting my stomach and ruefully shaking my head and she finally accepted I had eaten as much as I could and she sorrowfully removed my plate.

Food was to be one of my abiding memories of the trip. Soon after she got up, Mamy would take herself off to the *boulangerie*, or bakery, in the next street and be back before we were ready for school with a basket piled high with soft, richly sweet brioche buns, each of which was topped with tiny white sugar crystals. She produced a huge, screw-topped jar of peach marmalade to go with them and I was transported into gastronomic heaven. The peach marmalade turned out to be homemade from peaches donated by her nephew who owned a wholesale greengrocer business, with shops in both Hyères and Marseille. I can remember a young tousle-headed assistant calling in with trays of velvety-skinned, red-flushed peaches stacked one on top of the other. Quite possibly they were too overripe for the shop. Later in the holiday Mamy taught me how to make the marmalade and how to preserve the finished jars by pouring on a liquid paraffin that congealed as it cooled and would preserve the marmalade for years.

Several shelves of the kitchen held innumerable jars of pickled vegetables, all of them stored upside down; sliced green beans dotted with tiny red chillies, cucumbers in brine, sliced cooked batons of carrots, fat red tomatoes squashed tightly against the glass, vividly coloured jellies and jams made from strawberries, quince, raspberries and peaches. The kitchen was a hotchpotch of copper-bottomed pots and pans, sieves, colanders, round wooden tubs full of kitchen utensils, griddles, and yet more shelves full of crockery in lurid red, yellow and purple Provençal patterns.

One lunch time saw us all sitting down to '*bouillabaise,*' a kind of fish soup local to the region. Mamy had devoted the whole morning to sourcing the mussels, the sea bass and the prawns, and with her usual professional competence, set about creating the dish with a delicious combination of orange peel, fennel and garlic. The smell of it was total bliss, as was the sight of the large fish and prawn pieces surrounded by the irresistible tomato and saffron-flavoured sauce. I had never tasted anything like it in the whole of my sixteen years.

We must have arrived in Marseille before the start of the Easter holidays, as I remember several days at the local *Lycée* with Elodie. It was a short bus ride away. A massive old building on three floors, with casement windows and long, confusing corridors with green, half-glazed doors at regular intervals. Scrubbed straw matting was laid down the centre of the corridors, muting the sound of footsteps. One of the lessons, 'Philo,' was new to me. It turned out to be philosophy which I was surprised to find being taught in a school as I had always associated it with universities.

Also quite new to me was the way the lessons were delivered. I was used to teachers who walked around a classroom, explaining and correcting as necessary, but this was apparently unknown here. The teacher stood at the front of the blackboard and talked, with the students making notes or not as they fancied. Another lady walked around the room, whom Elodie explained was the *'surveillante.'* The classroom supervisor. Her job was to keep order, leaving the teacher completely free to teach. This lady was also present during break times, as I can recall some students being told off for going too close to the windows which were open as widely as possible in a vain effort to get a little cool air into the room. This was the third floor after all.

I have a hazy, mirage-like memory of Charlotte and Lydia huddled into a seat in front of me, Charlotte with her silky hair tied back in a broad navy satin ribbon, and Lydia with her mop of mousy curls. They were both convulsed with suppressed giggles at the strangeness of it all and bored, as we all were, by a lesson being given mostly in rapid French.

As well as being highly intelligent, Charlotte Maddox was just about the most gorgeous looking girl in our year group. She was the most beautiful girl in the whole school. She may well have been the most beautiful in the whole of the western hemisphere. She was just so utterly perfect in each detail of her face and figure. Tall, but not tall enough for people to remark on it. Thin without being scrawny.

Her long blonde hair was so shiny she looked like an advertisement for an expensive shampoo. Her eyes were of a rarely seen piercing, vivid blue. Even without makeup, which was not allowed for grammar school girls, her skin was as flawless as a five year old's.

'So, what's your family like?' Lydia was asking, *sotto voce*.

'Oh, they're not bad. Jeanne hardly ever says a word to me. But her brother....! You'd never believe it. He's seventeen, he's so tall even I have to look up at him, and *the* most perfect face. And you should see his muscles. He picked up my case like it weighed nothing at all.' She took a deep breath and glanced around furtively, making sure she was not overheard. 'The first day, he offered to help me unpack, and that took forever, he kept holding up every last thing I've brought....'

This elicited a low giggle from Lydia. She leaned closer to Charlotte, putting her mouth to Charlotte's ear and whispered. They both laughed out loud, only subsiding when the *surveillante* glared at them.

'Then he took me all round the house...' Charlotte continued in a low tone.

'Isn't that what Jeanne's supposed to do?' Lydia interrupted.

'He got in there first. He just told Jeanne that he was going to do it and she went off in a huff and disappeared. Actually, we spent most of the evening in his room, except for the meal. I didn't see her again until the next morning.'

'This is your chance, Charlotte,' she laughed. 'Don't waste it, you've only got two and a bit weeks before we go back. You never know what might happen. You'll be all over each other, he'll be whispering his undying passion for you by tonight. Oh, I forgot, he doesn't speak English....'

'We don't need to speak to each other,' she said loftily. 'We understand each other perfectly without any words.'

Lydia looked faintly amused. She made another whispered comment that was too low for me to hear, and then they both sat up straight, Charlotte fixing her eye on the teacher and Lydia staring insolently at the *surveillante* as she passed by.

When school was over for the day, Elodie and I caught the bus back to her house, but not before I had seen a tall, black-haired boy with rippling muscles visible through his navy tee-shirt take hold of Charlotte's hand and lead her to a powerful looking motorbike.

Lydia was at the front of the small crowd on the pavement, and turned abruptly away to hide the look of pure resentment on her face as Charlotte swung a long, graceful leg over the saddle. The boy looked back at her and laughed as she clung tightly to his waist. She appeared to be oblivious of the awed glances and jealous comments as the engine revved loudly and they roared off towards the main road.

Chapter 2
The Riviera

The Easter holidays began shortly afterwards, and Mamy was determined that I should have a good time while I was there. Accordingly, she had planned a trip along the coast for us all.

'We will go to Cannes,' Elodie told me, her eyes shining with excitement. 'And after, we will visit Monte Carlo and then Monaco.' I believe she was waiting for me to be thrilled, but as my life up until now had been confined to one of the less salubrious districts of Leeds I had never heard of any of these places and I failed to react as expected. To me they were just names. My geography at that time was as poor as my command of the French language.

Mamy was one of a breed of women who existed in large numbers fifty years ago in Mediterranean countries. A voluble matriarch who exerted absolute control of her family and brooked no argument. I saw Elodie try to assert her independence a few times, but she was beating fragile wings against glass. Once when we were shopping in the local market Elodie stopped by a clothes stall. She rummaged through the assortment of piled up skirts and picked up one in bright red with flounces around its hem, holding it against her waist and twirling to see the full effect of the swishing fabric. Here, Mamy intervened, snatching the skirt out of her hands and throwing it contemptuously back on the pile.

'We are not made of money!' she snapped angrily. 'Besides, red is a terrible colour for you and that is far too short. No granddaughter of mine is going to be seen like that. Here, I'll find one for you.'

She vigorously attacked the pile and thrust a brown, mid length skirt at Elodie. 'This one,' she said shortly, 'This will fit you. You can have this one or nothing. Take your choice.'

Elodie nodded miserably and the bored market stall holder wrapped it in crumpled tissue paper and handed it to Mamy who thrust it into her oversized straw bag. I was embarrassed as I watched her walking determinedly in front of Mamy and me, her hand going to her eyes every so often as she brushed away the hot tears.

Mamy was a highly volatile character and would envelop Elodie in a crushing bear hug one minute and slap her on the legs the next. Her husband Florian was the antithesis of this stout virago. I believe he used to work as a builder before he retired. The one occasion when I had seen him wearing a suit was when I was picked up from the *Lycée*. I never saw it again. Instead he was always dressed in a dull blue cotton bibbed overall with a long-sleeved shirt under it. Elodie told me that his hobby was fishing and I could quite see why. It would take him out of the house for a full day, and I expect Mamy didn't mind as long as he was home for his meals. He might even return with a catch which would find its way into her famed fish soup. He rarely spoke and when he did he was a faint echo of his wife. Underneath he had a wry sense of humour. I remember him pouring two drops of soup into my bowl while he put his mouth to my ear and whispered, 'Leave what you can't eat!'

Elodie explained that we would be calling to see her parents in Bormes-les-Mimosas when we went on the trip along the coast. Because I thought it a strange arrangement, she living in Marseille with her grandparents whilst her parents lived further along the coast, I was eager for details and tried to introduce the subject tactfully.

I waited until we were in her room, a neat, tidy space with a huge oak chest and almost ceiling-level wardrobe. Several paintings were hung on the walls; beautiful illustrations done in watercolours, pen and ink and oils. The ones that caught my attention were a group of animal studies: a mare with three foals, a cat in a basket with two playful, skittish kittens and one of a tit, beak open to disgorge food into the upturned beaks of chicks in a nest. The execution was detailed and precise, the colours muted but pleasing.

'These paintings are gorgeous, Elodie,' I said, moving closer to inspect them. 'I love the animal ones.'

'You like them?' She smiled faintly. 'Me, I am not very happy with the horse, I have not painted her very well. I wanted her to be with more movement but I could not get this effect.'

'What, you mean, *you* did these? But, they're brilliant! I could never paint like that in a million years. You could be a real artist!'

'This is what I would like to do if I succeed my bac. There is a special school in Marseille where I can learn to do the art properly but Mamy says I will gain no money for this. She says it is best for me to become a teacher of English.' She sounded defeated.

'But, that's not true!' I protested, staring at the faithful likeness of the glossy brown horse and foal which was delicately depicted with convincing anatomical realism. 'Lots of artists make good money, and especially if they're as good as you are. Doesn't Mamy know that? Honestly, you could earn a lot more producing work like this...'

She shrugged lightly. 'This I have said to her, but she does not want to listen to me,' she said gloomily. 'You have seen how she is. I ask her many times but she says to me that it is impossible.'

I was silent, knowing full well that I for one certainly wouldn't want to stand up against Mamy. I could usually persuade my own parents to let me do what I wanted provided it wasn't too outrageous, but this feisty French lady was a different matter altogether. I could imagine that any confrontation would end badly.

Propped up on the oak chest was a silver-coloured frame displaying a photo of a red-haired woman with a baby in her arms and a curly-haired, bearded man. I nodded towards the photo and asked lightly, 'Do you see much of them? Your parents, I mean?'

She paused before saying carefully, 'My father came to see me two years ago, but my mother, she was too....' She frowned as she searched for the English word, but not finding it, she said... *'occupée.'* She spoke very quietly with a slight frown on her face and looked away. 'But she sends me presents,' she said, brightening up. 'Come and see.' She unlocked one of the three top drawers in the chest and drew out a small wooden box. This too was locked and she opened it with a tiny gold key. On a bed of navy velvet reposed a gold coloured necklace set with shiny stones. I held it up, admiring the fiery brilliance of the deep red stones.

'So you can see, my mother, she always thinks about me. She is very kind and she gives to me many things,' she said wistfully.

I watched as she let the necklace slide slowly through her fingers before closing the box and very carefully locking it away again.

'Did your mother send you that one?' I asked, referring to the gold-toned necklace she was wearing over her tee shirt.

She nodded. 'Like this, I can remember my mother every day.'

I thought again about this word *'occupée.'* It is one of those odd words that sound as if the meaning is the same as the similar English word, although in French it has the sole meaning of 'busy.'

I looked forward to meeting these two; the father whose last visit was two years ago and the enigmatic lady who was apparently too busy to find the time to see her only daughter.

There was just over a week to go before we set off and meanwhile we romped and giggled our way through the long hot days, doing our best to evade Mamy when she waddled after us yelling instructions to put sun hats on, to walk in the shade, to be home for lunch on time, to tidy up, to eat more, to finish our desserts, to make our beds properly, to clear the dishes, and with both of us getting our legs slapped hard when we failed to measure up to her exacting standards. In today's society she would be deemed abusive, but fifty years ago in the Mediterranean this matriarchal attitude was the norm rather than the exception.

During this week we had group expeditions organized by the two schools. One was to La Sante-Baume, a mountain ridge spreading between the Bouches-du-Rhône and the Var departments with a summit over a thousand metres high. According to tradition, Mary Magdalene and other disciples including Lazare of Bethany were said to have sailed to the Mediterranean in a simple boat after being expelled from Palestine after the ascension, when Christians were being persecuted. On their arrival, while Lazare set about converting the entire population of Marseille, Mary herself retreated to La Sante-Baume and spent the rest of her days in prayer and quiet contemplation.

The excursion was not optional and neither was the arduous trek up to the summit. The hike started off with innocuous little winding paths through dense undergrowth, where you caught fleeting glimpses of vivid blue jays and heard the rustle of unnamed small creatures scuttling away. The paths twisted and doubled back on themselves, making the walk a lot longer than anticipated. Just when you thought you couldn't possibly take another step, the path got steeper and steeper until you were left gasping. The top was a long, long way up.

When you did get up to the summit there was a small grotto with statues, protected by railings. I visited it later in my life with my children, when a small souvenir shop had been opened and we bought several pretty little pink and turquoise soapstone boxes with hinged lids. I still have them.

We all took photographs of course; tilting our heads back to capture the sheer craggy limestone mountain face, of the statues behind their metal rails and of the view down in the valley from one of the stone parapets conveniently situated at intervals on the sloping track. And of each other too. But this was long before smartphones; we were still in the 'one day my prints will come' era, when you took your film out of your camera and entrusted it to one of the photo shops. If you had taken photographs in dim light you used a disposable flash cube which you slotted onto the top of your camera. You could specify whether you wanted a white border around your prints, or whether to go for a full set of prints with free miniature duplicates. A week or so later you made another trip to the shop and collected your prints in their bright primary coloured envelopes.

I didn't have too long to wait to see Elodie's parents as Bormes-les-Mimosas, even though inland, was to be one of the stops on our trip to the Riviera.

We travelled in what I later identified as a Citröen DS. It was comfortable and ideally suited for a long trip. The first port of call was Hyères, where Elodie's cousins Sarah and Francine lived.

Their house was very large and modern, painted a very pale pink, standing on a vast corner plot. I was fascinated by this garden, which boasted several palms and, wonder of wonders, a massive tree with branches loaded with tiny lemons. It was my first sight of both, as palm and lemon trees were scarce on the ground at home.

When I met them I found Sarah to be rather arrogant and haughty. She made no real attempt to communicate with me even though I really tried to talk to her in halting French. Her only response was a slight shrug of the shoulders and faintly raised eyebrows as if she had not the slightest idea what I was talking about. My French wasn't perfect, far from it, but I thought she could at least have made an effort. The younger girl Francine tried valiantly to establish some sort of common ground by asking me in broken English if I liked France.

It was their father who was the owner of several greengrocer's shops, both in Hyères and in Marseille, where Mamy obtained all the peaches for the marmalade, and accounted for the family's beautiful house on a wide avenue bordered by pine trees. Each of the cousins had her own bathroom, and they each had their own pony stabled somewhere nearby. It was all a far, far cry from my place of birth.

From Hyères we took a magical boat trip out to Porquerolles, one of the Îles d'Hyères, where I remember running swiftly through stunted pine trees, smelling the sweet fragrance that seemed to emanate from the very ground itself. Towards the beach the ground was covered with grasses and pockets of small sandy dunes, until I got my first view of the sparkling sea; turquoise, shimmering with a liquid diamond brilliance which deepened into a dark blue further out. I could barely even imagine actually living in a place where all this spectacular natural landscape was available within a few miles of home.

I was to visit Hyères again later in my life with my own children, but it was never again to be the magic of that first visit.

Bormes-les-Mimosas was to be our next stop, and I was looking forward to seeing these strange parents for myself. The visit lasted only two days but it was to be instrumental in crystallizing for me the processes which had shaped Elodie's character.

We arrived at a large, imposing white stuccoed villa in a side street off the main thoroughfare. Adjoining the main house was a two storey round tower, painted like the house in a pale blue. The woman who opened the massive oak door was a taller, thinner and slightly more haggard version of Elodie herself. Whereas Elodie's auburn hair framed her triangular face like a shiny copper bell, her mother's was curled and deeper red with touches of brown at the roots. She seemed all red. Her dress was white with large red flowers, her nails painted a gory crimson and her feet were thrust into mules decorated with red curling feathers. As I received the obligatory pecks on each cheek I was enveloped in an invisible, wonderful scent of a fragrant rose garden.

The salon was situated in the tower itself. The three red plush sofas, the heavy wooden bureaux and highly polished occasional tables were made to fit the curve of the walls. It was totally unlike anything I had ever seen. Each piece was a specially commissioned work of art. The centrepiece was a massive round fireplace set in the middle of the room with a tall stainless steel pipe outlet that rose to the ceiling. A curved glass door gave access to the interior of the stove, which was designed so that the fire was visible from all parts of the room. The hearth surrounding it was of a pale ivory veined marble and was set above floor level to allow for a stack of perfectly formed logs to fit underneath. Obviously it was a bespoke piece, made to fit the round salon. I had never seen anything like it and I gazed at it, fascinated, until Elodie's mother noticed my awed surprise and she laughed.

'It's beautiful isn't it? It cost us a fortune but it was worth every penny.'

I nodded in agreement, glancing briefly at Elodie who was smiling with vicarious appreciation. The room was undoubtedly stunning, and whoever had created it had taste as well as money. My mother would have been awestruck if I had been a guest here, rather than in Mamy's house. But the thoughts flittered gossamer-like through my mind like floating butterflies, landing here and there before alighting on a new idea. Where was Elodie's share in all this opulence? What were Véronique's priorities? Were expensive bibelots more ultimately satisfying to her than a normal relationship with her child?

Beyond the fireplace was a long, highly polished wooden table with eight chairs, their richly upholstered backs and seats in smooth red velvet.

Véronique saw my gaze directed now towards the windows, spanning the height of the double storey room and framed by heavy drapes, each held in place by bronze curlicues fastened to the walls.

She beckoned to Elodie and me to follow her around the room to see more of her treasures. Small oval niches were cut into the walls, each one lined in marble which matched the hearth. On each of these shelves stood a small bronze statue of a naked female figure, each in a different posture. Elodie tentatively reached for one, a delicately wrought slender woman with tilted head and outstretched arm.

'Don't touch that!' Her mother snapped. 'It's an expensive piece, we have it insured. In fact, they're all insured but I wouldn't want to try claiming for one if it gets broken.'

I couldn't see how a metal figurine could break by being held, but the effect on Elodie was immediate. Crestfallen and red faced, she pulled her arm away from the shelf and went to sit down by Papy's side, nestling against him for comfort while she left me to continue the tour on my own.

Later we were invited into the dining room for a meal. This was in stark contrast to the luxury of the salon, as if all the money and taste had been reserved to create an impressive centrepiece of the house. It was wallpapered in a dull brown that showed signs of peeling at the top corners. There was a small table of white melamine with scuffed brown chairs, and a massive bookcase which held surprisingly few books; most of the shelves were crammed with a paraphernalia of magazines, ornaments and small carved wooden trinket boxes as well as a collection of elaborately decorated figurines of men and women in costume. One, I remember was the stiff figure of a woman clothed in a long skirt in bright purple, blue and yellow, patterned like the fabrics I had seen in the market. She was carrying a basket of brown rolls and carried a long baguette under her arm.

If the salon had been Véronique's room, then this one, surely, had to be Elodie's. She had lavished as much attention on it as she gave to her daughter.

We had a simple meal of a lettuce salad, followed by fish and steamed vegetables. Mamy, I noticed, ate sparingly of each course, prodding at the fish doubtfully before parting it with her knife and extracting a few minute bones before eating it. When the main course was finished everyone had clean plates. Every last morsel of food had been mopped up with roughly torn off pieces of a doughy, delicious baguette. Except for mine. I had eaten as much as I could but my plate still had bits of fish and a few green beans left on it. These leftovers were a source of deep embarrassment to me as, quite inexplicably, everyone turned their plate over. I was bewildered by this. Should I turn my own plate over and let the food drip onto the table? On balance I thought not, so I waited for developments.

All became clear when Elodie's mother brought a cake from the kitchen and deposited a slice onto everyone's upturned plate. When she reached mine she smiled lightly, took my plate away and brought me a clean one.

The cake, a delicious confection of layers of puffed pastry and crème pattiserie topped with glazed apricots was obviously a bought one, as Véronique took it out of the box at the table. This brought an audible sniff of disgust from Mamy, even though she ate it.

During the meal Elodie's eyes scanned the room keenly with a slightly bewildered look, as if she were searching for something. At length, she turned to her father and said uncertainly, 'Papa, did you get the painting I sent you? The one with the ducks and ducklings? I can't see it anywhere...'

Even I could see the embarrassment on his face. 'What? Oh, yes – that painting. It was excellent, a really good piece. Yes, yes, I have it. I'm....going to have it framed. Just haven't had the time yet. But it's top of my list, I promise. Next week at the very latest.'

Elodie was struggling. I could see that she wanted to believe him, but it was equally plain that she was finding it difficult. Eventually the doubt on her face faded and she nodded slightly; a tacit acknowledgement that she had accepted his words. She turned her gaze towards the bookshelves, and grinned in appreciation of something she had spotted.

'There's Bobo up there!' she cried. 'Papa, you've kept him! Can I take him with me?' Bobo turned out to be a small brown furry bear, perched high up on one of the shelves which also held some of the wooden boxes.

'Finish your meal first,' he told her, 'and then get it. Yes, you can take it with you.' Immediately the meal was finished Elodie went to the bookcase. She reached up as far as she could but the bear was out of reach, even when she stood on tiptoe.

'Papa, I can't reach it,' she wailed. 'Can you get it for me please?'

'Elodie, if you can't reach it then get a chair!' he told her impatiently. 'You're old enough now to use a bit of common sense. Don't expect everyone to run around after you as if you're a baby.' At that she flushed and her eyes filled with tears. She was dragging the heavy dining room chair towards the bookcase when Mamy interjected.

'Florian, you get it down for her, will you? She'll fall off that chair.'

Papy, looking most unlike his usual self, dressed as he was in a jacket and brown trousers in place of his habitual blue overalls, obligingly walked over to the bookshelf. His tall frame reached the bear easily, but it was behind a pile of magazines. In reaching for the bear, he dislodged the pile and it clattered to the floor, the magazine pages fluttering open as they tumbled. He started gathering them up, and Elodie was instantly by his side, resting back on her heels as she started to gather up the haphazard mess. Piling magazines on top of each other, she stopped suddenly, with an exclamation that was part dismay, part horror. From between the leaves, she pulled out a sheet of cream paper. It was disfigured by overlapping coffee and wine ring stains, but clearly, it had once been a painting. A pond scene, with ducks and ducklings.

Papy pulled her gently to her feet and put his arm around her as he led her back to the sofa where she sat beside him, Mamy moved closer to be beside her while she cried. Until this moment I had never seen Papy other than genial and slightly aloof, but his white knuckles as he clenched his fists clearly expressed the depth of his fury as he gazed first at Pierre, then at Véronique. Neither of them spoke, although the atmosphere was as charged as if a summer lightning bolt had struck.

After a few minutes of acutely agonized silence, whilst Elodie's parents' expressions ranged from frank annoyance to exasperation, we trooped back to the salon. Conversation was staccato and desultory until Mamy, gazing round at the room, said, 'Véronique, this room could do with repapering. You should get Pierre to do it for you.'

'Wallpaper costs money,' her daughter replied crossly. 'We haven't any extra to pay for decorating. And Pierre can't hang wallpaper.'

Mamy sniffed 'If it was mine I wouldn't let the place get so dilapidated. That paper hasn't been changed for years.' There was no reply. After a contemptuous glance at Mamy, Véronique angrily snatched up a glossy magazine and flipped through its pages without reading it. Papy said nothing at all but hugged Elodie a little closer to his side. She nestled against him, burying her face in his shoulder.

There were no hugs when we left soon afterwards, just a ritual pecking of cheeks all round before we were on our way. Elodie struggled with her feelings for many hours as the car sped along, gazing out of the window and barely replying to anyone's remarks.

The trip was broken up into nights spent with relatives and our next stop was Cannes. I have a photograph of myself and Elodie stretched out side by side on the beach which I believe Mamy had asked someone to take, as there she is, sitting slightly apart from us, looking towards us with her habitual suspicious expression. In the photo I am wearing a hot pink bikini and Elodie is in a dark navy costume. Later, when we had changed behind the screen of a huge towel that Mamy held up, we posed by some railings on the other side of the road from the pristine whiteness of the Carlton Hotel. After Cannes was Antibes, where an old friend of Papy's lived. As I recall, there weren't enough beds for everyone and Elodie and I slept on the floor. It was a fantastic trip, for both me and Elodie, who only left Marseille to go on their annual holiday to Puigcerdà, just over the Spanish border.

This visit to Bormes-les-Mimosas was one of the more memorable incidents of my whole trip. Whenever Elodie irritated me, which she did with monotonous regularity, I really tried hard to remember the scene, and to be more understanding of a character shaped by blatant, unrelenting rejection. I very rarely succeeded.

Then it was on towards Nice, and after that we wended our way towards the Italian border. That was when all the commotion began. I had vaguely clocked signs to the Italian border from my seat in the back, and as we got nearer and the number of kilometres to the border grew smaller, I felt a growing disquiet. Italy. It was a different country wasn't it? And what did people need to visit a different country? They needed a passport. And I hadn't got one. Not with me, at any rate. My passport was back in Marseille. I knew exactly where it was, in the top drawer of my bedside chest. Which wasn't a lot of help. I felt myself getting redder and redder, and the situation growing more and more tense as the kilometres flew by. I knew I would have to say something.

So I did, and Mamy erupted.

'But you knew we were going to Italy!' she screamed. 'You are with us and you have no passport! If the police stop us they will say we have kidnapped you! I will go to jail!' The words were unfamiliar but the tone of voice and her outraged expression were enough to convey her general meaning. She was livid, and there was no stopping her once she got going. An avalanche of reproaches was being directed my way. By this time Papy had stopped on a grass verge, Elodie was crying, I was crying, Mamy was still screaming and the whole trip was just ruined.

'*Why* didn't you bring your passport?' she yelled at me. 'You knew we were coming here!'

Well actually no I didn't. I genuinely, categorically, did not know. Ok, so the word Italy might just have cropped up in the conversation at some point, but if it had then either I hadn't heard it or realised its significance.

It occurred to me in later years to realise that *none* of this was my fault. It's incredibly easy to make as if you understand when you haven't a clue what people are talking about. It involves an eager nod of the head, accompanied by a bright smile and a little noise in the throat that can be interpreted as assent. So there was naive little me nodding and grinning at every blessed thing they said and generally making as if I knew what they were talking about. Which I didn't. Not in the least. I was catching one or two words here and there but that was as far as it went. Now all my play acting had come back and bitten me on my derrière.

Another thing was, why on earth didn't someone check that I had my passport on me before we set off? I came from Leeds, for heaven's sake. Passports were not a part of my daily life. Nobody there carried a passport with them the whole time. Why would they? Britain is an island, and in the sixties there were very few people who took holidays in other countries. Later on I dismissed it as a culture difference, with French people always carrying some kind of identification with them, which British people didn't as it was not a requirement of daily life.

It came to me later on that she had quite possibly been genuinely frightened of being stopped with a child in the car who had no identification. The gendarmerie carried guns. They were not known for their affable chats about the weather or for genially providing you with directions. They acted first and asked questions later; if indeed they bothered asking questions at all. This was not *Dixon of Dock Green* territory.

Quite pragmatically Papy swung the car around and we started on the long, long journey back, with Mamy bawling at me practically the whole way home.

Strangely, from that moment on, it seemed as if I became part of the family instead of a visitor. In practice, that meant that my status as a guest was totally gone, as she yelled at me just as often as she did at Elodie, which was practically every other minute.

The incident eventually made its way into the realms of legends past and every subsequent trip to Marseille was peppered by conversations beginning with, 'And do you remember when you forgot your passport!'

At the end of the three weeks it was time to say goodbye. I was taken back to the *Lycée* and the waiting coach at the appointed time where I met up with the rest of my group, all hugging and kissing their hosts and vowing eternal friendship. There was a lot of sadness and cries of 'See you soon!' before we the coach gathered speed and we finally left Marseille.

Chapter 3
Correspondence

Dear Stephanie,

I do wish you were still here. It was like having a sister and it is so quiet here without you. There is nobody to talk to. Mamy is just the same. She never lets me do anything I want. Everyone I know, all my friends, they buy their own clothes, their parents give them the money, but for me, I cannot do this. It is always Mamy who says what I must wear and how much I must eat. Papy would like it if I had my own money every week like my friends but Mamy does not want to listen to him. She says I will buy rubbish things. All she ever thinks about is cooking and my studies. I always have to get good marks and if they are bad she hits me and says I did not try hard enough. She wants me to work at my English, she says it will be good if I can become a teacher of English. I have not seen my parents, I do not know when I will see them again. I hope you are well.

At soon, Elodie

I would like to say that I felt just a little pity for her, but it wouldn't be the truth. At best, I skimmed over her letters, feeling very little, if any, concern for a girl of my own age who was leading such a troubled life. The main thing that caught my attention was her strange way of signing off. It was years before my own French reached dizzy heights and I realised that the literal translation of *'à bientôt'* (see you later) is 'At soon.'

Dear Elodie,

I was sad to go home, I had such a fantastic time with you. I saw so many places that are nothing like my home. We do not have palm trees here, or lemon trees like the ones in the garden in Hyères. When I was in the garden I picked a lemon from the tree to take home with me as a souvenir. It has gone hard now but I still keep it. One day I would like to have a tree like it but there is no chance while I live in the UK, it is simply too cold. We do have beaches but it takes ages to get there, and when you do go they are not like Porquerolles, the sea is always grey, not blue, and it is usually freezing. I expect you will be back at the Lycée now. I hope your studies are going well for you. If you have any homework in English then perhaps I can help you with it. Would Mamy let you telephone? I know she wants you to get high marks. (She used to hit me too, do you remember that awful time when I forgot my passport?) I am sorry you have not seen your parents, but perhaps you will see them in the next holidays.

With love from Stephanie x

Dear Stephanie,

I am well. I am at the Lycée again. I work hard for my English and I have good marks now, they are much better than before. Thank you for helping me when I rang you up about the difference between the present perfect and the present perfect progressive. I think this is very difficult in English, we do not use this distinction in French. Mamy is pleased with my marks. I must tell you, there is a problem with one of the students. He is called Antoine, do you remember him? He was the brother of Jeanne, the penfriend of Charlotte in your group. He had to see the proviseur, I think you say headmaster. He says to his friends that Charlotte keeps on telephoning to him. People at the Lycée laugh about this and they say that they know the reason. Me, I had an argument with a girl because she was saying terrible things about him. I shouted at her and I pulled her hair and then we started fighting. I was so angry! Antoine is not a bad person as everyone is saying. My mother has telephoned to me. She did not speak very long but I was very happy, she says that she and my father will think of coming to Marseille. I wish you were still here with me.

Why do you put x on your letter?

With love, Elodie

Dear Elodie,

Sorry! The x means a kiss in English. It is a short way of saying 'je t'embrasse,' (I embrace you). Yes, I remember Antoine, and there is a problem here too! There is a rumour going round at school that Charlotte is pregnant. She was very sad on the way home, she hardly stopped crying for the whole journey. No-one knows for certain though because when we started school after the holidays she had left. Her friends say that she is not at home but no-one is saying where she is. I think the only person who knows is her best friend Lydia but she refuses to tell anyone. Mrs Thomas has left too and we *have another French teacher. She is nice but gives us a lot more work than Mrs Thomas did, she says our French is hopeless. I will let you know if I hear anything about them. It is good that your mother telephoned. Perhaps she will arrange for you to visit her again. Do you still have Bobo?*

I have lots of photos from France now, I am sending you this one from our visit to Notre Dame de la Garde. Do you remember it? Please write to me soon.

Love, Stephanie x

I did indeed remember Antoine. Before we boarded the coach for the return journey, Charlotte was clinging to the tall, dark-haired teenage boy we had seen her with at the *Lycée*, and she was sobbing her heart out. Lydia and a few other girls were surrounding her, trying their best in murmured tones to comfort her but to no avail. She got herself onto the coach finally, and waved to him with the tears running down her cheeks as the coach edged slowly into the Marseille traffic. Who had thought it was a good idea to put a drop dead gorgeous sixteen-year-old girl in a family with a seventeen-year-old boy?

The photo I had enclosed was to remind Elodie of our visit. A couple of days after the visit to La Santa Baume came a reminder from Mrs Thomas. We had to assemble at the Vieux Port, from where we would walk up to the much famed Basilique de Notre-Dame-de-la-Garde. What fresh hell was this? Another group forced march which involved yet another heat stroke inducing climb.

We were sadly out of luck, as only two years earlier there had been a funicular taking tourists to the top. In later years a bus and a small tourist train were available, but we had hit the period when if you wanted to see the church up close, you walked up. We didn't specially; there was much low voiced muttering about being able to see it quite well from where we were, thank you very much, but were forced to walk up anyway.

We set off in the early morning, with our teachers cheerfully remarking on the freshness of the day, completely ignoring the looks of pure malevolence being shot in their direction. An hour and a half later they were not so sanguine; the heat was intense and we arrived at the site exhausted.

We were almost too hot to register the spectacular view over Marseille. The dizzying panorama of the red roofs of houses, innumerable apartment buildings, winding roads and the far distant hills only merited a few desultory clicks of the camera before we all trooped inside. I believe that for most of us the most remarkable attribute of the building was the protection its thick walls provided against the intense heat outside.

We were given a guided tour: the stunning main church was pointed out with its vast marble pillars supporting arches of banded red and cream, the awesome gilded ceiling, glowing with intricately decorated gold circles. The Roman-Byzantine style of mosaic and small stones was indicated with much excitement and waving of hands towards the various splendours.

The tour was in French; not a single English member of our group understood a word, with the possible exception of Mrs Thomas who was listening with the gentle smile and interested expression of one intent on demonstrating her superior understanding. To this day I have a 'seen one, seen them all' mentality towards churches and cathedrals. This one was undoubtedly as spectacular as advertised but frankly I was bored.

Elodie and I were towards the back of the group. We glanced at each other and no words were necessary. A slight nod, and we slipped away into a chapel which held tiered rows of lighted candles below a wall made of small stone squares, each with an inscription on it. In the corner was a life size gilded Madonna and child. After wandering over to them for a quick inspection I sat down beside Elodie. I was wondering again about her parents.

'Have you always lived with Mamy and Papy?' I asked curiously.

She hesitated. 'No, not always. When I was a baby, my father worked on Martinique. It is a French province in the Caribbean, and I was with them. But I became ill there. The climate was not suitable for me, so they brought me back to Marseille. My father worked on.....'

She stopped as I quite evidently hadn't understood. Later, with the help of a dictionary and several complicated diagrams, I worked out that he had been in charge of a water desalination plant.

'Now, he is the owner of a perfume shop in Bormes-les-Mimosas and my mother, she works there also.'

I was immediately transported back to Bormes-les-Mimosas and the heavenly scent that had enveloped me with her mother's peck on the cheek.

Elodie sat completely detached for a moment, her small face sombre and her eyes fixed on the statue of the Madonna. To begin with she had the eyes of a lost waif, of a frightened animal, and I was puzzled when the stare turned to a look of pure scorn. Recovering herself shortly afterwards, she began to talk determinedly about the kind of films she liked, and we discussed the cinema until it was time for the gentler descent.

This was to be the last of the group organized tours, and for the rest of our stay we were with our hosts.

Dear Stephanie,

Thank you for your photograph. I remember the visit very well. Nearly all of my class had already visited Notre Dame with their families but for me, it was the first time I have been. That day was so hot, wasn't it? As winter approaches here, you would hardly believe how cold it is! Papy stays indoors instead of going fishing. He and Mamy keep having arguments. Mamy thinks it is time that I lived with my parents, but Papy does not agree with her. He says they will be too lonely if I leave. I remind them that I will be leaving anyway when I go to the university. I work hard for my English. Mamy says that she wishes you to come back to Marseille next year. I hope you will come.

But, I am very happy because my parents will come to Marseille, they will come next month and they will stay for two weeks. They will stay in the upstairs of the house. Like that, my mother can have her own kitchen. Please tell me, did you like my parents when we visited them? You did not say when you were here.

At soon, Elodie

I was nonplussed at this. I had definitely formed my own opinion of her parents; especially of Véronique, her mother, but they were my private memories, not to be shared and certainly not with Elodie.

I hardly knew what to think about her parents' visit. Could it be a preliminary meeting with a view to Elodie going to live with them? It was a possibility I supposed, but I resolved to say nothing to Elodie. Even if it was a visit with a purpose, it struck me as rather odd, a bit like viewing goods on approval. The one thing I was pleased about was the fact that Véronique would have her own kitchen. The mere thought of Mamy being forced into sharing her beloved kitchen with anyone made me shudder. Gang warfare in La Busserine would seem like a gentle spat in comparison.

Dear Elodie,

Sorry I haven't written for a while. First, yes I would love to come to back to Marseille with you next summer! Thank you for inviting me, it will be great to see you all again. I haven't heard anything more about Charlotte. How did your parents' visit go? Will you be going to stay with them? I liked their house very much, it is unusual. Can you tell me more about the little dressed up figurine? I saw a lot of them in the shops.

Love, Stephanie

Dear Stephanie,

I am so pleased you will come to Marseille again! Mamy wishes that you stay with me for all of the summer. She says like this, I can practise English with you. I hope you will tell me my mistakes!

My parents came, but it was not a good time for us. My mother said I did not have enough clothes. She took me to the shops with her and she bought me three dresses. Mamy did not come with us. I like the dresses, they are very short, which is the same as the other girls wear, but when we were at home, Mamy said they were terrible. My mother was shouting at her and she said that Mamy does not let me choose anything for myself. I was very sad to hear them shouting, and then my mother said she and my father would not stay any more, but I cried and I said I wanted her to stay. She did not want to listen to me, and so they went home. But she gave me a very beautiful necklace, and, I was very surprised, my father gave me some oil paints! They are very good quality, and so I was very pleased with them. My father said that I must listen to Mamy and do as she wishes. Mamy does not want that I wear the dresses, she has taken them away.

The little figures you asked me about, they are called Santons de Provence. They are very famous here. Many people have them. Sometimes they are figures for a nativity at Christmas, my parents have many of these but they are for Christmas only. The figures on show in my parents' house are just figures of the region in the costumes of before times. I think she has many more but perhaps they are put away, I did not see them all when we visited.

At soon,
Elodie

Chapter 4
The Return

The 'French Girls' as they were dubbed, made their return two week visit to Leeds in the summer. The shorter time scale was due, I believe, to time commitments on the part of their English teacher.

I was just a little nervous about it, feeling that Leeds and its surroundings was not much to offer Elodie in return for my own visit. I remembered her excitement before we set off for our long tour of the Riviera. 'We will go to Cannes,' she had said excitedly, 'then to Monte Carlo, and Monaco....'

Although I didn't yet know our own itinerary, my imagination was working full pelt and imagining the horror of it all.

'We'll be going to *Barnsley,*' I would say with a little thrill in my voice. 'And then onto Doncaster, and Scunthorpe, and we might even get as far as *Grimsby.* Just think of that!'

It didn't have quite the same élan, quite the same magic, the same sophistication to it.

Definitely apprehensive, I quizzed my mother on the subject.

'What are we going to do when Elodie comes here?' I asked. She laid the iron on its heel and placed a freshly ironed tee shirt onto a pile which she placed into my arms.

'Just nip upstairs with these, love, will you, and put them away for me. Save my poor legs.'

Reluctantly, I did as she asked, even putting the clothes in the right rooms. Two were Dad's shirts, and I crept into his room thinking he was asleep. Instead he was sitting up, in the middle of the double bed, with the crumpled duvet tucked up to his chin.

'Steph, while you're here, could you get me a glass of water, love, and pass me those tablets?' On his bedside table was a packet of tablets with only two left. I extracted one and went to the bathroom to fill his glass. On my return he was sitting on the side of the bed in his pyjamas, back hunched and holding his head.

'Dad, what's wrong?' I was more concerned now than I had ever been. I had never seen him other than cheerful and this new persona was worrying me.

'It's nothing,' he muttered as he tilted back his head and gulped the pill down. 'Just a rotten headache, that's all. It'll pass. Nothing to get upset about, d'you hear?'

'Are you *sure?*'

He nodded weakly, before swinging his legs into bed again and lying down. 'Just need to rest, that's all. Turn the light off when you go out.'

Not at all convinced, I clicked off his bedroom light and frowned as I put away the rest of the clothes.

Mum was still ironing when I came down again. 'Dad's not very well, is he?' I began.

She looked at me sharply. 'What makes you say that?'

'He never goes to bed during the day – and he's got a headache, I could tell it was a bad one.'

She picked up one of my school shirts and began pressing it, saying lightly, 'Well, everyone gets headaches from time to time.' And, echoing Dad's words, 'It's nothing to worry about, he'll be back to himself in a day or so.' She changed the subject far too abruptly.

'So, have you thought about what we're going to do when Elodie arrives next week? Her grandparents were so good to you when you were in France, taking you to the Riviera. We'll have a think about it after tea. Some of the other parents are taking their French girls on holiday with them. Claire says they're taking theirs up to Scotland...'

Claire was one of the bridge group, and I could see the thought processes as they flicked through her mind. Whatever happened, our efforts would have to at least match those of other parents, and if at all possible, exceed them.

It was almost nine o'clock before she broached the subject again, when we were in the lounge. Dad had not put in an appearance at tea time. 'What do you think she might like best?' she asked, a touch concerned. 'You know her. What is she interested in?'

'She likes shopping,' I said hopefully. A shopping trip might be worthwhile, I thought. I could think of several things I wanted. Those new jeans I had seen in Schofields for instance....

'Oh, I don't think that's the idea at all.' Mum was definite on this. 'We're supposed to show her British culture while she's here. That's what the letter said, wasn't it? She can go shopping any time she wants in Marseille, surely.'

Well actually, no, she couldn't. She could only buy clothes on Mamy's approval and their tastes nearly always clashed. My hopes of a shopping trip faded away.

'She's really good at art,' I remembered suddenly. 'She's done some fabulous paintings. We could go to an art gallery, she might like that...'

'Yes, it's a good idea,' she said. 'But that will only fill a morning or an afternoon at the most. We need to think of something else as well.' She hesitated, before saying, 'What about a coach tour? Your dad has an appointment on the twenty-third,' she said lightly. 'It's only a follow-up on his results so he won't mind if I don't go with him for once. It will just be me and you two girls. I've got a catalogue somewhere.'

Dad's hospital appointment caught my attention for a moment, before I was distracted when I leafed through the colourful brochure offering a bewildering selection of tours. I giggled as one of them proposed *'A luxurious 14 day Mediterranean holiday. Visit Provence, take in the sights of Monte Carlo and Monaco. Wonder at the beautiful Riviera coastline, experience the magic of an optional excursion to the Isles of Porquerolles.....'*

'We could take her back home,' I giggled. 'Tell her we've got a real surprise for her.'

'Oh, Steph, do be serious,' she said, exasperated. 'Here I am, trying to do my best for your friend and all you can do is come up with ridiculous suggestions... Look, what about this one?'

The page showed a tour of North Yorkshire. 'It starts from Leeds bus station,' she said. 'Then it goes on to Harrogate, then Thirsk and Pickering, and it includes two nights in a hotel in Scarborough. On the way back we stop for lunch in York and then we're back at the bus station the same day. Would she like that, do you think?'

She saw the doubt on my face and continued, the offence already showing on her face. 'It might not seem like a huge adventure for you,' she said shortly. 'You've been to all these places before. But look at it from Elodie's point of view. It will be a different country for her. She's never been here before. And Yorkshire is one of the most beautiful counties in England. She'll be able to compare it with France, won't she?'

That was what I was afraid of. Elodie might be a stranger to England but could we really hope to compete with the South of

France? With the impossibly beautiful scenery of the Riviera? Of the golden beaches and crystal turquoise waters of the Isles of Hyères? I was highly doubtful and it showed.

'Stop being so negative, Stephanie,' she said, getting really cross. 'We'll do our best for her, she can't ask more than that. Oh, and I forgot to ask. What does she like to eat?'

I was in deep waters here. 'She likes *bouillabaisse*,' I began. 'We often had that. And paella...' A slow smile crept over me as I remembered that first, disastrous meal in Marseille.

'Oh, of course. Paella. I'll get a few packets in before she arrives. Some Chicken Supreme as well, that's quick and easy. And if she likes home cooking then I can always make us a stew. And what was that other thing you said?'

I was horrified. I could never in my wildest dreams imagine my own mother going to the market and cooking all day, as Mamy had. For my mother, food had to be filling and nutritious, and the quicker it was prepared and eaten the better. I thought of Elodie's reaction to the twenty minute dinners we were used to, instead of the two hours that were dedicated to most meals in France, and my heart sank.

'She likes *bouillabaisse*,' I repeated.

She was confused. 'She likes what? What's that?'

'It's a kind of fish soup,' I said helpfully. 'Her grandmother makes it. She spends all her time cooking...'

'All day? Surely not. No-one cooks all day – well, I hope my food is good enough for her, I'm sure. We can't all spend our waking hours stewing over a hot stove, but we always eat good quality food in this house.' She was aggrieved at the suggestion that our food might not make the grade.

I knew why she was irritated. My mother was the type of person who always wanted 'The Best.' I had long known that it vexed her that our own part of Leeds was not considered to be 'the best.' We lived in Headingley, in a neat street of houses that would later acquire uniform black painted front doors and looped railings in front of each house, making the area smart and desirable, but which at that time were perfectly ordinary, dull brick three-storey houses with cellars. She would have preferred a house in Alwoodley, for instance, one of the preferred neighbourhoods of the wealthy. Still, she did what she could within her limits. Her hair was regularly permed by a hairdresser whom she considered to be exemplary in his skills, and she was happy if her clothes bore a designer label and came from a shop with a double-barrelled name, preferably wrapped in tissue paper and in a long box.

She was annoyed at my unspoken attitude, my gut feeling that Yorkshire might not come up to French Riviera standards. In her view, there shouldn't be any lingering doubts about it. Yorkshire would triumph, naturally.

In the event we decided on a North Yorkshire coach tour, staying overnight in The Crown hotel in Harrogate before continuing on to Thirsk, Pickering and Scarborough the following day. The journey back would take us through Malton and York where we would have time to explore the city and have lunch before the return to Leeds.

'That sounds ideal!' Mum said, pleased. 'It will take us through some wonderful countryside. She won't have scenery like this at home, she'll be delighted. And as we have a few hours in York we can show her The Minster....'

We greeted each other with the awkward politeness engendered by absence, by a slight nervousness on Elodie's part induced by the unfamiliar surroundings and by my mounting unease that we could not offer her the sights that her family had organised for me. She was wearing, over her brown pullover, a necklace that I recognised as one of her mother's presents – a gaudy, bright gold-coloured chain with red stones.

It was a good hour before we were in my room and chatting away as unreservedly as we had in Marseille. Elodie gave the room her full inspection, going over to the desk that Dad had installed for my homework, complete with a reading lamp and bookshelf above it. She looked at the dressing table which Mum had chosen; a kidney shaped piece in walnut with three angled mirrors, a footstool covered in deep blue velvet and a pretty frilled royal blue valance reaching the floor.

'So, your parents?' I asked, after she had completed her visual tour. 'Have you seen them since their last visit? And how is Mamy?' I was eager for her news.

She came to sit beside me on my bed, her plump legs crossed like a contemplative Buddha.

'Mamy is just the same,' she told me gloomily. 'She has always the bad temper. And for my parents, I do not see them at all since they came to visit. For you, this is not the same, you have both parents, and I can see that they both love you very much, even though your father is ill.'

'Ill? What do you mean?' I asked sharply. 'He isn't ill. Mum told me he's got prostate, that's all. He'll be better soon, my mum said.'

She stared at me, looking surprised, before she said slowly, 'But – this thing you speak of, it is a cancer,' she went on. 'It is a serious problem for your father, many men die from this illness. Your mother, she does not tell you this?'

I was shocked to the core, and furious. 'That's not true!' I said vehemently. 'You're making it up, you're just teasing me...' I had a sudden vision of my father, who had lost a considerable amount of weight recently and looked far more haggard than usual, but I had not given it much serious thought until now. Like a slightly nagging tooth that is ignored until the pain forces you to do something about it, I supposed that I had had brief moments of growing unease, and I hated her at that moment for forcing me to confront the inevitable. 'I'm going to ask Mum. She'll tell me.' I wriggled off the bed and almost ran towards the door.

'Stephanie, no!' She caught up with me before I could leave and, catching hold of my hand, pulled me gently back to the bed. 'Please stay here. Really, I had no idea that your mother has not spoken of this to you. If she has not told you of the seriousness for your father, this will mean that she does not wish you to know. It will be better for her if you do not ask, this will give her only more problems. She wishes to protect you...'

She put a tentative arm around me, and said softly, 'This is not a good situation for you, but it will be worse if your mother thinks you will worry. You are lucky to have such a mother who wishes only for what is good for you...'

'Of course I'll worry, now,' I shouted. 'Why couldn't you just keep quiet about it?' I was close to tears now and trying hard to stop myself from rushing downstairs and confronting my mother.

She turned away, but cast furtive glances at me from time to time as if to gauge my feelings. 'It may not be as bad as I say at first,' she continued hesitantly. 'I think not all men will die from this. Your father may be lucky.'

I didn't answer, still being too unsure of my voice, and finally she said, 'At least you have both your parents living with you. Mamy has told me now, why I do not live with my parents.'

Sitting on the bed, but still half wanting to go and confront my mother immediately, I raised my eyebrows questioningly, aware that my expression was cold but a small part of me was interested. Was I going to hear the full story at last? When she saw that she had caught my interest, and to deflect my thoughts from my dad, she continued. 'It was when my mother met my father,' she said slowly. 'Before they were married, my mother discovered that she was pregnant with me. I think Mamy must have been very angry with her, because she told her that she would have to leave Marseille.'

'And did she?' I avoided looking at her and my voice was curt. I was still angry, but she carried on as if she hadn't noticed.

'Yes. She and my father went first to the north of France. I was born in Allonne, it is near to Beauvais. They lived with the parents of my father. I think they lived there for three years, and then we all went to Martinique. My father told me that he had a good job there, and he earned much money for all of us. He told me that we lived in a very beautiful house, but I have no memory of this. I became ill there. My father said that I was outside in the garden and the sun was hot and it burnt me. My mother said I cried every day and she did not know what to do. She took me to a doctor and he told her that he would find another person to look after me because my mother did not look after me properly. My father was very angry and he told my mother that he would not let another person look after me. He said that he would take me back to France, to Marseille, for Mamy and Papy to look after me. He said that at first Mamy said that she was too old and she did not want to, but he told her that if I stayed on Martinique, the doctor would tell the authorities to find another person to take care of me, or I could go into a home for children who have no-one to care for them. My father did not want this, so Mamy said that I could stay in Marseille with her and Papy.'

She stopped, and she brushed away angry tears.

At that time as a teenager, her story saddened me just a little, if only for the brief moment when I thought about it. Later, as an adult, it occurred to me to question the total randomness of birth. *Why* were some people born in the slums of third world countries, or with deformities of body or mind, or into hideous slavery, when others were born into countries where life was stable, and into lives of total ease and luxury? What or who decided that I would be born in the twentieth century, and others in the fifteenth? Was it relevant?

Did it matter? Was all human life, independent of initial circumstances of birth, made up of roughly equal parts of joy and misery? I thought not, but as I was wrong about most things, I was quite willing to believe that I was wrong about that too.

As she had so recently turned my thoughts, the only practical course of action at that particular moment was to try to deflect hers, and so I broached one of the subjects that we both had in common. I turned towards her.

'And what about Antoine?' I asked. 'Did you ever hear anything else about him? I know Charlotte left school but I haven't heard anything since.'

'Ah, yes, Antoine...' She stopped, confused. 'He is still at the *Lycée*, we have met several times. But, he does not want to pursue his studies for the bac. So he will leave the *Lycée* soon to become an apprentice, he wishes to study the electricity.'

She smiled to herself as if remembering, a secretive, almost triumphant smile which completely excluded me. 'He is very nice, we like each other very much,' she went on. 'In fact, I did not say in my letters but....' She sounded excited and I raised my eyebrows in anticipation. 'We have been out together, several times. Sometimes we go to his house and sometimes we join with his friends. Me, I prefer when we are by ourselves, this is better for us...'

'But Elodie,' I spluttered. 'He's the one who got Charlotte pregnant! You do *know* that, don't you? What sort of a boy gets a girl pregnant and then leaves her? Charlotte has had to leave school. From what I've heard, he doesn't want anything to do with her. Honestly, it's been the talk of the whole school since we got back from France. He's left her to have his baby on her own. What sort of louse does that make him? Surely you can't...'

'It was not he,' she affirmed stoutly. 'It is not his baby, it could have been another boy. He has told me everything. He did nothing with Charlotte....'

'What other boy?' I asked scornfully. 'Charlotte was Jeanne's penfriend, she was living in his house for three whole weeks, remember. She loved him, anyone could see that when we left Marseille. She was in tears, she was desperate to be leaving him – it must be his...'

'She is not a good girl, this Charlotte!' she interrupted vehemently. 'Mamy knows well the parents of Antoine. She says he is a good boy. She does not mind if he takes me out, she gives her permission. She invites him to my home and we talk together. Mamy does not object if I see him. She likes that he eats her food, he is polite with her, she likes that he admires me. She says that he is a clever boy and he will have a good and secure job one day. She has told this to me. And he will make much money...'

'And does she realise that he got one of our girls pregnant?' Suddenly my clannish impulse rose to the fore. Charlotte was no friend of mine, just the opposite in fact. I had never really managed to conceal my jealousy of her, but now she was in trouble and in my mind she became one of 'our girls', to be protected and defended as the need arose.

'She does not believe this, it is not a truthful story. He has told his parents it is not him, he is not the responsible one, and they know that Charlotte went out with Jeanne every evening. They stayed out until after midnight, she met other boys when she was in Marseille.'

I was doubtful. I could only think of Charlotte as I knew her at school. Attractive as she was, she naturally she made other girls jealous, but as far as I knew she wasn't the sort of girl to sleep around with boys whom she barely knew. I could think of some girls in my class who might – Lydia, for instance. But then Charlotte *was* pregnant, and she hadn't got that way by staying in the house all the time. Unless, of course, the boy was in the house with her all the time. To me, that sounded the most likely scenario.

I could see that this conversation was not going to end well. *Mamy likes that he eats her food....* That spoke volumes to me. Anyone who got through her gargantuan plates of food would have her approval, I could quite see that. Plus, she knew his parents. It was quite evident that she was eyeing up Antoine as a suitable match for Elodie. She would eventually have shared grandchildren with his parents, which would suit her admirably. All this was about what Mamy wanted, and as I well knew, what Mamy wanted, she invariably got. Elodie was playing into her hands as she had done all her life.

There were footsteps on the stairs and my bedroom door swung open to reveal my mother, her glossy brown hair freshly permed and wearing a smart navy dress with bands of cream lace at the edges of the sleeves and the hem.

'Are you two girls ready for lunch?' she asked brightly. I could hear the slight nervousness in her voice. She would be worrying herself sick over the food, I thought, and I just hoped that Elodie would appreciate the effort she had put in. I was beginning to have a little more empathy with her, now that Elodie had forced me to confront the seriousness of my father's illness.

'Come on, Elodie, we'll talk later,' I said, standing up and leading the way downstairs.

Lunch was hardly the success that my mother had hoped. Elodie barely touched her plate of lamb chops, which were accompanied by a festive touch of roast potatoes instead of mash, as well as the normal peas and carrots, which Mum had sliced in batons instead of chopping into rounds. She pushed away her half eaten plate and nodded her head decisively when my mother asked her if she had finished. She didn't even attempt the dessert of lemon meringue pie, which was made from the inevitable packet.

My mother's face tightened, and I felt a wave of annoyance towards Elodie, who wasn't showing the least appreciation. I looked at her small triangular face, now with a slightly sneering expression and her lips tightened in an obstinate thin line. So the food might not be up to Mamy's impossibly high standards, but she was behaving like a spoilt princess. It was lucky that Dad was not there. He would almost certainly be present at dinner and if she continued in this vein, I could imagine him utterly ditching any entente cordiale that was going and telling her to clear her plate and stop being a brat. His patience was severely compromised at the moment.

After the conversation with Elodie about my dad, I took to looking warily at Mum from time to time, trying to spot any signs of incipient sadness. After a few days of this if was plain that she had noticed and didn't care for it.

'Stephanie, have I developed adult acne or something? A red nose? Mascara running – what?'

'Nothing. Not a thing, I said hastily. And, as I was backing away, I said anxiously, 'Mum – look – if you're worried, you know – about Dad, I mean, would you say?'

As soon as I got the words out I realised their futility. If she *was* worried and wanted to keep it from me then of *course* she wouldn't say. To my surprise, she said, 'Look, Steph, sit down, will you? No, leave that,' as I clattered the dishes out of the dishwasher onto the worktop. 'That can wait.'

I left the dishes alone and sat at the table opposite her. She regarded me with the hint of a frown, as if judging whether to say anything, and if so, how much.

'First off, Steph, I *really* don't want you to worry about any of this. Let me do the worrying, alright?'

I was confused, and slightly panicky. 'So what's to worry *about?* You can tell me, you know.'

She hesitated, and then, resolutely, she said, 'The thing is, Steph, your dad has a type of cancer....' My eyes opened wide. So Elodie had been right after all. 'When I told you he'd got prostate, well, that's what it is, a cancer of the prostate....'

'And what's the prostate?'

'It's something that men have,' she said quickly. 'It's a gland near the – well, it's just a gland really, and it can get bigger when men get older. Women haven't got one...The point is, your dad's prostate has a cancer in it, but the hospital is monitoring him very carefully, and just now there's nothing at all to worry about...'

'So – you mean, there might be in the future?' I hazarded.

'It's not very likely. Not at all, in fact,' she said firmly. 'So, now I've told you everything, you can stop staring at me to see if I'm about to burst into tears, because I'm not. And your dad's going to be fine, so there's no need for you to worry about it at all.'

With that, she stood up and started putting the dishes away in the cupboards.

The coach tour began two days later, and as it progressed I grew increasingly irritated with Elodie's attitude. Her teenage strop manifested itself in all kinds of subtle ways. The countryside was flat, she said. There were no mountains like in Provence. She grudgingly acknowledged that the fields were very green, but added acidly, 'This is because you have no sunshine here, only rain.' To be fair, it was a grey day with a fine mist of drizzle blurring the view slightly. The coach was too cold for her, but she refused the extra cardigan my mother offered her. She loved the sumptuous Crown Hotel but the food was not like Mamy's.

'Really, you eat *jam* with meat?' she asked incredulously, when she was handed a pot of redcurrant jelly to accompany her slices of roast lamb.

'It's traditional British cuisine,' my mother interjected smoothly. 'Just like you have traditional French foods. Stephanie tells me you eat a particular fish soup...?' She left the question open-ended.

'Ah, yes, the *bouillabaisse*,' she agreed. 'But we do not eat something sweet with it...'

'For heaven's sake, Elodie, if you don't want it then pass it over to me,' I said impatiently. 'No-one's forcing you to eat it.' I was fast losing patience with her pickiness and general sulky attitude. I put it down to her unease at being in the UK, at being away from Mamy and having no-one to direct every passing moment of her life, but I was finding it increasingly hard to tolerate. She was a completely different person from the one I had known in Marseille. It was not simply a matter of her churlish behaviour that made me sharp, made me take more notice of what was happening all around me. I had a huge worry to avoid thinking about.

The tour was not, I felt, a complete disaster, but neither was it a resounding success. Once we were home, I thought things might improve but I was wrong.

After a quick supper of fish and chips, which Elodie actually said was very good before she flounced off to the lounge with a French magazine she had brought with her, I decided to help with the washing up. 'I don't know why she's being like this,' I said as I dried the underside of a casserole dish. 'She was never this bad in France...'

She looked across at me, concerned by my tone. 'I wouldn't worry about it, Steph. She's probably homesick. Don't forget all this is new to her. She won't be able to follow our conversations either, she must feel left out. And she isn't dressed like British girls either. That jumper she wears is frightful, the sleeves are too long for her, and it looks terrible with those plaid trousers she's wearing. I'd love to take her to Marshall and Snelgrove and find her something decent. But her grandmother might object, I suppose. And why on earth she wears that ghastly cheap necklace with it – it doesn't go with her outfit in the least....'

'Why d'you think it's cheap?' I asked curiously. 'She told me it was gold, and the stones are rubies...'

'Oh, come, now, Steph! Anyone with half an eye for jewellery can see that it's not real gold. And the stones are way too big to be real ones. The crown jewels don't have rubies that big. Either she's telling fibs, or she genuinely can't tell real from fake. In any case, it doesn't suit her in the least. Poor child, no wonder she's feeling lost.'

'And what about me?' I retorted indignantly. *'I* felt lost when we were in Marseille. I had no idea what anyone was talking about most of the time. It's no different!'

As she stacked the dried plates into the cupboard she looked over her shoulder at me, saying patiently, 'That's part of the whole experience. It's character-building – putting young people in a situation where they have to think for themselves – find ways of expressing themselves in unfamiliar surroundings. Both you and Elodie will be better for it.'

She may have been right, but whether either of us would become better people was definitely questionable.

Chapter 5
News

When we were young and at school Elodie and I wrote letters to each other. We each wrote in our own language and as the years passed, each of us became a little more fluent. Later on the letters had morphed into emails, and today's communication, when it happens, is via Facebook and Instagram. Her address is written down in my address book but I use it only at Christmas when we exchange cards. We are on each others 'friends' list, although our friendship has now degenerated into the spurious friendship of the internet. There are no more secrets to discuss, no more giggling together, no more shared excursions. The only attention we ever pay each other is to 'like' a post, which is rather sad.

Many of the letters and emails from the earlier years have been lost. I have tried to reproduce them, based on my rather hazy memories of what passed between us in those days.

Dear Stephanie,

I have some very good news to say to you! I am very excited because I will go to live with my parents! My mother has said to Mamy that she wishes that I spend several weeks with them. I will go at the beginning of the next holidays and I will stay for three weeks. I hope that my parents will like it when I am with them. I know that I will like to be near them too. My mother says to me that she will still work in the parfumerie, but I will be able to help her. I will love to work with her and I am sure I will love to work with the perfumes.

How does it go for you with John? I hope you are happy with him as I am with Antoine. Also, I have the results of my bac! I am so happy because I have a good mark and this means that I can go to the university. Many of my friends have succeeded in the bac too, but Antoine was not concerned with the bac as he had already decided to do his BEP in the électrotechnique because this is interesting for him. I am still with him, we did not go out together during my bac but now we can be together much more. He takes me to the nightclub in Malpassé. Mamy says I can go there but she tells Papy to come to meet me to take me home. This is not a good situation for me, I have eighteen years now! Please give my love to your parents, I liked them very much when I was with them. Please tell me, how is your father with his illness? You are very lucky. You have spoken about John in your emails, are you still with him? I am looking forward to receiving your news.

Love, Elodie

This puzzled me a little, since she had shown no sign whatsoever of liking my parents when she was with us. And why should she think I was lucky? They were just my parents after all.

Dear Elodie,

How great that you have passed your bac! I always knew that you would. You will have a fantastic time when you get to university. My father is not very well unfortunately, he is very thin now and he has stopped working at the bank. He says he has pain in his back so he spends a lot of time resting at home. I worry about him and I know that it is difficult for my mother but she tries to stay cheerful. Sometimes I wish that she would tell me how she feels but she never does, I think she is afraid that I will worry about him. About John, yes we are still together, he is very good for me, he never gets into a panic like I do! I have met his parents too, we went to their house last week. He was really quiet all evening, and he told me later that he had never taken a girl home before! Do you think this is a good sign?

Love, Stephanie

I had only briefly mentioned John to Elodie, mostly from a desire to hide my own, growing love from a potentially hostile world, and most certainly from the probing questions that I knew Mum would ask. Personally, I didn't care that he was a trainee quantity surveyor and not a hedge fund manager or a consultant in some prestigious hospital, but I knew that his modest ambitions would not spark any interest with her. He was the son of Claire, of the bridge group, and I met him each time he arrived to pick up his mother from a card party. He would arrive early, long before the party had finished, and we waited in the dining room until the last game was over. We spent many hours together. Hours that convinced me that I wanted him so much that I was afraid to admit, even to myself, that my life would be empty without him. He was serene where I was liable to wild mood swings; calm and rational in the face of my impetuous decisions which were mostly based on my instincts at the time. He was intelligent, and this, to me, was hard to come to terms with, but deep down I knew his mind to be superior to my own. It wasn't his appearance that had attracted me to him. To be frank, he was not an immediately attractive man, being ungainly in movement, with a long loping walk, and slightly hunched shoulders. His redeeming features were his hair, which was a smooth glossy nut-brown and his large, deep set eyes which often sparkled with good humour. He had a set of the bushiest eyebrows I had ever seen, which could lift readily to point out added meaning to his often pithy statements. But whatever the state of his outward appearance, of the intellect of his mind, I knew that for me there would be no-one else in my life to match him.

I heard nothing more from Elodie for several months, before the next letter arrived.

Dear Stephanie,

Please, tell me what I can do. My period is late!! Sometimes it comes one day late, or even two, but now it has been one week and I do not know what I can do. I keep hoping and hoping that it will come but it does not. I cannot tell anyone about this. My mother would not be of any use to me, and Papy would not understand. I do not dare to say anything to Mamy because she would be very angry with me. You know how she is. Please, is there a solution? Perhaps you will know something. Please email me very soon.

Love from Elodie

This was totally unexpected, and I had no practical answer to give her but I tried my best. At least I answered her, a couple of minutes after I had received hers and posted it the same day.

Dear Elodie,

Listen, you have to stop panicking! I know you must be very worried, but sometimes there are false alarms. It might not be as bad as you think. Wait a few more days, and your period might come. Sometimes mine can be up to a week after I expect it. (But please tell me, could it be possible, with Antoine?)

Love from Stephanie.

First of all, I was exaggerating when I said that my period was sometimes a week late. Two days was my normal variation, and even that hadn't happened very often. But with my usual avoidance of unpleasantness, I was trying to be reassuring, whilst at the same time with the near certainty that she must be pregnant. It also occurred to me that I was the last person qualified to advise Elodie on the necessity of avoiding panic. If I had been in the same situation my world would have been spinning. I'd have bitten the heads off anyone who addressed a single word to me. But then, advice is easy to give.

Dear Stephanie,

My period never came. I have told Mamy. I thought she was going to kill me, she was so angry! And then she started crying; oh, she cried so much! She says she has been a bad mother and now she is a bad grandmother to me, and that she had not brought me up to be a good girl, and that Antoine would have to marry me. She is frightened of what her friends will say about me, and she is afraid that they will all blame her. She has been to see the parents of Antoine. They were together for one whole evening. Papy went with her but she said that I must stay at home. It is true, it is with Antoine that I am pregnant. In one way I am very sad, but in another way I am happy that I will have his baby. Mamy has told my mother that I am pregnant. My mother has told her that it is not her business and that I was never a good daughter. This makes me very sad. I would have been a good daughter to her if she had ever been with me in my life, but she was never there, it was always just Mamy and Papy.

Love, Elodie

Dear Elodie,

It seems to me that you have to accept the situation. I think it is such a shame that you will have to leave University. Mamy must be sad about this too. I don't suppose you would consider a termination? In the UK this would be an option, but I am not sure about the laws on this in France. Have you spoken to Antoine about it?

Love, Stephanie

Dear Stephanie,

I cannot believe that you are advising me to kill my own baby! I would never do such a thing. Not for one minute did I think of this. I have not spoken of this to Antoine as I know what he would say. He would definitely not wish this. He thinks as I do, that if a baby is started, no-one should kill it. So, we have decided that we will marry as soon as we can. He has bought me such a beautiful ring, it is three emeralds with diamonds. We think the wedding can be in August when I will be on holiday. We will invite only a few friends because of the cost. Antoine's parents tell us that they will pay for a small party afterwards.

You said that I will have to leave the University, but this is not true. I will stay at home until the baby is born, and then after, Mamy and Papy will look after it for me and I will go back to the university until I have my licence, and then I will have a job as an English teacher. Mamy says this is the best solution for everyone as Antoine does not yet earn very much money. He would like to set up a company of his own but he cannot do this until some years have passed. He likes working for Monsieur Coste though, even if his salary is not very good. He says he is very happy that I will have his baby and he hopes it will be a boy. After we marry his parents will give him money so that we can rent an apartment, close to his parents. It will be in Allonne which is in the north of France. Mamy and Papy say they would prefer if we were closer to them, but they have little money to spare for the rent of an apartment.

It is only two months now, but I am being sick every day and this is horrible. I cannot leave the house. I have visited the doctor many times but he says that it is a part of being pregnant and that it will pass if I am patient. But I do not wish to be so patient! I wish for something to stop me from being sick every day. Do you know if there is something that I can do? Please tell me if you know anything that will help me.

Love from Elodie

'I don't know why you still write to her,' my mother said, exasperated, as she put my dad's soup on a tray preparatory to taking it up to their bedroom where he was resting, as he had been for the last few days. 'She's just using you as a sounding board. She's not a friend, she's an encumbrance. Anyone would think you were her mother, the way she leans on you. And another thing, what's preventing her from looking after the baby herself? Why let her grandparents do it? They must both be well into their seventies now, they're hardly of an age to cope with a baby.'

'Oh, please, Mum, she's not that bad. I'm pretty sure the arrangements for the baby are only until she graduates and finds a job, it's not forever. In any case, we were good friends, once.'

'That was years ago. And what did she ever do for you? You really need to move on. And if you were such good friends, where's the invitation to her wedding? Why you need her in your life now?'

'She invited me to go on holiday with her, didn't she?' I said defensively.

'Yes, but only so that she could practise her English with you, and even that was probably her grandmother's idea. Seriously, Steph, let her go. Some people will just feed off you and never give anything back. Honestly, I wouldn't have let you go to France if I'd known you were going to get mixed up in all this....'

'I'm not *mixed up* in it!' I flared. 'It's not *me* who's pregnant! She's only telling me what's happened, that's all.'

Mum looked crestfallen, and I immediately regretted my outburst. 'I think it's more that she needs me in her life,' I said hastily, trying to make amends but not, in fact, succeeding. 'Just think about it. Who else has she got? Her mother's got no time for her, Mamy bullies her. It's only Papy who really loves her, and what does an old man understand about a teenage girl?'

'He'll know even less about babies, you can be sure of that,' she said testily. 'It's quite ridiculous of Elodie to expect people of their age to cope with a baby while she takes herself back to university. Extremely selfish of her, if you ask me. History seems to be repeating itself as far as she's concerned. If she was as unhappy with her grandparents as you say, then she's hardly doing the best for her child in handing it over to them, is she? It seems as if all she's thinking about is herself and the baby will have to fit in with it, the poor child.' With that, she added a spoon to the tray and set off upstairs.

I didn't hear from Elodie for months afterwards. I tried my best to forget about it, supposing that she had been offended by my suggestion of terminating the pregnancy, or my assumption that she would abandon her studies. I honestly couldn't place myself in her situation and imagine myself having to make that decision. I would probably have agonised over it for months until it was too late to do anything about it. I could see that Elodie, living in a Catholic country as she did, might take umbrage at such a suggestion, but I had given her my opinion and I wasn't about to either take it back or defend it. That was what I thought and I had said so. Whether she was offended or not, she remained silent for many months afterwards and I couldn't bring myself to contact her. If that was the way she wanted, then it was fine by me. This is what I told myself, but inside, in the inner recesses of my mind where I refused to look, I was hurt. I was bitterly disappointed that our friendship could end like this. Since there was nothing that I could do to help her in a practical sense, I did my best to close my mind to it and got on with my own life.

Chapter 6
The Apartment

'Stephanie! Come here a minute, will you?' The voice was urgent and I hurriedly closed the bridal magazine which had absorbed most of my attention since John and I had fixed the date of our wedding.

Mum was in the dining room, picking up and discarding several squares of white satin and brocade rectangles and laying the chosen ones out in neat squares on the table. 'Oh, there you are. Now then, which one are we having, do you think? Personally, this cream brocade is my favourite, but I wanted to know what you thought before we go ahead with the order.'

If things had been normal I would have told her brusquely to back off and let me decide on my wedding dress myself. I wasn't fourteen any more and I was well able to make decisions on my own. But things were far from normal and I had to bite down hard on my lower lip to stop myself from shrieking at her.

I made a half-hearted attempt, which I knew would be futile even as I said it. 'But Mum, I thought we'd decided already. I really don't want a dress making specially. There are plenty of them in the shops. Look, why don't we go together to Leeds and I'll show you the ones I like?'

'A bought dress? From a *shop*? Are you crazy Steph? Really, let's do the thing properly and have you looking your very best. This brocade is my favourite. It will suit you, and we'll have it made by the best dressmaker we can find. I've already been asking around.' She turned towards me and reached out for my hand. 'Steph, this day has to be perfect for you. If he were here, your father would want you to....'

'I know, Mum,' I muttered wretchedly. I didn't need it put into words. The grief of my father's death nine months ago was still an aching, raw wound that hadn't even begun to heal, especially for her. In her own blunt way, Elodie had prepared me for the possibility, and now that I had half forgiven her, I could even be grateful to her for preparing the ground for what would definitely have come as even more of a shock than the event engendered.

'Alright then,' I conceded. 'I'll have the cream brocade and we can decide on the style of it together.'

She hugged me, with eyes bright from unshed tears, and I was guardedly pleased that I had made the effort.

Ostensibly as a pair, but with Mum taking up her familiar role of organiser, we decided on the venue, the flowers, the bridesmaids, and the catering, with Mum choosing each course. The wedding was so important to her and I agreed to her choices time and time again, knowing that keeping herself busy was the most effective antidote she knew against a loss that had all but destroyed her.

I married John in the autumn of 1974 and Elodie was not on the guest list.

We had two girls in three years. Pamela came first in December 1976 and sixteen months later Janice joined her and I was as busy as a mother with two babies always is. The arrival of the two new lives helped to grow a thin, fragile piece of skin over the gaping hole that constituted Mum's mental injury, although it was a hollow underneath which would never heal over completely. I wouldn't say that I completely forgot about Elodie, just that I was far too embroiled in my own life to give her much thought.

The years passed with no communication, and the girls grew up. Pamela eventually became a breastfeeding consultant, and Janice worked for a prestigious accounting firm in Leeds. Both of them had long standing partners and busy lives. After many holidays in the various regions of France John and I had thought for many years about moving there. He loved it as much as I did, and our finances were robust enough to allow us to buy a house outright, leaving us mortgage free. We both thought the time was right to realise our dream and begin a new life in France. I sent Elodie a quick email, letting her know of our decision, just in case she might still be interested. I didn't really expect any reply, and none was forthcoming.

We decided to take things very slowly and buy an apartment first. We could always let it out, use it for holidays and find out if we really liked the region before committing to a life there. A coastal apartment in the Languedoc region appealed to us. Why didn't we settle on Provence as our destination? It was the region I knew best after all, even though it had been years since I had heard from Elodie. Provence was our first choice until further research and a bank balance reality check showed that property in the Languedoc was half the price. The Languedoc won. Easily. It looked enchantingly beautiful, with historic hilltop villages set against the sombre backdrop of the Montagne Noire, wide meandering rivers and seemingly endless vineyards.

The Mediterranean beaches would be in easy reach of anywhere we chose to live, and we were looking for somewhere not too far from Carcassonne airport.

At that time, the airport was nothing like it is today. Our first flight confirmed that it appeared to be a one-man operation. The plane was guided to its final parking spot by a bloke waving his bats around, and then he slung his bats somewhere and started unloading the baggage onto a trailer, which he then drove to the terminal building before flinging them onto a small conveyor belt. When we arrived at security, he popped up again behind a small window, this time with a severe expression and a peaked cap, ready to check our passports. We assumed that when he had finished, he would change out of his uniform, start cleaning up the plane and refuel it himself before he guided it back out again on its return journey.

We had booked a hire car and looked vaguely around for some sort of desk. There wasn't one, so we looked for someone to ask. There was only one person available and he was still in his official guise examining passports. We waited patiently for him to finish and then enquired about our car. He directed us to a small building next to the terminal. If it didn't resemble a car hire office, there was one good reason for that. It was a garage. There was one car up on a ramp with a man's legs poking out from underneath it. Seeing no-one else to ask, we politely coughed to attract his attention. He wriggled out from underneath the car, his bright blue overalls streaked with oil.

'*Voiture*?' I asked hesitatingly.

He was clearly a man who was more at ease with cars than with humans. He flapped his arms at us, effectively shooing us out of his garage, before lowering the ramp and backing the car out onto the forecourt, missing our luggage by a couple of centimetres. He got out of the car and thrust the keys at John. '*Voiture*,' he replied shortly.

Today if you hire a car at Carcassonne airport you go into a separate building, you fill in a lot of forms, pay a hefty deposit and after a lengthy car inspection you are handed the keys. Life used to be so much simpler.

As we were both working full time, myself as a teacher and John as a quantity surveyor, we were short on time. So short in fact that we decided to go and look for an apartment one weekend in February. On Friday we flew out, on Saturday we made an offer on a first floor apartment in St. Pierre la Mer, checked out of our Novotel on Sunday morning and were back at work on Monday.

The apartment came ready furnished but not equipped, so we consecrated the whole of the Easter holidays to getting it ready for the summer's peak letting season. I had a long, long list of needed equipment.

A week later and the apartment was complete. We spent the rest of the holiday getting to know St. Pierre and the neighbouring Narbonne Plage. Each time we set off, our downstairs neighbour leaned on his gate and said a friendly *'Bonjour.'* His name was Jacques and he knew everyone and everything that went on in the resort. Unusually for a block of holiday apartments he lived there all year round. By the end of our visit he had told us which restaurant was the best, where to do our shopping, the name of the plumber he used and every detail of his grandson's life. He was proud of his small garden, which was a home for his battered bicycle and which was planted up with bright ranunculus and sea lavender.

On our return to the UK were ready to let the apartment out to visitors. Fortunately the estate agent who sold it to us was a letting agent too, and so we passed all the arrangements over to him. He would take care of everything for us, from welcoming the guests, collecting our rent, to cleaning and replacing any necessities. We would have nothing to do until the end of the year when he would present us with a list of the clients who had rented and the money he had collected from them minus his own 25%. It was all going to be so simple.

And so it proved to be, until the first problem arose. We were comfortably at home watching T.V. when the phone rang. The voice on the other end sounded distraught.

'Is that Stephanie?'

I was cautious. So many calls turned out to be scams these days.

'Who is this, please?'

'My name's Jane. Jane Fisher. We haven't met, but I'm supposed to be renting your apartment this week. Your agent gave us your name and phone number.'

'Oh, I see. And what can I do for you?'

'We're here,' she said urgently. 'We've arrived in St. Pierre but the agency is closed! We can't get the key to your apartment. What shall we do?'

I could picture the scene. A couple phoning from their car, in the dark, for it was now half past ten in the evening, both of them highly agitated at the prospect of no accommodation. What on earth could we do from the UK?

I panicked. And when I panic I do the job properly. I do it wholeheartedly. I put my soul into it. My mother was the same. There is no half hearted panicking on my side of the family. I tremble. My whole body freezes. My heart goes into overdrive and my adrenaline goes off the scale.

'Just a moment please,' I heard myself squeaking. I gently put the receiver down and tiptoed into the lounge to find John. Why I tiptoed I really don't know. Nor do I know why I whispered when I got there. It wasn't as if she could hear me or see me, but my body said otherwise. My panicking body told me that she could hear and see everything I said and did.

'John!' I whispered. 'They've arrived and they can't get in.'

Did I mention that I am also completely incoherent when I panic?

John was understandably confused.

'Who can't get in? Is it one of the girls?'

'No,' I squeaked. 'It's the apartment. They've arrived and they haven't got a key. John, what on earth can we do?'

What did she expect? We had a set of keys ourselves but no way of getting them to her. I briefly gave it my best shot: Hire a jet. Send a racing pigeon with a bunch of keys strapped to its leg. Put them in an envelope marked 'please deliver within the next ten minutes.' None of those ideas seemed entirely plausible.

John himself is not given to panicking like I am. If he does panic, he panics very calmly and rationally, with a quiet reflection that a master of yoga would envy. He does it so quietly that it barely qualifies for the word. He is also extremely practical.

He looked at his watch. 'It's getting on for half past ten,' he said in surprise. 'What are they doing at this time? The agency shuts at seven doesn't it?'

'She's still on the phone!' I whispered. 'What can I say?'

'Steph, you don't need to whisper,' he said reasonably. 'She's nearly a thousand miles away. She can't hear you.'

'I know,' I whispered back. 'John, we have to do something. We can't leave them standing there in the dark. It might be raining for all we know.'

He was pragmatic as always. 'They'll be in a car. They won't be in the rain either. It never rains in August. Tell them to book into a hotel and go to the agency in the morning.'

Of course! Why didn't I think of that. Relief flooding through my body, I picked up the receiver again.

'You are late, you know,' I said with a touch of reproof. 'Didn't the agency tell you they closed at seven?'

'We couldn't help it,' she said. 'We had a flat tyre on the way down. It took us ages to get it fixed.'

'Well, there's not much you can do at this time of night. You'll have to find a hotel and then go back to the agency in the morning. They open at....'

'We've *been* to the hotel, they're full,' she wailed. 'And there isn't another. We'd have to drive for miles to find one.'

A second, male voice took over, a steadier one this time, more determined and serious.

'Now, listen,' he said. 'We've paid to rent your apartment for a week. There's no way we're going to drive for miles and pay for a hotel. It's your responsibility to get the keys for us.'

'The agency told you how to get the keys. It's not their fault if you didn't turn up on time,' I retorted. 'Yes, I know your wife said you'd had a flat tyre, but did you think of phoning the agency to tell them?'

'We don't speak French well enough to explain a flat tyre,' he said shortly. 'Now, how do you suggest we get into your apartment tonight?'

'Just a minute, please,' I squeaked, as I gently placed the receiver on the seat and tiptoed to the lounge to find John.

'Have you told them to go to a hotel for the night?'

'They've tried that already. The hotel's full. And he's bleating on saying it's our responsibility. John, what do we do?'

John now started showing signs of panic. It was evident in the way he slowly reached for the remote control and lowered the sound on the TV. Soon he would be sufficiently panicked to turn it off altogether.

He considered carefully, and then said, 'Why don't we phone Jacques? He'll know where the agent lives and they can maybe find his house and ask him to get the key for them.'

Jacques! He could be the answer to all this sorry mess. If anyone could help us, he was the man.

I crept back to the hallway. 'Can I phone you back in a moment?' I asked.

The wife had taken over again. 'No!' she shrieked. 'You won't ring me back! You're just going to leave us....'

'No, I will ring you back, I promise. It's just I have to ring someone first...'

Not being able to cope with much more, I gently replaced the receiver, before I furiously leafed through the address book at the side of the phone.

Jacques... Jacques. Hurrah, his number was there and I dialled rapidly. I was certain that he would be in. He never went out in the evenings. To my relief he answered almost immediately.

I explained as best I could. Some clients of ours were outside the agency and it was closed.

'Bien sur,' Jacques murmured. 'C'est la nuit.'

So, as it is night, we thought you might know where to find Monsieur Lecroix.' I paused. Do you have his address?'

'But today is Saturday,' he replied prosaically. 'He won't be at home. On Saturday at this hour he will be in the restaurant with his wife. He will have taken the key with him. You know, the one by the marina?'

Of course. Everyone's habits were personally known to Jacques. I just hoped he was right.

I thanked him and prepared to dial again.

'Jane? It's Stephanie here. You need to find the Restaurant de la Mer, it's by the marina. Go in there and ask for Monsieur Lecroix. He should have the key.'

'Really? We know where that is, we passed it on our way in. Thank you,' she said, and the conversation ended.

Half an hour later the phone rang again. My panic levels rose and I tentatively picked the phone up.

It was Jane. 'He was just where you said, in the restaurant!' she said in surprise. 'And he did have the key. Thank you so much, we didn't know what to do!'

'No problem,' I lied. It had very nearly turned out to be a huge problem, but thank God for Jacques, I thought.

Chapter 7
Renting

We rented the apartment out via the agency for the next year, until we decided that we were ready to make the move ourselves. Both the girls had busy lives with their respective careers, and Mum had sadly passed away from a sudden heart attack three years earlier. I missed her acutely and had to stop myself from giving icily dismissive replies to anyone who said sympathetically that it was a release for her, as she had found life so tough after she lost my father.

It took us a good nine months to sort out our affairs in the UK. We finally sold our house to the couple from hell who came back for third, fourth and even fifth visits, each time bringing their ungovernable five-year-old son who raced around creating havoc, whilst his mother remonstrated with him, doubtless filling the child with unspeakable terror.

'Mummy would really appreciate it if you didn't jump on the nice lady's beds, darling.'

'Mummy would love it if you stopped picking the nice lady's flowers.'

'Mummy would be so pleased if you didn't take things out of the nice lady's cupboards, sweetie.'

The nice lady was ready to belt him one round the ear and nothing but a fear of jeopardising the house sale made me desist. I sometimes wondered what the child would be like as a teenager.

'Mummy would really appreciate it if you stopped throwing bricks through the neighbours' windows, sweetie....'

We decided to make a leisurely drive from our home in the UK.

We had prepared incredibly well for France. We set off on 6th March, a Friday. The previous year we had bought a French car, a small Citroën, on the basis that it would make the transition easier if we got used to the car before we were confronted with a left-hand drive and the French road system at the same time. On the way to our apartment I thought smugly of all those people who foolishly made the leap into the unknown without due diligence, with no idea of French life, of the tax system, of the healthcare, the jobs market, the insurance... I had a mental jolt and looked across at John.

'John, you know when we insured the car in Narbonne?' I began.

'Steph, I'm driving,' he said tersely.

When he is driving, John is the kind of person who answers any communication with gestures such as a shrug, or raised eyebrows, or a grunt that has to be interpreted as either a 'tell me a bit more' grunt or a 'stop bugging me' grunt. He is not the kind of person who can drive and chat at the same time. His hands grip the steering wheel tightly and his face has a look of great concentration. He definitely doesn't like being interrupted, so that our journeys are all completed in near silence. But I felt this was important so I persisted.

'Yes I *know* you're driving,' I retorted. 'I'm sitting in the car with you aren't I? But we need to talk.'

'I can't talk when I'm driving. Can't it wait?'

'No. Pull over somewhere.'

'We're on a motorway,' he said urgently. 'I can't just stop.'

'Well, wait until we get to an *Aire* then, and park up.'

'I want to get there before it starts getting dark. You know I hate driving in the dark.'

'It's not going to take long but we need to look at the car insurance. Look, there's a sign, *Aire de Laurageais* 5 kilometres. Pull in there will you and I can check the certificate.'

Very reluctantly, to make up for any future time wasting, he speeded up until we arrived at the *Aire*. All French motorways have them. They are convenient roadside stopping areas funded by the tolls. Some are large enough to warrant a bridge over the motorway and their own petrol station, cafe and shop, whilst others are no more than a rest place for weary truck drivers. This was one of the larger ones on the Canal du Midi. It had a restaurant and I would have loved a coffee and a hot meal, but John was adamant; time was running out. We parked at the end of a series of long bays each containing a lorry and its driver. Some were smoking, some were eating but mostly they were asleep.

John was resigned by now. He leaned back and laid his head against his head rest. 'Right, we're here. Now, what about the insurance?'

'Let's have a look at the certificate.' John slid his seat forward and found the paper. He smoothed it out on his knees. 'Oh,' he said, after rapidly scanning its contents. It was only one word, but it was the kind of 'oh' that meant that he knew that something was very wrong. The insurance ran out on Friday March 6th at midnight.

'Why didn't you check it before we set off?'

'Why didn't *I* check it? Why me? You could have checked it yourself.' I was very irritated by his assumption that the insurance was my responsibility.

'Alright, alright. *We* should have checked it then,' he admitted.

'So what are we going to do?' I asked flatly.

'There's only one thing we can do,' he said. 'We have to get there before midnight of course.'

'Can we do it, do you think?' I asked apprehensively. Driving without insurance was the last thing we wanted to do.

'Oh, yes. We're not too far off now. Three hours at the most and it's only two o' clock. I wanted to get there before dark in any case.' He sounded confident and I was slightly relieved.

'Well, take it steady then. Don't be driving like a maniac just to get us there.'

Resignedly, he started up the engine and we were on our way again. Cinderella couldn't have been more anxious than we were. We had to get to the apartment before midnight.

As he had said, we really had plenty of time and it was around five o'clock when we arrived.

It was still light, and the apartment was exactly as we remembered it. A small fitted kitchenette, a lounge area with a sofa bed, a round wooden dining table and four chairs, a large bathroom tiled in beige, and a double bedroom.

The insurance company was in Narbonne, an easy thirty-minute drive away. That is, for those people who were driving an insured vehicle, which we weren't.

'We can go tomorrow,' John said, and at that I protested.

'We are *not* driving uninsured!' I stated very firmly. 'The one day we do that will be the day we run someone over and kill them and I am not going to start our life here with you in a French prison for manslaughter.'

He saw that I was serious and capitulated. 'Oh, alright, have it your own way. We'll go first thing Monday morning then. There's a bus stop on the main road. There's bound to be a bus for Narbonne.'

Monday morning arrived and we were up bright and early, clutching the insurance papers and very eager to get into Narbonne and sort everything out.

We arrived at the bus stop and consulted the timetable. We rubbed our eyes and blinked and we looked again. We ran our fingers up and down the rows and columns of figures. We shook our heads in disbelief. It had to be a mistake. Finally John spoke very slowly.

'Steph, it's true. It really is. The next bus is Wednesday.'

Sadly, we made our way back to the apartment.

On Wednesday morning we set out for the bus stop again, even more anxious this time. Would a bus actually turn up or was the timetable a blatant lie and there were no buses at all? Thankfully a packed single decker arrived only two minutes after the official hour and we prepared to set our affairs in the order they ought to have been.

The few empty seats were soon filled. At one stop a gang of teenage boys boarded. They were great hulks of lads; tattooed skinheads boasting metal objects inserted into various orifices of their bodies where metal objects were never meant to go. John and I looked at each other nervously, both of us wondering the same thing. Would we get off this bus alive? Would they start a fight maybe? Start swearing and singing and insulting people with loud guffaws of laughter? Brandish long knives and start stabbing the passengers?

Our British attitudes had surfaced yet again. The boys found seats, sat down quietly and conversed discreetly with each other. When we reached Narbonne they got up and politely ushered all female passengers in front of them before descending the steps themselves after courteously thanking the driver for a good journey.

We knew roughly where the insurance office was located even though we hadn't visited for a year, and as we were in plenty of time before the long lunchtime break, we were optimistic that we would sort out the papers in record time.

We pushed open the heavy glass door and looked around in bewilderment. There were two desks, each occupied by a woman clerk. Filing cabinets were ranged all across the long wall behind them, with photocopiers, telephones and office paraphernalia all clearly in view.

But that wasn't all. The office resembled a crèche. In front of one of the desks was a wooden train set, complete with toy houses and a metal train being pushed along the track by a child in dungarees. In one corner a little girl had ranged her dolls in a precise row and was dressing and undressing them in turn. Another boy screeched past us on his toy pedal car, narrowly missing driving over John's foot. One of the women clerks, the only one not occupied by the children, looked up at us with a professional smile, showing teeth of an unnatural whiteness.

'Can I help you?'

It was then that she noticed our air of bewilderment. We weren't at all sure that we had found the right place.

'It is Wednesday,' she informed us brightly, as if this information would clarify everything for us.

Suddenly it dawned on me. Of course! French schools closed on Wednesdays. The children had been brought to work as there was no alternative provision for them. Briefly, I pondered such an occurrence in the UK – minors racing around behind bank counters, clients tripping over toys in solicitors' offices, youngsters shouting down tannoy systems at railway stations. It was an unnerving train of thought and I turned my attention back to our insurance documents.

A few rubber stamps and signatures later, all was satisfactorily sorted and we left clutching the valid document, vowing never to do any business in France on Wednesdays.

Chapter 8
House Hunting

House hunting in France is exhausting, demoralising and can easily involve hundreds of miles of fruitless searching for houses that have been long since demolished, have no proper address and appear on no maps. And that's only for the estate agents. Once you add ill-prepared English clients into the mix, you have a certain inducement for taking early retirement, with or without a pension. The hopeful clients speak limited French, they have no idea of what they are actually looking for and they expect to be driven around for hours, looking at totally unsuitable properties and then they demand to know what else you have on your books.

We were those English clients. Our wish list was enough to send the local estate agents demented. In fact, word may have got around, as a suspicious number of estate agents seemed to be 'just closing' as we approached the door. We had visions of desks being suddenly cleared, files set on fire and the unlucky agent sneaking out of the back door.

It seemed simple enough to us. We wanted a house in the country, but near enough to a large town to satisfy all our shopping and restaurant needs. It was imperative that we were close to the seaside, but equally, a mountain view really ought to be on the agenda. We needed a garden large enough to grow fruit, vegetables and flowers, but small enough to be easily manageable. And it would need to have a watering system already in place. A pool would be ideal too, but wasn't essential as long as there was plenty of space to install one.

Amidst all the confusion about what we really wanted, we were clear on one thing at least. The house had to be ready to move into. We were down to earth, canny Yorkshire people, and never going to be the types to fall in love with an isolated derelict barn and transform it magically into our dream property. So our list was quite reasonable, we thought, and surely most estate agents would have files full of desirable houses.

Not so. The basic problem with 'ready to move into' was that some people were prepared to move into a property as long as it had external walls and some semblance of a roof on top of it. We were shown around lots of those.

We saw one house which looked fine, it had everything we wanted, except that it was a village house with a flight of stairs which would have taxed the stamina of an experienced Everest mountaineer. When we finally made it to the top floor, we peered into its gloomy depths and could just make out, at the furthest end, an extremely large and bulky cart which was propped against a wall. Happily the horse which went with it was not in evidence.

It turned out to be the house of a *vigneron*, or wine grower, as most of them were, and he had decamped leaving his cart behind him, to be inherited by the next lucky owner of the property.

We climbed dispiritedly downstairs.

Another house was, on paper, everything we had ever dreamed of. Four bedrooms so as to have lots of room for family and friends, and a large garden for John, who was fond of cooking and was desperate to have his own vegetable plot where he would grow all kinds of exotic vegetables unavailable to us whilst living in the UK.

The owner took us around his garden first, which was impressively neat and well tended, with rows of vegetables visible from a distance. We were thrilled with it, and as if to seal a bargain, he picked two large smooth skinned orange fruits from a tree, one for each of us and waited for the approval which would surely come. We had never come across them before and we bit into them doubtfully. They tasted of slightly bitter marmalade. The owner told us they were kaki, which we later identified as sharon fruit. We beamed our approval and he nodded and grinned with us. Evidently the visit was destined to be a great success. He led us reluctantly away from the garden and into the house.

It all fell apart the minute we entered the door. The four bedrooms were there all right, but the owner had forgotten to mention that he had tacked three of the bedrooms on all by himself, to accommodate his increasing family. The three patched on rooms had corrugated tin roofs and were noticeably tilting at an angle to the main house. They did at least have windows in them, if a hole in the wall without glass can actually be classed as a window. We didn't think it could, so we reluctantly voiced our concerns to the estate agent. The owner looked disappointed but somewhat resigned, as if he had been through this whole scenario many times before, as indeed he probably had. Sadly, we left, but not before we had been plied with more sharon fruit, several choice lettuces, some very large and dirty bunches of carrots and a bag of artichokes. Looking as if we had just raided a rather large greengrocer's, we returned to our flat and consoled ourselves by cooking enough vegetable soup to see us through the year.

When we were sick of soup we ate out in the fish restaurant close to our flat in St. Pierre la Mer. We could see immediately why Monsieur Lecroix made it a weekly treat. The food was way beyond sumptuous, and its proprietor was a testament to the excellence of the cuisine. She was a colossal mountain of wobbly flesh as wide as she was tall, and she wheezed mightily as she wended her slow way from one packed table to another, taking orders. Her son did the cooking, using double cream as his main ingredient in every dish, and she supervised her clients. She treated everyone as if they were recalcitrant children, making sure that every succulent morsel was being eaten. If you left anything on your plate she would glare at you balefully before snatching it up with an audible sniff and banging it down in the adjoining kitchen with a resounding slam that was audible throughout the whole restaurant. You either accepted this treatment or you left. Most people accepted it as the price they had to pay for eating what seemed to us to be the best food in France.

We suspected after a few visits that it may have been a performance, carefully honed to create a caricature of herself in the area. If so then she really needn't have bothered. The food spoke for itself.

My particular favourite dish was a filet of dorade which was accompanied by a herb and cream sauce. It came with small, perfectly cooked potatoes that gleamed with a golden butter glaze and vegetables so fresh they might have been picked a few minutes before they landed on the plate. John invariably plumped for the *bouillabaisse* which he said was delicious. The minute he offered me a spoonful and I tasted it, I was transported right back to Marseille. It came up to, and dare I say it, even exceeded Mamy's. She would definitely have approved. We braved the place several times over the next few months, each time leaving a little heavier than when we arrived.

Between eating out and cooking soup we continued our hunt for the elusive house. One possibility on paper was the house of a woman who lived on her own, and who depended on nothing and no-one for her existence. She appeared to have made all her clothes herself. She was around sixty with a shock of grey hair that had never seen the inside of a salon, and a wizened face that was likewise a stranger to skin care. She was dressed in a strange combination of woollen garments that covered her body rather haphazardly. The shapeless cardigan had bits of wool poking out in places, as if she had sheared a sheep and spun and carded the wool on her own before she knitted it up. We wouldn't have been surprised to see several merino sheep wandering around.

The place was heated by way of a massive iron stove on the ground floor, with ingenious vents at various strategic locations on the upper storey, so that the whole property could be adequately warmed with a couple of sticks of matchwood. We were quite impressed, and added the house onto our 'possibles' list. The garden was, as advertised, very large, with a stream gurgling at the bottom of it. The estate agent got very excited about this, and pointed out all the advantages of having your very own source of water. We still didn't get it, as we were incredibly resistant to the idea of a country where rain was a rarity.

As promised, the garden was large, flat and appeared manageable. But we were very puzzled by it. There was a bare patch of earth in the middle, surrounded on all four sides by three tiers of cages, each of which housed an animal. In the open square in the middle several scraggy chickens pecked dispiritedly at the bare earth. The lady owner beamed at us. She had evidently been advised that our command of the French language was limited, so she resorted to the method most used by the French when they wish to convey information to the English. She started shouting at us.

'Pour manger!' she yelled, pointed at one of the rabbit hutches. 'Manger!' she repeated, making extravagant gestures with her hands shovelling food into her open mouth.

Finally we got it. These were not much loved, furry pets to be handled with love and reared with care, they were her larder. There were enough chickens and rabbits to feed a single person for years. The owner let us know that she would be moving in with her lately widowed sister. She beamed at us both and added, 'If you buy, I make you gift. The animals, they are all for you!' Somehow we couldn't deal with that and we left.

So, onwards and upwards, we thought. We had an appointment to view another likely looking house, about half an hour's drive from Carcassonne. From its description, a reasonably modern bungalow with a conservatory and large garden, it seemed ideal, and so we embarked on yet another trip in an estate agent's car.

Despite it being late October it was still very warm. We were hot even in our summer clothes and sandals, and the estate agent was evidently hot too, but he was a consummate professional, and dressed in a slightly shiny brown suit, polished brown shoes and a somewhat garishly striped red and green tie which he constantly fiddled with. He led us to his car and we were shortly en route looking for a house which he was sure was still available. Once out of the town, his car sped along the long straight roads, where tall plane trees gave temporary avenues of deep shade before we emerged once more into the glare of sunlight. Beyond them were the disciplined straight rows of vines. Denuded of their heavy bunches of grapes after the harvest, their leaves were now beginning to wither in great swathes of golden brown, russet and crimson. We caught glimpses of crumbling stone windmills and tumble-down shacks which the estate agent identified for us as '*capitelles,*' or basic accommodation for the *vignerons* who sometimes had their homes high in the Montagne Noire. Here and there a field of sunflowers flashed past, their identical yellow heads inclined at an angle to catch the rays of the hot summer sun. It was so warm, in fact, that I started wondering about the local climate.

'Does it ever get cold here?' I asked curiously.

He half turned round, taking his eyes momentarily off the road so that we swerved dangerously close to an oncoming tractor. 'Yes, of course,' he said. We clung onto each other as the car swerved violently over to the verge, missing the tractor by a couple of centimetres.

I wanted to know more. 'So when does it start getting cold?' Coming from the UK where it could be colder in June than in February, I was not ready for a country with predictable weather patterns. I was equally unprepared for his answer.

'The fifteenth of November,' he replied with surprise, in a tone that clearly indicated that I was an idiot for asking and I really ought to have known better.

I had a sudden irresistible urge to ask him to be more precise about it. Would it get cold in the morning, say around eleven a.m or would it be maybe late afternoon, or perhaps in the evening, about tea time? I didn't believe him for one second. How could anyone predict the weather to such a degree? Later on, when we were finally settled in France, I recalled his answer and acknowledged that he had, amazingly, been perfectly correct. (Always trust your estate agent, he's lived in the place a lot longer than you have). Some years, winter might start a day or so earlier or later, but generally speaking, the date was unfailingly around the fifteen of November. After a gloriously hot summer, you would wake up one day to a lowering sky and a definite chill in the air, and winter would have arrived.

With hindsight, we realised that we should have had more faith in French estate agents. Unlike their British counterparts, their profession is highly regulated. Under the *Loi Hoguet* which was passed in 1970, French estate agents must possess a *carte professionnelle* (licence), which has to be renewed annually. The licence is not easily obtained, and estate agents need to provide evidence that they are professionally competent, either by holding one of various diplomas in French property or by demonstrating practical experience over a set period of time.

So, we ought to have trusted him, but the fact was, we had brought our British attitudes of deep distrust in estate agencies with us into France, where they turned out to be highly misplaced.

He was equally correct about the rainfall, and again, we failed to have any faith in him whatsoever. And how wrong that turned out to be.

'If you wish for a house with a large garden,' he said laconically, 'then the house we are going to see will not be suitable as you will need more rainfall. If you like, I can show you a house about five kilometres away, where the rainfall will be greater. This will be better for you.'

We looked at each other with raised eyebrows and shrugged. How could it be possible to expect a difference in rainfall over such a short distance of five kilometres?

We took absolutely no notice of what we thought of as an absurd statement, and finally agreed the sale on the house. With a huge conservatory. With a large garden. With no pool. With practically no rainfall whatsoever. Within an hour of the Mediterranean. With a view of the Pyrenees. Within a hamlet with no facilities. With severely limited French. With no real knowledge of life in France. But, we were delighted. We were here, we had done it, and this would be the dream come true. It was to be our home for the next seventeen years.

Chapter 9
Settling In

So, this was it! We finally had the keys from the previous owners, Gregoire and Yvette Damery, who had dropped them off at the *notaire's*, or solicitors. John opened the door and we walked into the kitchen. We stopped, eyes wide with horror. Where the kitchen had previously been was a bare room with a sink in the corner, and that was it. No cooker, no cupboards, no worktops, nothing! Hard to believe, but the owners had stripped the kitchen and taken it with them.

Neither of us spoke for a minute, the shock left us reeling. We were dumbstruck. Utterly stunned. No-one moves house and takes the whole kitchen with them. It just isn't done. No-one could be that miserly, could they? But it seemed that they could. That was the grim reality. We had bought a house with an empty room. Nowhere to cook, nowhere to put our pots and pans or crockery. Bare walls with faded dull brown paintwork where the cupboards used to be. In one corner was a stained, rusty sink and I was certain the Damerys would have taken that too if they had been able to prise it out of its housing.

John's eyes narrowed and his mouth was a grim line. I looked at him nervously. He is normally cool and doesn't upset himself over trivialities but this was a step too far for him. His angry thought processes were clearly visible on his face. He would march round to the *notaire* and insist that the kitchen be returned or we wanted compensation for it. In the UK he would have been round at that solicitor's door like a shot, charging into the office, thumping his fist on the desk and generally making a huge drama.

And therein lay the problem. We were no longer in the UK. There would be no barging into anyone's office. The *notaire* spoke no English and John spoke no French. There was no way in this world that my own French was up to a ferocious argument. I knew the right words, but arguing with someone like a *notaire* demands a certain fluidity of speech. It means sharp retorts, fierce arguments, swift and deadly repartee and shooting off loaded phrases like swift silver bullets, and I simply wasn't up for that.

'There's nothing we can do,' I said resignedly, after a long stare at the four walls. My own fury was slowly dissipating and being replaced by sadness. 'It was a lousy kitchen anyway. I hated that brown. At least this way we get to choose our own.'

'And we get to pay for it,' he retorted darkly. Still, he did see my point. The now defunct kitchen had been a bit scruffy anyway, with units apparently dating from the nineteen thirties.

'Listen, we were always going to update the kitchen,' I urged. 'We'll just have to do it a bit sooner, that's all.'

'Like tomorrow,' he growled, and I knew that I had won. I went into Gone with the Wind mode. 'Tomorrow is another day,' I said pragmatically.

We hadn't brought much furniture with us, thinking that a fresh start merited some new furnishings, and in any case, most of our possessions dated from the time of our marriage. We had beds, a microwave, kettle and coffee pot, an antique glass fronted china cabinet inherited from John's late mother and a wicker sofa and chairs that we installed in the conservatory.

All our other belongings were in boxes stashed on top of one another; the place resembled a very badly organised warehouse. We were slowly ripping off Sellotape, dejected when we unwrapped packages of crockery which had no home until we bought a kitchen. We were stacking them for the time being on top of the microwave. I was so annoyed at the state of the place that I carelessly put a plate on top of the pile and it fell off, smashing onto the tiled floor and shattering into pieces which flew in all directions.

Momentarily I was stunned, and then suddenly, it was the final straw and the floods broke. I sobbed my heart out.

John put his arm around my shoulders and looked into my eyes. 'Darling, just stop it. It's a sodding plate. We can buy another. There's no need to cry about it.'

'It's not that,' I sobbed. 'What are we *doing* here? Look at the bloody place. There's nowhere to put anything. I haven't got a kitchen. How can we cook? I'm not washing up in that filthy sink. I don't know why we ever came. The whole place is a mess –there's so much to *do*...'

'Listen, sweetheart, it's only the beginning,' he soothed. 'Even if we'd moved to a new house in the UK things are never perfect to start with. You always have to do some work to a new place. We'll get it sorted. Stop crying.' He was calm and reasonable about it all and my sobs died away but I was still upset. This wasn't how it was meant to be. It was supposed to be the start of a wonderful new life, and just look at it. Bare brown walls with fragments of chipped plate all over the floor, half unwrapped boxes, rolled balls of sticky tape littering the floor, plates balanced precariously on top of the microwave...

'I don't even like the wallpaper in the lounge,' I muttered, a little restored now but still obstinately fixating on the things I hated.

'Steph, you didn't like the wallpaper when we first looked at it,' he said reasonably. 'We were always going to redecorate, weren't we?'

'It had better be soon, then,' I said sulkily. 'I'm not living with that paper a minute longer than I have to...'

He knew that I would come round to my usual self shortly. Wisely, he left me to myself and collected the largest fragments and then gathered the smaller ones into a paper towel. The kitchen bin was still in a box somewhere so he deposited it in a corner before he went on ripping off tape and setting glasses on the floor in neat rows.

Over the next few days we unpacked more boxes and installed the two fabric sofas and two revolving armchairs into the conservatory, which was huge, with walls that were solid halfway and then glazed to the roof. A few plants were already there, left by the previous owners, but when we came home from our daily shopping trip, I was puzzled.

'John, have you moved that iris plant? I'm sure it was here when we went out.'

No, he hadn't moved it. Why would he move a plant? He was just as puzzled as I was. We put it down to one of those inexplicable mysteries and forgot about it. Until the next plant disappeared. This time it was a large pot of geraniums, which had definitely been just in front of the larger sofa. I checked all round the room, quickly scanned the brown tiled floor, glanced round the windowsills which lined three sides of the room. Nothing. The plant and its pot had definitely gone.

'This is weird,' I said, frowning. 'Someone's been in here. Plants don't walk off by themselves. D'you think we should call the police?'

'Over a pot plant?' Don't be daft, they'd laugh you out of the station...'

'It's not the plant I'm bothered about,' I retorted. 'It's the fact that I know someone's been in here while we were out. The only people to have a key would be the Damerys. Unless they gave a spare key to one of the neighbours.'

'They can't have done. We should have the only keys, they're obliged by law to hand them all over on completion.'

We accepted the strange situation as it was. There was no damage to the house, just a couple of plants gone missing, and as John had said, the police were hardly going to launch a nationwide investigation over a geranium.

Matters came to a conclusion a few days later. Gregoire and Yvette were strolling along the back lane, and I hurried out of the open conservatory doors to meet them. I didn't exactly accuse them of stealing, I merely asked them if they knew what had happened to our plants.

'Yvette, she wanted them back,' Gregoire told me in a matter of fact tone. 'So me, I came to get them for her. If you had been in I would have asked you for them but there was no-one there.'

I was astonished and it showed. 'But,' I gabbled, 'the house was locked! How did you get in?'

He winked at me, his florid face creasing into what passed for a smile. 'Your conservatory...' he began.

'That was locked as well,' I said firmly. 'We lock all our doors when we go out.'

He chuckled. 'It is easy to open these doors,' he said. 'I can do it with a small screwdriver....' He took a small red screwdriver out of his back pocket and showed it to me with a brazenness that just left me completely amazed. The paperwork had been signed off, the money exchanged, the house was legally ours, and yet he seemed to be looking upon it as some kind of shared ownership where he could still come and go at will. It was intolerable.

'The house belongs to us now,' I retorted, 'and you have no right whatsoever to break into our property.' John strolled over to see what the fuss was about.

'It was Monsieur Damery who took the plants,' I told him grimly, even though Gregoire and Yvette were still standing by the gate.

Yvette looked a little sheepish, but Gregoire was still trying to laugh it off as a pleasant joke.

'Tell them, Steph,' he said. 'If they enter this house again without permission we're going straight to the police...'

I was about to translate but the couple had heard the word 'police' and knew what it meant. They regarded John with just a little alarm and Gregoire took a step forward. Leaning towards us, he said, 'There is no problem with us, you understand. We wish to be your good neighbours and friends. We will not come to your house again if you do not wish it.'

With that they walked away, deep in conversation with each other. From the snatches I overheard, Yvette seemed to be remonstrating with her husband and we went inside before they were out of sight.

We decided to chill out in the conservatory. It had been a stressful day and we both needed the comforting glass of red wine that John brought.

'What a day!' I laughed. 'At least we've solved the mystery of the missing plant pots. Let's hope tomorrow's a bit more peaceful.'

At that moment my mobile rang.

'Elodie!' I exclaimed. I hadn't heard from her for years. Both of us led busy lives as teachers, there hadn't been the opportunity. I was delighted. Happy to hear a familiar voice in the middle of the chaos. Just the sound of her voice lifted my spirits.

'No, I'm fine,' I lied. 'How are you? And Antoine?'

Her next words left me reeling.

'But,' I stammered. 'Elodie, we've only been here a few days. We haven't even done all the unpacking. Everything's still in boxes. There aren't enough beds....'

John was staring at me, evidently fully aware of the gist of her call.

'Put her off!' he hissed urgently in a low voice. I frowned at him with a 'wait a minute' gesture of my head and then returned to the lunacy that was developing on the other end of the phone.

I did my best. I really did. More explaining that we were not ready for visitors. That we had no kitchen, that we needed more time to get used to the place, to stock up on food, to unpack the rest of our boxes, to make the beds. None of it was any use. I held the phone away from my ear but I caught her final cheerful words... 'Till tomorrow then....'

'She says they'll stay in a *gîte* in the village,' I told him glumly. 'They've already booked it for three days.'

'She must be insane!' he cried. 'No-one visits someone who's just moved in. And we haven't got time to entertain them. Look at this place, it's a total mess! Why on earth didn't you say no?'

'I tried. Honestly, I *told* her about the house. I said we'd got no kitchen, we were still unpacking. She just wouldn't listen. You know what she's like....'

'No, I don't,' he replied truthfully. 'She's your friend, not mine. I've heard a lot about her from you but we've never met.'

'It might not be *so* bad,' I continued hopefully. 'I mean, she doesn't expect to stay with us or anything. They just want to visit, that's all. We don't need to feed them, we can go to a restaurant.'

He was not at all mollified, and continued to grumble intermittently for the rest of the day about the insensitivity of some people. We continued to unpack as fast as we could, as if the phone call had lent an additional urgency to the task.

We were up early the next day. Despite our initial consternation, part of me was glad they were coming. It would lend a feeling of belonging to our fresh start in a new country. At least we knew someone who lived here, which is more than can be said for most people who make the leap into French life. I only remembered Antoine as he was the last time I saw him, aged seventeen, and I had never met their daughter. I calculated. She would be getting on for her fourteenth birthday now.

We kissed, both of us possibly exhibiting more excitement than we actually felt. It was the Elodie I remembered, but a taller version now. The same auburn hair, although cut shorter, with a severe fringe and precise shaping around her ears. The same freckles sprinkled over her face. She was much slimmer though, and with an air of sophistication enhanced by her high heeled sandals, deep burgundy nail polish and ultra-smart red skirt teamed with a thin white polo necked jumper. I had a sudden flashback to the adolescent Elodie pleadingly holding up a red skirt to Mamy in the market so many years ago. Evidently her penchant for red skirts was more easily satisfied now. I looked down at my trainers, feeling very shabby in them and my worn jeans, which I wore constantly while everything was in such turmoil.

Her daughter Lucie was tall, with a slight stoop as she stood awkwardly between her parents. She reminded me vaguely of her grandmother Véronique, with the same reddish hair of the family, but softened into a wavy auburn mop inherited from Antoine who still had his tight black curls. Unlike Elodie as I had known her as a teenager, her daughter was stick thin; her legs were so spindly it was difficult to see how they carried her weight.

After a short tour around the house we sat in the conservatory, it was the only room with enough seating for everyone, and even there, unpacked boxes littered the floor, some spilling their contents out from burst sides onto the tiles.

Antoine was looking around him with an unpleasant sneer on his face. 'There is much work to do here,' he said unnecessarily. He nodded towards the piles of boxes. 'These boxes, some of them are coming apart. 'And in your garage,' he went on. I looked at your fuse box; it does not conform to today's standards, you will need to replace it. Probably all the wiring as well.'

I resisted the urge to slap him in the face. He was an uninvited visitor, for God's sake, nobody had asked him his opinion on the state of our electrics.

'The boxes have had a long journey,' I said acidly. 'As we have. And we knew about the wiring when we bought the house.' I looked pointedly at John, hoping that he would back me up with a choice comment, but being John, he merely shrugged slightly.

Elodie too waded in with her unhelpful comments. 'The house is very small,' she remarked. 'There is so much to do here. All the rooms need decorating. I thought you would be moving to a good district too. This is just a hamlet. Where will you do your shopping? Carcassonne is too far away.'

'It's half an hour's drive,' I retorted defensively. 'Besides, we have three villages nearby. Peyriac has a food shop. Rieux Minervois has a good supermarket too, and there's Caunes. We don't have to go to Carcassonne.'

She shrugged maddeningly. I tried my best to be rational, to not allow myself to get upset by her attitude but it was a huge struggle. I forced myself to think of all the times we had shared; the holidays together, the secrets we had confided in each other, the memories we both had of Mamy and Papy. But, I reasoned, many years had passed since then. Mamy and Papy were both long since dead and maybe we had both changed. This was certainly not the Elodie from years ago.

It was a poor start and it got even worse. The busy restaurant we went to was one of our all-time favourites, but it was quite evidently not a patch on anything they had in Marseille.

'No, Lucie, not the pork, there is too much fat in it,' Elodie sternly told her daughter, in between denigrating the restaurant. 'You can have the mushroom omelette.'

'But I like pork,' Lucie protested mildly, and this statement brought an onslaught of loud remonstration.

'Don't you ever listen to a single word I say? I've just told you, you cannot have the pork! You'll finish up as big as a cow,' she raged. 'It's the omelette, or you go without. It's your decision.'

Sulkily, Lucie agreed to the omelette, and as she directed her daughter's choice of food, she put me in mind of Mamy and her controlling ways. Even after she ate the omelette, Elodie refused any dessert for her on the basis that she had already eaten enough. At the end of the meal, the moment before the bill was placed on the table, Antoine got up and went outside to light up one of the many cigarettes he had been smoking all evening. Elodie similarly whisked Lucie and herself off to the toilet. So, that left myself, John, a smiling waiter by our table and a bill for the five of us. Highly reluctantly, John peeled off a number of twenty euro notes. We were too furious to leave a tip, even though the meal had been excellent with impeccable service.

The visit was not a success. We were both tired and irritable, Elodie and Antoine found nothing to their liking, hinting strongly that we were mad to come to France and we were relieved when we finally waved them off two days later. Throughout their whole stay Elodie seemed to be obsessed with Lucie's weight, nagging her endlessly over the number of calories in every bite the poor girl took.

We remained friends of a sort and kept in touch, although spasmodically. By this time the letters of years past had morphed into emails but our relationship took a deep dive until many years later.

Chapter 10
Neighbours

We are not the type of people to introduce ourselves. We thought it unlikely that the inhabitants of the village had been waiting for their lives to be completed by our presence, but I did feel compelled to go round to our next door neighbour's house and let them know who we were.

So it was with a sense of trepidation that I first walked the short distance between the houses. Would they accept an English couple living in close proximity? Would they be polite but distant, immediately signalling tacit disapproval of our arrival, or would they be ready to like us?

I had no need to knock at the door, since a diminutive figure with a shock of rough black hair was ensconced in a rocking chair on the porch, surrounded by huge tubs of scarlet, pink and white geraniums and pots of begonias. On a wall which separated the porch from the vegetable plot beyond were further pots of flowers; dwarf palms, brightly cascading petunias, miniature pale pink roses and masses of phlox. Beyond the wall was a vegetable plot of pristine tidiness: I could identify row upon row of lettuces and I saw carrot tops gently waving in the light wind but many of them were strange to me.

Hesitatingly, I introduced myself. The old lady raised herself out of her rocking chair and greeted me with the traditional two kisses and poured out a stream of words, presumably of welcome, although I understood not a single word. I was greatly alarmed. I spoke French. I knew I did. I had seen to that for years before we arrived, so what was the problem? Was it her accent? Could she be speaking in a local dialect that I had yet to understand? Did everyone speak like that?

She was now holding up her hands and counting on her fingers, and from that I understood that she was telling me her age. She was seventy nine. But I *knew* what seventy nine was in French. It was *soixante dix-neuf* and I knew I hadn't heard that. Some of her words were vaguely familiar but still it was impossible to follow her conversation.

I later learned that Madame and Monsieur Bellini were Italian. The husband, after thirty years in France, spoke French with a local accent, whereas his wife had never entirely mastered the language and she spoke with a curious mixture of French and Italian, though the couple had raised their four boys in France. It was a relief to me to learn this since I didn't have a single word of Italian. Over the years we understood each other better, using gestures and facial expressions to convey meaning and I gradually became accustomed to her odd speech.

She was an incurable, excitable gossip and I gained a lot of local knowledge from her, even communicating as we did. Monsieur Bellini was a staid, placid and stoical man of great pride and seemingly inexhaustible knowledge of plants. John was greatly indebted to him for hints on when to plant his vegetables.

Coming across John planting his carrot seeds, he was horrified. *'Les grains,'* he said decisively, 'The seeds, you must wait.' He waved a bony arm towards the sky. 'The moon, she is full. You wait and when she is new, then you plant the seeds.' He wagged his finger at John. 'Remember! Not before!'

He dispensed this nugget of information along with many others on the same theme. Potatoes and onions should be planted after the full moon; lettuces need lots of light so you wait until the moon is full again before planting. All this was new to John but he followed the old man's advice and sure enough, whether due to planting time or not, we had great crops.

I grew to be fond of the couple. They were both proud people who never accepted a favour without giving one back. A visit was considered to be a service; a sort of offering; a gift from one neighbour to another and sure enough, a few days following any visit we would wake up to find a row of freshly picked lettuces on the kitchen window sill. Anything that is perceived to be of value can be used as currency, and lettuces and other plants were the currency of the day. In our lives in France we saw wine used as currency, in lieu of euros. On a visit to the doctor, a man entered the waiting room with two crates of red wine. On hearing that the doctor was in consultation, he asked me to be sure to tell her that she should be sure to refrigerate the wine as soon as possible. This was his payment to her. He had plenty of wine, but maybe not the 23 euros fee for an appointment.

On one visit I accidentally walked in on the Bellinis when they had visitors. That was so unusual that I began to make my apologies and withdraw, but Monsieur welcomed me warmly by taking my arm and leading me to a vacant chair. Sitting around the table was a group of men and women, alike only in their wrinkled faces and gruff, guttural local accents. Some were leaning their elbows on the oilcloth, hands grasped around tiny glasses of Monsieur Bellini's famed *cartagène,* a local liqueur of torpor-inducing alcoholic strength made from the grapes in his garden. None of the company was known to me so I couldn't join in the conversation. Instead, I listened, and very quickly the group of them started discussing someone's birthday and the presents they had bought. I didn't recognise the name of the person they were talking about and she was not a local as far as I knew.

'We bought her some records,' one of the elderly guests stated proudly.

'We gave her a stereo,' said another, and I was convinced that this was going to be one of those 'my-present-was-more-expensive-than-yours' kind of chat, but I was wrong. The discussion continued.

'Is she still doing her dancing, then?'

'Oh, yes, she wouldn't give up her dancing. She goes every week, never misses. You know how she loves music. Gets her out of the house as well, she meets her friends.'

'And her walking group, is she still with them?'

'Of course, she still loves walking. She keeps saying she'll give it up but she hasn't so far.'

There was a slight lull before one of them asked, 'How old will she be this year?'

The talk died down as they all appeared to be calculating, some of them counting on fingers before the next lively discussion started.

'Will she be a hundred and four this time?' someone queried.

'No, she can't be. She's a hundred and five if she's a day...'

'That's not right, because she's twenty years older than I am, so that makes her a hundred and four.'

'Well if you ask me, she's only a hundred and three because she was ninety when Phillipe died, and that was thirteen years ago this July.'

'Rubbish! She was only eighty-nine when he died. I know that for a fact because I was eighty-seven and she's two years older than me.'

No-one was quite certain and the argument went on until I left them to it and went home shaking my head in disbelief all the way. I never did get to hear the correct age.

One of the first visits we made was a chance encounter. A narrow path, strewn with rough loose stones, led from our back gate before taking twists and turns and finally straightening out into an arrow-straight path leading to woodland. It was here that the wild boar made their nocturnal ramblings, tall trees with massive trunks soared overhead, their canopy of green creating dense pools of shade, interspersed with patches of dappled sunlight. Further on, the woodland grew thinner and finally gave way to meadows of wild grasses dotted with tiny seeded oaks. The sense of total isolation was liberating. In the distance, crouched low amongst the vines was a large farmhouse. Even from a distance it had a neglected look and we went closer, thinking it to be uninhabited.

We were wrong. As we approached we saw a tiny, frail, thin woman appear from a side door. She was loaded with a pile of washing which she slowly and carefully pegged onto a sagging line. Spotting us, she raised a hand in greeting. We felt obliged then to go and introduce ourselves.

On close inspection, I realized that she was younger than I had first thought. Mid-sixties, perhaps. Her hair was a cloud of silvery grey curls, her face lined and weathered, with large darker patches giving her a slightly piebald look. Her bare arms were as bony and thin as the rest of her frame and it was quite amazing to think that her twig-like legs could ever support a human body, even such a diminutive one as this.

We explained who we were and where we were living, and she pinned out one last, faded green cotton shirt before introducing herself as Dominique and welcoming us inside.

We followed her from the bright glare of the sun into a cool interior room with huge rough grey stone walls. Placards, faded photographs and texts hung from each wall. In the centre of the room was a scrubbed table, worn away and riddled with knife cuts, like an ancient butcher's chopping block. It was evidently a table for eating as well as for preparing food, as there were four wooden backed chairs with rush seats placed around it. Dark brown cupboards were set above a rusting cooker with years of grease burnt into the rings. Behind the table was a sort of bureau whose surface was almost hidden by mounds of tattered papers, unwashed plates and cups, a matted hairbrush and several bowls of vegetables waiting to be washed and prepared. Dominique made us tea which she poured into glasses.

'*Le thé anglais,*' she smiled as we took the glasses. 'The English tea. But it is not the five o'clock tea as it should be. For this we are too early.'

To label this concoction of pale brown liquid '*English tea*' was an abomination of the term, since it resembled no cup of tea I had ever drunk. Nor did we drink it out of glasses in the UK, but we dutifully took cautious sips and tried our best to ignore the faint jagged cracks in the glasses and look appreciative.

When she spoke her voice was barely audible, and John was leaning forward on his chair, trying to catch her meaning.

'It is so good to have new neighbours,' she whispered. 'You will be very happy here, I am sure...' She stretched out her wraith like arm and touched me lightly on my bare arm.

How exactly she had gained this certain knowledge of our future happiness, I couldn't say, but I found her words oddly comforting, to say that she was a stranger and we had never met. There was something calming about her presence that I was unable to explain.

'So, you are married?' she asked. Suddenly I stiffened. Why on earth would anyone ask that? And if she was in any doubt, she only had to look at my left hand which sported both an engagement and a broad gold wedding ring.

I confirmed that John and I were married, the surprise evident in my voice.

'And you are baptised?' she went on, hopefully.

Ah, now I had it. The woman was a religious freak. I began to regret coming here, and yet still, she had a mesmerising effect which seemed to keep me glued to my seat, instead of allowing me to get up gracefully, make some tactful excuse about needing to rush back home to feed the non-existent budgie, and leave.

'You are very welcome here,' she went on. 'You are Catholic? We have a wonderful church nearby in Laure, and the priest is a great friend of ours. He will be very pleased to meet you both.'

John felt the urgent need to interject here. 'No, we're not Catholic,' he stated firmly. 'And we really do need to be going now. Are you ready, Steph?'

Her face changed, but so fleetingly, the expression of sadness had disappeared even before I had fully registered it as such, and it was replaced by a gentle smile. 'You will come again,' she said in her low voice, 'and we will be good friends. The Lord does not look on you with any ill because you do not share our faith. He will be there to guide you in your lives and watch over you in everything you do....'

John grasped my elbow and hoisted me to my feet. 'Well, thank you so much for the tea,' he stated crisply as he led the way outside.

His eyebrows were raised. 'Phew, what was all that about?' he expostulated as soon as we were out of earshot. 'She's a maniac; a religious fruitcake. Best to keep away....'

'Oh, I don't know. She seemed quite kind. She probably doesn't see many people, it's a bit isolated over there.'

'Well, you can go back if you like but don't expect me to come with you. She looks half demented if you ask me.'

I did go back. In fact I went to the farm many times, mostly on my own, and got to know the family well over the years. Dominique came from an aristocratic background and had married for love, against the wishes of her family who still lived in a château in the Loire.

'Gustave was very poor when we married,' she explained to me one sunny afternoon. We were sitting outside, on deckchairs which were placed firmly in the long, uncut grass which surrounded the farmhouse. 'When we bought this farm, we had no windows. Not for five years. We could not afford the glass for them.' Her voice never rose above the whisper we had heard from her at first. 'And for the beds for the children, we had mattresses on the floors.' She paused, then went on, 'It is my dream, that before the good Lord takes me, that one day I will sleep in a bed. I will say goodbye to my mattress.'

She sighed, as if such a possibility was a luxury way beyond any reasonable expectation. In a roundabout way, and over the course of many months, I learned more about the family. They were a strange mixture of outward benevolence, mixed in with a fair amount of grasping whatever they could and from wherever they could. They were not well liked or respected in the community, it seemed. I learned that Dominique and Gustave were first cousins, which went a long way to explaining the mental health problems of many of their offspring. Their nine children were poorly dressed and even more poorly fed. They had always been encouraged to ask for food and clothes from neighbours which did nothing at all to enhance their popularity.

Whenever I visited, there were always one or two itinerant workers who were evidently not French. One of them was a bent, black-haired gentleman who was supposedly 'employed' to help on the farm. He spoke very little French. On one visit, he glanced around him furtively and then beckoned me to follow him. He was evidently bent on showing me where he lived, and I followed him to a tiny stone outbuilding. He limped over to it, pushed open a battered wooden door and I went inside. There was no sign of any sanitation, no heating and the only decoration was a roughly-hewn crucifix which was screwed to the wall above his lumpy mattress. Against a wall at the far end was a battered wooden chest of drawers. The gossip in the village was that Gustave and Dominique had taken him in as an illegal immigrant, offering him food and basic shelter in return for work. How true this was I never found out, but it seemed to fit in well with the poverty of the family, the vastness of their farm and the need for labour to keep the place functioning.

Worst still, I heard whispered rumours in the village that Dominique routinely inspected the bedsheets of her invitees, presumably to look for any signs of private behaviour that she thought of as unacceptable and a sin against God. What she did about it if she found any was anyone's guess. In my mind she was one of the fervent Christian martyr types, and although I felt no connection with her lifestyle, I continued to visit and ignore any mention of religion as best I could. My sole justification, if I ever really sought one, was that I was new to this region, and it simply wasn't my place to enquire too deeply into my neighbours' affairs, however much I disagreed with them.

As we had no common language I was unable to have a conversation with the old gentleman so I never found out how he felt about this arrangement, which was, in effect, blatant slavery. He lived there for a number of years until one day when I visited, he was quite simply gone. No explanation was ever forthcoming about his whereabouts, and I made no enquiries.

As an aside, the story was similar for their goat, a mangy-looking animal which was kept on a chain at the entrance to the farm, where it subsisted on grass and any food which happened to be thrown its way. It was there for years until one day, it too simply disappeared. This time there was an explanation. Of sorts. The dog had eaten it, apparently.

The farm always housed various workers who came for the experience of living on a rural, organic French farm, helping with the activities in return for board. Many of them came quite legitimately, sent by a scheme named Wwoof. These people were a world away from the bent old man who had now disappeared into the ether. They were a cheerful, energetic and enthusiastic bunch of youngsters, eager to add to their life experiences and their CVs by helping on the farm. Their duties ranged from picking figs, planting trees, driving tractors and spraying the vines, to cooking and light housework.

The general consensus among the villagers was that these workers were being exploited on a massive scale, but once again, it was not my place to interfere, even if I had known the correct organisation to report it to, which I didn't. I had enough to do to sort out our own affairs, without pushing my nose into someone else's. I shrugged mentally. If that was how they wanted to work then as far as I was concerned, that was their own affair and nothing to do with me.

The husband Gustave was a tall, long-nosed fellow with crooked front teeth, the beginnings of a beard and a sun-wrinkled face which was always smiling. It was said that he was lazy, but as time went by I realized that this was untrue. He was not lazy, just simply disorganised. He had a huge respect for nature, and organised his farm on strictly organic principles.

He implemented a system for his vines whereby he stuffed fresh dung into cow horns before burying the horns in selected positions in his vineyards. After a full winter, the horns were dug up and the contents were diluted with water to obtain a weak solution of manure that was sprayed over the vines. Even the small quantity generated, I was told, made a huge difference to the quality of the terroir, and subsequently to that of the grapes themselves.

His main problem appeared to be an almost pathological inability to finish a job once he had started it with huge enthusiasm. Consequently, half his vines were riddled with mildew as they had not been sprayed, fields would be half planted with a new variety of tree until he ran out of steam and abandoned yet another well-intentioned project.

I am quite sure that one winter's day, he had fully intended to cut logs for the immense fire in the salon at the farm. When I went in, I was met by an unbelievable sight. I was stupefied. A massive log stretched the whole length of the room, with one end a bright red glowing ember in the fire. As it burned down, Gustave strode over to the other end of the room and kicked and nudged at it with his foot until the embers fell into the grate and another fresh section of log took its place. I honestly tried my best to conceal my feelings, but I just couldn't get over what I was witnessing. To this day, the log in the salon remains a very clear memory. I have never once heard of anyone else doing this. On second thoughts, maybe his reputation for laziness was justified.

Clothilde was one of the daughters from the farm, and I met her when she was waiting to collect her younger sister from the school bus which deposited its pupils at a stop opposite our house.

I saw her as she walked up and down by our back gate; tall, thin to the point of emaciation, with gangly legs and feet clad in shabby, Roman type leather sandals. Light brown wispy hair floated to her shoulders. Her head was down and she was totally absorbed in a small book she was holding, muttering to herself as if trying to absorb its contents by heart.

On seeing me, she looked up and smiled vaguely. I waved at her and she waved back. Taking this polite exchange as an invitation to approach, she rested her forearms on our gate and beckoned to me.

'You are English?' she asked. Word had apparently got round.

I admitted this and she appeared pleased and eager to ask the next question.

I was quite prepared to be interrogated about our precise location in the UK, or other matters relating to our foreignness, but I wasn't ready for the question that came.

'What do English people think about the Virgin Mary?' She was very eager to know.

I was totally nonplussed. I could see by now that the small book she was carrying was a bible, so it seemed that my answer might be quite important to her.

I am not a Catholic, or a Hindu or a Sikh or an Anglican, or a Baptist or any of the other multitude of configurations that go under the name of religion. If pressed I would probably fall into the agnostic category, without being even very positive about that. I am willing to believe that there may, just possibly, be some kind of existence or entity which our senses are incapable of perceiving. After all, microbes exist, bacteria exist but I seriously doubt whether they are capable of any kind of understanding of the human world as we know it. I wouldn't wonder if we ourselves are similarly unaware. But until I am magically endowed with the equipment to perceive, I will persist in my unbelief.

I was loath to offend her, as I no doubt would have done if I had said that as far as I knew, the vast majority of Brits didn't spend an inordinate amount of their time wondering about the Virgin Mary. I'm not saying there were *no* people in the UK who wondered about the Virgin, I'm just saying that I hadn't met any of them. Or maybe I had and they were wondering in secret. Or maybe I was going around with the wrong crowd.

'Moi, je L'adore,' she continued with a rapt expression I had already gathered that, and I began to wonder how we would get on, given our differences.

The best thing, I felt, would be to ignore the question entirely and stick to my usual mantra of never discussing money, politics or religion with outsiders. Religion comes at the top of that list.

Clothilde, on the other hand, *was* religious. As one of the nine children from the farm, she had never stood a chance. This is just *my* opinion, you understand. It may not be yours and naturally you are perfectly free to disagree with me. But as I see it, when you are indoctrinated in early childhood into a set of beliefs, and those beliefs are reinforced daily by those whom you love and trust, it is a rare human being who stands out against them, and she was no exception. Her whole life was devoted to the Catholic church and its teachings.

I later discovered that she was nineteen and jobless, relying on her state benefits and suffering periods of deep depression. As far as I knew there was no significant other in her life, apart from the Virgin Mary who fulfilled that function admirably. As the years passed I grew to like her more, notwithstanding her religious beliefs which in no way coincided with my own, such as they were.

Personally I lean towards the more practical aspects of life – will that fish be enough for dinner or should I make a dessert? Will we have time on Saturday to go to the garden centre, get the car cleaned and do the shopping? Will John ever get round to marking out the plot for the pool? Only a limited portion of a person's life can be taken up with pondering the imponderable before the demands of daily life take precedence, and trivial little items like those do tend to make up the minutiae of my life.

Later on, Clothilde became a good friend and we passed many hours together, both of us managing successfully to avoid the contentious subject of religion.

Chapter 11
The Harvest

In the Aude, as in many other regions in France, the grape harvest is the culmination of a year's relentless work. As we didn't have many vineyards in Leeds, I was unfamiliar with the sheer amount of time, expertise and back breaking toil that goes into producing a bottle of wine. Naively, when I did think of it, which wasn't very often, I fondly imagined that the vines were planted, then left to themselves in the hot sunshine until the time came to pick the grapes. I couldn't have been more wrong, as we were about to find out for ourselves.

I became extremely familiar with all the problems of wine growing as they were the principal topic of conversation amongst the neighbours. The only period of respite for *vignerons* is immediately after the harvest. The leaves change colour, turning from fresh green to palest brown to deepest hues of ruby, scarlet and orange before they slowly shrivel and drop, leaving the stark gnarled and twisted stems lining up like a battalion to face the onslaught of winter. They are hardy, these vines, with roots that penetrate the earth to depths of up to several metres, to suck up every last bit of nourishment that the stony earth can provide. During the harsh weather of winter they shrug off hailstorms, ice crystals and heavy deposits of snow until they emerge triumphant in the early spring when the tiny shoots appear and they continue a cycle that has lasted in this region for over two thousand years.

The work starts at that moment and carries on all year until the grapes are picked. The vines have to be sprayed every two weeks to protect against the deadly diseases such as phylloxera, powdery mildew and black rot that can ruin the grapes.

Our house was on one side of a busy *départementale* road; opposite us on the other side was a large house with a turret. It was the home of Marc, Sophie and their son Bernard. Sophie became and still is, a dear friend and it was through these people that we learned about the tough life of wine growers.

A few days before the harvest begins, samples of the grapes are taken to be analysed for the balance between their sugar and acid content. It is a finely honed balancing act. The hot sun increases the sugar content by the day, therefore the grapes should be picked when it is at its highest. But wait too long and the grapes will begin to shrivel; indeed, a quick walk through the vines shows some of them past their best with skins already starting to shrivel. The *vignerons* have expert knowledge passed down through many generations and their experience tells them the exact moment to start picking. After the harvest the grapes are taken to the local cooperative in Rieux Minervois, where a patient line of tractors wait their turn to tip the grapes into one of the huge vats. Each grape variety has its own specified vat: Merlot is deposited into one, Carignan in another, Sinsault into another and so on. Each *vigneron* is paid according to the sugar content of his grapes. In addition to the financial recompense, the *vignerons* also have the right to purchase bottles of the resulting wine at extremely low prices.

The stultifying heat of the shimmering September air combines with the pungent aroma of fermenting grapes. The fermentation process is ever present in the heady air of the local supermarket, the car parks, the pavements and the roadside cafes. The local *collège* is unfortunately situated within a few metres of the wine cooperative, meaning that most of the pupils stagger out of the place at home time practically drunk on the fumes. Still, it does serve as an apprenticeship, as most of them will be smelling the aroma as *vignerons* for the rest of their lives.

Once the harvest is over, the cooperatives then take over, blending the wines, bottling and labelling them and arranging for distribution. In former years the wines from the local area, Minervois and Corbières amongst others, were of a low quality and reserved for the locality who drank them as table wines. Gradually the quality improved, until the wines were considered suitable for national and international distribution.

This is life as a *vigneron* in the Minervois. For many generations of families, this was their way of life. But for Bernard it was never going to be good enough, and he decided to set up on his own, producing organic, or *bio* wine. It was a hard slog for him. It takes many years and a lot of money to set up on your own. Machinery has to be bought, you need somewhere to store the bottles, a labelling machine, boxes to pack them into, and above all, you do all the marketing and distribution yourself.

He was lucky to have formidable allies in his parents. To finance him they remortgaged their house. There was enough land to build a substantial wine cave and install several plastic *cuves*, or vats, for storing his wines.

Amazingly, to us at any rate, even though he owned the land he was not allowed to plant any variety of grape he wanted. The local government decided which grape varieties he was allowed to plant, and in what quantities. We concluded that this was the famed *'liberté, égalité, fraterneté'* in action. This would be the *égalité* bit, ensuring that all the local *vignerons* got a fair bite of the cherry, or of the grape in this case. It seemed to us as if an awful lot of the *égalité* was in play here even if it was a bit short on the *liberté* bit.

Another friend of ours, Odette, was the secretary on a huge wine estate a few kilometres away in Trausse Minervois. This operation was light years away from Bernard's, and the estate was large enough to be able to supply wine to a large UK supermarket. She told me about the lorry arriving to collect the pallets of bottles. The contract they had to sign ran to seventeen pages and it was loaded with provisos. One of the clauses stated that until the very last bottle had been unloaded at the UK warehouse, the Minervois domaine was responsible for the whole shipment, and any damage or loss occurring would be their responsibility. It was evidently worthwhile to comply with the draconian conditions, as the supermarket order was way in excess of anything they could sell on their own, despite the wine being of a very high quality. They had their own grape picking machine, which was a luxury denied to many *vignerons* in the region, who either hired a machine for the harvest or picked by hand.

And this was where John and I came in. Bernard was preparing for his all important first harvest and he needed a team of people to pick his grapes. Anyone in the village who still had the use of both legs was asked, and no-one refused. There was no polite *'refusal will cause no offence,'* because in this case it simply wasn't true. Refusal would have resulted in massive friction, and since they were our friends as well as our nearest neighbours we agreed.

'It'll be an experience,' I enthused to John. 'Imagine, us picking grapes in the south of France! Lots of people would just love to get the opportunity to do that.'

As this was France, there were many forms to fill in, but once all the formalities had been completed we were ready to begin.

Bernard picked us up in his blue Jumpy van at the ungodly hour of six in the morning, while it was still dark.

'We must be in the vineyard and ready to pick,' he announced, 'as soon as the sun arrives.' We could tell he was tense. This was it, this was the final grand culmination of his year's ploughing, spraying, staking, pruning, ripping out old vines and planting new ones. It was a massive deal to him and we were all aware of the huge responsibility as he instructed us in our duties.

There was a cohort of villagers present. John and I were in battered shorts and trainers, but many others wore long trousers and even jumpers, against the mild pre-dawn chill. As the morning wore on they would discard their top layers, leaving them on the ground where they were inevitably covered in sticky grape juice.

Bernard had advised us on our footwear. It needed to be closed at the heel and toe to prevent accidents, with air holes to afford some protection against the sweat that would build up. We nodded sagely and we had duly rushed off and equipped ourselves with the correct type of trainers.

There was a very faint lightening of the sky towards the horizon; the distant Pyrenees became visible as dark grey looming shapes; they were barely distinguishable from the awakening dawn sky. Bernard and a couple of others began unloading the *'cagettes'* or plastic crates, from the back of the Jumpy. They carried them into the rows of vines, dropping an empty *cagette* every few metres. Meanwhile, Sophie and Marc delved into a plastic bucket and handed out a pair of secateurs to each person. We were warned about how sharp they were, and of the absolute necessity of cutting off only bunches of grapes and leaving the vineyard with the same number of fingers as we had arrived with. It had happened in the past, they told us sternly.

We set to work. Each person was assigned several rows of shoulder high vines, and we snipped bunch after bunch of the dewy grapes, dropping them into the increasingly heavy *cagette* at our feet which we dragged along the row with us. Bernard strode the lengths of his rows, piling up three full *cagettes* in his strong bare arms and striding to the edge of the vineyard to load them onto his waiting tractor.

Work was interrupted after about an hour or so, when most people were finishing off a row. Sophie opened the back doors of the Jumpy and produced breakfast. She had wisely provided bottled water which we poured over each other's hands to wash away the sticky grape juice which had stained hands, shoes and clothes. There were hard boiled eggs, crusty baguettes, yellow Normandy butter and slices of cold meat, along with strong coffee poured from flasks and for those who wanted it, paper cups of wine.

Seven o'clock in the morning was an unheard of hour for John and I to sample the wine and we were amazed to witness Bernard and some of the others drinking it with every appearance of enjoyment, even at that early hour.

As the morning wore on, the August sun was overpowering, making sweat and grape juice mingle and run down our faces. Trying to wipe it away was futile and only made our faces unbearably sticky. John and I were in our forties in those days and reasonably fit, but after a lengthy session of constant bending to drop in the full bunches of grapes, and the unaccustomed manual labour of dragging the steadily loading *cagettes*, our backs were protesting. Standing straight and stretching was a temporary relief, but as the morning wore on and the sun rose higher in the sky, our stamina was sorely tested. Believe me, grape picking is not romantic or for the faint-hearted. It is a pleasurable, euphoric experience for up to about ten minutes and after that it is a dogged, relentless slog to finish your rows of vines.

We were puzzled by the sight of helicopters which repeatedly passed low over our heads, and asked Bernard if he knew why they were there.

'Photographs,' he said briefly, looking up at them. He put down the *cagette* he was carrying and explained briefly. 'They fly over the vineyards during the harvest. I have registered the number of pickers I have in my team, so they take photos of all the vineyards, and if there are more pickers than those registered they will fine me because I have paid no tax for them.' He grinned at us. 'This is why you filled in the forms before we started. This is how it is done.' He picked up two more *cagettes*, loading them on top of the first and leaving us to continue the everlasting snipping. To this day, whenever I hold a pair of secateurs I get an urge to find a vine and start clipping. Despite the fact that there are literally millions of vines in the region, the locals still paid for grapes in the supermarkets, even at harvest time when the grapes were ripe. This, we learned, was because of the difference between grapes for making wine and those for eating. Wine grapes are measured according to their Brix level, which is the measurement used to assess sugar in grapes. Eating grapes have a measure of approximately 18 and are seedless, whereas wine grapes when they are ready to be harvested have a level closer to 25, as well as being full of seeds.

Work continued day after day in different vineyards. One which is a clear memory was early in the morning as dawn was breaking, deep in the countryside where the vines grew close to a massive swathe of reeds which towered over our heads. The air was completely still. The pickers stood silently, and there was a tense atmosphere of determination, of anticipation. We were doing this for Bernard, to help him on his way to becoming a successful *vigneron* whose organic wines would be drunk around the world. Notwithstanding the back breaking toil that it truly was, to be part of this team, completely surrounded by vines heavy with innumerable clusters of smooth black grapes, looking upwards to a cloudless sky with the ever present Pyrenees mountains to the south and the sombre hills of the Montagne Noire to the north was in all honesty one of the most unforgettable, surreal and magical experiences of my life.

The only real disadvantage to Bernard was the fact that he lived in a tiny community of *vignerons* who relied on the local cooperative to process their grapes, distribute the wine and pay them enough to live on. He was doing far better than this and there was the inevitable jealousy. His mother Sophie came across to our house one afternoon in a fine indignation, her round face reddening with emotion.

'Bernard's tractor,' she began breathlessly, flinging herself onto the sofa. 'He cannot use it. Someone has sabotaged his tractor! He was on his way into Rieux and his tractor, it died, it makes a terrible noise, it did not want to start. I knew how this would be, I told Bernard right from the start that people would not want him to succeed.'

'It might have just broken down?' I suggested hopefully. But no. Sophie knew what was at the root of it all. She shook her grey head vehemently. 'When a tractor makes this noise,' she said, 'it is the petrol that is not pure. Someone has put sugar into Bernard's petrol. They do not like my son,' she cried. 'They cannot make wine as good as Bernard's! His success, it is too much for these people here...'

'Oh, but Sophie, no, surely it can't be that!' I protested. 'Look at the way everyone helped him to pick his grapes. I'm sure no-one wishes him any harm.'

John looked up from his laptop with raised eyebrows, evidently following the gist of her words.

'You do not know these people here,' she stated darkly, as if daring us to disagree. 'Yes, they picked his grapes with him in his first year, but they wanted him to fail, so that they could say, *even though we helped him, he could not do it alone.* Many people thought this. I have seen it myself in their faces, I hear it in their voices when they ask me how he is doing. He has worked so hard,' she continued, and I could see that she was on the verge of tears. 'It is not fair, it is not just that people treat him like this. They look as if they are helping him but then they work against him in secret. He cannot transport his grapes without a tractor. They know this. It is all jealousy, I tell you.'

I was silent. Human nature being what it is, I could see that she had a point. Bernard was not only massively succeeding, he was doing it right under the nose of his neighbours who were in the same business. It was not a recipe for harmony.

Whatever his private feelings may have been, Bernard mastered them and appeared to be on friendly terms with most of the village. His best revenge was to be as successful as possible, and he knew it.

'You'd think,' John said after Sophie had gone, 'that he'd have been prepared for a certain amount of jealousy and taken some precautions.'

'What could he possibly have done?' I retorted impatiently. 'He hasn't got enough space for his vats *and* a garage. The tractor's out in the open day and night. Anyone could have sabotaged it. Well, poor Bernard. I hope he can get it fixed.'

'Why doesn't he open a little shop in the village?' I had once suggested to Sophie. 'After all, he's ideally positioned on the edge of a main road...'

But she shook her head. 'We have discussed this, many times,' she told me, 'and Bernard would like to do this, but it is too expensive. If he opens a shop there are many rules he must follow. He must have access for those in wheelchairs, he will need to provide a toilet for his visitors, and he will need to employ someone to serve. This, he cannot do by himself. But maybe in the future, he will think about this.'

At the time of writing this book, Bernard still has no shop, but he is now in his eleventh year and recognised as one of the best producers of 'bio,' or organic wine in the region. He attends the most prestigious wine fairs in France, the USA, Japan and the UK, gaining contacts and orders from these and many other countries. Year on year, he expands his wine portfolio, introducing new grape varieties and increasing his storage capacity, secure in the knowledge that the quality of his wine reflects his ever increasing expertise and meticulous attention to his vines.

Chapter 12
Traditions

Our first Christmas was fraught with problems. The French have their own Christmas traditions, such as the *bûche de Noël*, or Christmas log, which is essentially a chocolate swiss roll decorated with cream and sometimes topped with tiny nativity figures. They are delicious and we bought one, but it was intended for Boxing Day. On Christmas Day itself I wanted a cake. A proper, traditional fruit cake loaded with nuts, sultanas, currants, laced with brandy and covered with marzipan and icing. I also wanted a Christmas pudding, but there were none in the shops, as we lived in France well before the supermarkets had shelves devoted to international cuisine. When they did get round to it there were frequent errors, as we discovered when we found Birds custard powder, Fray Bentos pies and Heinz soups proudly displayed as produce of Italy. Still, it was a start.

As there were no Christmas cakes to be bought I decided to make my own, but once again I was stymied by the lack of large packets of mixed fruit, dark treacle which was an essential, dark brown sugar and cakes of marzipan.

Sophie told me where I could find the sugar, but the treacle remained elusive, as did the marzipan, except for very small slabs divided equally into blocks of pink, green and white. The French are very fond of nuts during the Christmas holidays, so there was no shortage of those, and dried figs and dates were easy to come across too. I made my cake with the ingredients available and it was a success. The Christmas puddings came thanks to various UK friends who decided, separately and without consulting the others, to send us one. We received five the first year, until we tried as tactfully as possible to discourage this practice. I offered one to our doctor, who smiled and politely declined as she had many English patients and had already accepted three puddings.

The tree was no problem either, except that in our hamlet we were the first to put one up, as Christmas is far more of a religious holiday than its UK counterpart. We bought a large artificial tree, on the basis that disposing of a real one might be a problem. The lights and decorations were equally easy to source, and we put the tree in the conservatory where it sparkled and was much admired, especially by the Bellinis next door. Madame must have bullied her husband, as one afternoon he set off for the woods carrying a large saw, and returned towards dusk dragging a huge fir tree behind him. I believe we were the only two families in the hamlet to have one.

We were used to gaudy displays of Christmas lights in the streets in the UK too, and after a fashion, it was the same in France. Our hamlet merited one shooting star at the entrance to the village and some lights wrapped around the lamp posts. Oxford Street need not have worried.

The French have their own Christmas traditions, naturally, and equally naturally many of them involve food. *Le réveillon* is one such: a long meal for family and friends which can go on for up to six hours. Generally there are two of these, one on Christmas Eve and the other on New Year's Eve. They are not cheap, and go a long way to explaining why French families always have large dining tables. A fairly standard *réveillon* would begin with nibbles such as tiny salted biscuits or short crunchy cheese sticks, followed by a starter of either foie gras, lobster or fresh oysters, followed by a main meat course, which can be anything from turkey, pheasant, beef or goose. A vast selection of cheese would be next, followed by the *bûche de Noël*. Each course would be accompanied by the finest wines the family could afford to buy, or in the case of the inhabitants of our hamlet, by wine they had produced themselves. Some households such as Marc and Sophie's across the road, liked to be exotic. I remember her getting terribly excited about the squirrels she would be cooking one year. That was just a little too extreme for us, and we stuck to our normal turkey, which was easy to find in any supermarket. It was Sophie who made me realize the intensity of family rivalry at Christmas. They alternated hosting with Marc's sister in Lyon, and she was loud in her condemnation of the preparations.

'Just imagine,' she said indignantly. 'We will be thirty-two for *Le réveillon*! Ridiculous to try to cook for so many. She starts preparing at least two weeks before and they have to bring out trestle tables to fit us all in. She thinks she is the world's best cook, but I can tell you, two years ago when we were there she had overcooked the turkey and it was as dry as a bone. I would not have given it to a dog.....'

As much as she purported to despise such a flurry of culinary activity, when it came to their turn, her own kitchen was a hive of frenetic activity in the days before her guests arrived and she could barely force the lid down on her chest freezer. She had invited John and me to share the meal with them, but I had the distinct impression that we were not meant to accept. In any case, we would have felt dreadfully ill at ease amongst family members whom we had never met, and conversation would have been, at best, polite and stilted with forced smiles all round. We would have acted as a damper on the whole proceedings, and I could hear the relief in her voice when I declined as tactfully as I could.

I was never in Marseille for Christmas, but I imagine it would have involved a marathon cooking extravaganza from Mamy. In my mind I was back there, hearing the screech of her voice, watching the surprisingly rapid, deft movements of her large body as she chopped, sliced, seasoned, fried and boiled; always either cooking a meal, preparing the next or shopping for supplies. She was exactly the same when I joined them for their yearly holiday to Puigcerdà, except that the space she had to work in was far more cramped.

Chapter 13
Puigcerdà

I have only a few clear memories of my time with Elodie in 1971 in Puigcerdà. The rest is a confused jumbled memory of narrow streets decorated with red and yellow Catalonian bunting flags, with the massed peaks of the Pyrenees mountains towards the horizon.

It was here that I found out about her stay with her parents. It had not gone well, and she recounted it to me as we were on our way to the only butcher in the village, with instructions from Mamy to bring her four lamb steaks. As soon as she began speaking I could see immediately how completely devastated she had been.

'I could see the minute she opened the door that she did not really want me there. I was wearing one of the necklaces she had bought me. You remember? The one with the rubies? I thought she might mention it but I do not think she even noticed. The only thing she said was that I had put weight on. That first evening, she had me doing all the washing up – the whole sink was full and there were dirty pots on all the work spaces, it took me over an hour to finish it all. Then she told me they were expecting some friends over, and would I help to prepare the vegetables for the meal. She said 'help her', but she left me on my own to do the whole lot. I had to peel the potatoes and the carrots, and she wanted the beans slicing. She even made me slice them thinner when she saw them. Honestly, Steph, I was exhausted. And when their friends came, I was not even invited to eat with them. She left me a couple of sandwiches and a drink in my room, and that was all I got. I was supposed to stay for three weeks but I had had enough after four days. I sneaked out to a phone box and I rang Mamy. She sent Papy to come and get me. All I wanted to do was to go back home.'

She stopped; her shaky voice indicating the tears not far away, and I put my arm around her. 'Stop thinking about it, Elodie,' I said. 'Please. It's only upsetting you.'

She shivered suddenly even though the sun was hot that day, and said, 'I will do as you say, I will try to forget about it....let us see if the butcher has any of those steaks left. I hope he has or we will both be in trouble!' She gave a faint giggle at that and by the time we reached the butcher, she was her usual self, for which I was very thankful.

It may have been Bastille Day, or possibly a summer celebration for the many tourists, but at any rate the large lake which was central to the village was to be the scene of a firework display in the evening. To that end, the fireworks were lying in the grassy verges all around the edge of the lake ready to be detonated later on.

They must have been well hidden, because I didn't notice them as we strolled around the lake. The first thing I was aware of was when Elodie grabbed my arm in a painful grip, shouting 'Run!' She dragged me away from the lake and a second later the ground exploded where we had been standing only moments before. We ran as fast as we could, still holding hands until we stumbled and slithered along the rough ground, before we sat up and our faces turned from red, to blue and to vivid green as we watched the fireworks detonate into a dazzling display of bursting coloured lights in the blackness of the night. She let go of me at last. As everyone knows, standing too close to fireworks is extremely risky. Planting yourself on top of them is sheer lunacy. Health and safety was certainly more lax in those days.

My other sharp memory floods back to me from time to time. Puigcerdà boasted, as well as its traditional small shops and vivid tall apartments, an open square where the local dance, the Sardane, was performed. It is danced only in Pyrenean villages and symbolises the independence of the Catelonian culture from that of mainland Spain. I remember a stage, resplendently hung with red and yellow material, where the musicians were tuning up. There were flutes and others I could not name. The discordant notes filled the air, rising and falling in volume and dying away as a conductor strode onto the dias and faced his small orchestra.

A group of people was converging in the centre of the square. They formed a rough circle, edging backwards as more people, men, women and teenagers joined them. The women laid their handbags in the centre of the circle. Mostly they wore a kind of espadrille sandal, although some of the men wore ordinary shoes.

Elodie grabbed me, and propelled me with her towards the gathering. Before I had fully realised what was happening, I was standing between her and a man, who held my arm aloft whilst Elodie did the same with my other arm. The musicians were ready by now, and suddenly the air was filled with the piping notes of a melody. The dance began. The steps were completely unknown to me. Elodie, familiar with the place from her very early years, knew what she was doing. My only option was to watch her closely as she performed the tricky sequence of steps, rising and falling on her heels and toes, eyes straight in front of her and her expression serious. The circle moved round in a clockwise direction, before reversing the sequence and beginning again. To me, the steps seemed at variance with the beat and piping of the flutes, but gradually, as I copied as best I could, some semblance of the rhythm of the dance became easier, and I was soon rising and falling on my heels and toes with the rest of them. Forward then back, arms held high, facing forward, moving in synchronization with the circle.

At the end I was smiling faintly. I had got it at last. Finally the music died away and there was a scatter of applause from seated visitors.

To this day, well over fifty years later, I am pleased that I once danced the Sardane. In a gesture of friendliness, Elodie later bought John and me a painting of Sardane dancers, with arms raised, standing in a circle in the foreground, with the peaks of the Pyrenees forming the background. It still hangs in my living room today.

Chapter 14
Drought

The year was 2003. It was a year that will live long in my memory, and one that I never want to live through again. Most of the population of France will never forget it either. That year was the hottest European summer on record since 1540. It began in May, with a series of long, hot days normally associated with the peak summer heat of July and August. The sky was a dazzling, completely cloudless deep blue, and the sun was relentless, beating down mercilessly onto the landscape; onto the animals, onto the people, drying up the rivers and burning the grass until it turned to hard straw with vicious spikes which crackled and hurt the feet.

Inside and out, it was the stuff nightmares are made of. If you are too cold, there are solutions. You can add clothes, you can light fires, you can turn up the heating. But when you are too hot and there is no air conditioning, there is literally nothing you can do. Wearing thin white cotton clothes only helped minimally, before the sweat soaked through them and you had to change.

In Paris, a refrigerated warehouse had to be used by the undertakers to store bodies, as there was not enough room for them in the normal facilities. It was mostly the elderly who were affected, who lived, like us, in houses without air conditioning. In our case, it had been on our list of jobs to do, and how bitterly we regretted not having done it already. We were to add the air conditioning the following year.

We spent almost the whole of the summer outside, in the one place that offered any shade, which was by the barbecue close to the tall pine trees which made up the perimeter of our plot.

Earlier in the day we had showered. It was useless even bothering to get dried, as ten minutes later, our bodies were running once again with rivulets of warm sweat that got into the eyes and mouth, tasting of weak salt.

John and I spent much of the time looking hopefully up at the sky, waiting to see just one tiny wisp of white that might bring rain and an end to the suffering. It never came. I have never lived in a country where water is scarce, and I experienced a feeling of utter panic, in case the drought really did mean that there would no longer be water available for my body. It was such a primeval feeling that even now, many years later, I find it incredible, and slightly shaming that I once felt like that. Perhaps because our bodies are three-quarters water, the thought of your cells dying for lack of it throws the mind into turmoil.

Very occasionally, clouds did appear overhead and we waited in anguished hope for a fall of rain. The sky would almost blacken with clouds, whilst the thunder rumbled in the distance and the lightning flashed around us, but not a single drop of rain fell from the sky. Eventually the clouds would dissipate, leaving us in a raging, swearing and utterly impotent desolation. John is normally calm, but he was more than once reduced to helpless, heartrending sobbing as the heat built up around us and threatened to overpower us completely.

We were not the only ones affected. The villagers of Caunes-Minervois took an unprecedented and desperate step to alleviate the suffering of its people. In the abbey were housed a series of holy relics, normally kept in dark boxes to preserve them, and only taken out on extra special ceremonial occasions.

These relics were taken from their boxes and mounted on purple velvet cushions. The clergy donned their white, golden decorated robes and led a solemn procession around the village, offering up prayers and singing hymns, imploring God for mercy and asking him to send his life-giving rain.

We had never seen anything like this in our lives. It was surreal; it was something that belonged in the fifteenth century. It was an event that only served to further deepen the nightmare of heat that was all around us.

It didn't work.

The *canicule*, or heatwave, lasted for months. I can remember driving into the village for some essential supplies. The car was actually one place where we could escape, if only temporarily. By switching on the air conditioning and leaving the car running for a few minutes before getting in, it was cool enough to drive in. Touching the steering wheel before it had cooled down was out of the question and would actually burn your hand if you tried it.

On the long straight road which led into the village was a pharmacy, equipped with a thermometer which gave a shade temperature. I looked up at it and I stopped the car. I knew for a certainty that if I didn't have photographic evidence of this, that no-one would ever believe me. The thermometer was showing a shade temperature of 45°.

Another escape route was to drive high up into the Montagne Noire. About half way up was the *Gouffre de Cabrespine*. One of the largest and deepest caves in the world, as deep as the Eiffel Tower is tall, it offers visitors a true experience in itself, with the interior lit up to reveal dripping stalagmites and stalactites in lurid colours of turquoise, amber and ochre. In that scorching summer of 2003, it was positively thronged with visitors. Most of them had been there many, many times before and had known every blessed stalagmite in the place since early childhood. But, and this was tremendously important, the temperature inside was a wonderful, heavenly fourteen degrees. This temperature was ideal for storing wine, and several *vignerons* in the region paid to have their barrels of wine matured there. It was a refuge, for us as well as for our neighbours. Nearly every visit brought you into contact with someone you knew. You greeted them with sheepish kisses, each party knowing full well why the other was there. We would have paid ten times the entrance fee just to have an hour's worth of coolness.

The heatwave finally broke in early September, but not before it had claimed the lives of well over fourteen thousand people in France alone.

Chapter 15
Waterworks

Make no mistake, living in the South of France gives you cachet. It comes immediately, like a free gift along with your French address. There's not much point in denying it. The minute you tell people, 'I live in the South of France,' your cachet level shoots right off the scale. People are impressed. You need to adjust your face into an expression of careless nonchalance in case people say you are showing off. (They will say it anyway as soon as they leave you, but it helps to make the effort).

Just to really boost your status to stratospheric levels, you then let people know, nonchalantly of course, that you have just installed a pool. Then wait for the gossip to go around, which doesn't take long. A few minutes at the most. You won't actually hear it yourself but you know what's being said.

'They've just moved to the South of France. It's a villa, with a pool,' they say...

Their own faces take on the exact nonchalant expression of yours, just in case the showing off accidentally rubs off onto themselves for talking about it.

What nobody mentions, or even thinks about, is that there is the South of France with a capital S and then there is the south of France, meaning that southern part of a country where the land meets the sea. The South of France with the capital S is synonymous with large yachts, imposing stuccoed villas with price tags that would buy you a fair chunk of Kensington, Olympic-sized swimming pools and glamorous model types in designer clothing who look and smell divine.

That is what springs to mind when you tell people you live in the South of France. Actually, that image bears very little resemblance to the place we had actually moved to. Our own part of the country was definitely in the south of France category. With a very small 's'. A land of vineyards, of lonely *vignerons* working the land, where a sudden hailstorm can blight the lives of entire villages. The surrounding countryside with seemingly endless vineyards, spectacular golden beaches and the sombre distant Montagne Noire was every bit as spectacular as anything Provence could boast, but it was a calmer, non pretentious place, where normal people went about their daily humdrum lives and had no deep seated ambitions to buy a yacht.

But, this was actually the south of France, and here we were, in a house without a pool. The garden was huge, being roughly three quarters of an acre. There was plenty of room for one and we knew exactly where we wanted it. Down towards the end of the garden, in a spot where the trees would not overshadow it and it would be in full sunlight.

There was no shortage of swimming pool companies. We looked at Piscine Plus for a while, then Dejoyaux, and there was Union Piscines in Carcassonne. Then onto the scene came Cash Piscines, and we decided to pay them a visit. They are located in a small *zone industrielle* not too far from the centre, with an impressive showroom full of boxed up pools, a great range of equipment; giant sieves for removing floating leaves and insects, impressively expensive automated cleaning systems, kits for testing the ph and chlorine levels, and vivid inflatable accessories ranging from plastic ducks to sit-on whales with improbably grinning faces.

Cash Piscines specialise in above ground pools, which was our choice. An in-ground pool would have had the advantage of looking better, but would come with the huge disadvantage of costing many thousands of euros. There was also the question of tax. An in-ground pool is taxable, whereas an above ground one is deemed to be temporary and movable, and is therefore tax exempt. Although exactly how one would go about moving a swimming pool is open to question. Most people install them and then leave them where they are. No-one gets a pool with the idea of shifting it a few centimetres to the left once a month.

We bought the pool in much the same way as we had bought our apartment. That is, quickly. Once I know what I want there is no hanging around, I go for it. We chose an 8 metre by 4 metre one, on the basis that it was large enough and deep enough to actually swim in.

We paid for it and waited expectantly by the counter, eyebrows slightly raised questioningly. The assistant smiled nicely. 'Was there anything else you wanted?' he enquired brightly, as if we had just bought a pound of carrots.

'Well, when can you deliver?' I asked politely.

His eyebrows shot up as if I had asked for something quite impossible. He spread out his hands in a gesture of helplessness. 'But, Madame, we do not deliver,' he said in a pained tone. 'Do you have a van? A car?'

Well, yes, of course we had a car, but who in their right minds expects to fit a swimming pool into the boot of their car? Even one packed up in a box. Two boxes to be precise, one for the pool itself and the other containing all the equipment that went with it, such as the blue corrugated plastic pipes and the pump.

Not being frequent buyers of swimming pools, we failed to realise that we had gone about this in completely the wrong way. Real French people, when they buy a pool, consult the immediate family first. Then they ask the opinions of all their extended family including all the cousins and as a second thought, most of the neighbours, just in case anyone feels left out and it causes bitter feuds for generations to come.

Then five, ten or maybe fifteen people all get together and decide between them whose van will be best to transport the goods, whose equipment can be borrowed to dig out the required plot and who is best at laying concrete. It is a village affair and no-one is quite foolish enough to attempt the whole process on their own.

Except for the British, of course, very few of whom have ever bought an outdoor swimming pool in their lives. The rare British people who don swimming gear and leap into an unheated pool, even in the height of what passes for summer in the UK, are either extremely hardy or severely mentally challenged. Possibly both. So, in general, we just don't do it. And then we find ourselves at a disadvantage when it comes to getting a newly purchased pool back to our French home again.

We backed off for a moment to consult.

'What are we going to do?' I asked. I was back in my whispering mode once more. This time it was probably immaterial as it was unlikely that the shop assistant spoke English, but I kept my voice low all the same.

John was at his unruffled best. He was calm, he was utterly unfazed as he voiced the only practical solution.

'Tell them that if they can't deliver, we'll cancel the order,' he said stolidly. 'There must be a cooling off period like we have. Go on, you can do that.' He ushered me with a wave of his arms back towards the assistant.

So I did my best. In what I fondly hoped was a firm, clear voice, I made it quite clear that the swimming pool would be delivered or our next visit would be to our bank to cancel the payment.

Matters moved on as swiftly as we had expected. The manager had a friend. His friend had a van. The friend and the van were both at our disposal and he was certain that matters could be arranged to our specifications for a small fee.

'The way they do business here is appalling!' I was outraged as we walked towards the car. 'Why not just have a price structure in place – you pay for the pool on its own, or you pay a higher price for pool plus delivery, or you have a ready to swim price. A sort of *Prêt à Plonger*. I am sure that's how British shops would do it.'

'Ah, yes, sweetheart, but most British people don't have outdoor pools, do they? I mean, our weather's not exactly ideal for it, is it?'

Finally the pool was delivered. It was installed onto the concrete base and we watched as delighted as children on Christmas morning as it gradually filled up. The disadvantage was that it filled up with water from the kitchen tap which we fed into the pool by dint of joining three hose pipes together. Our next water bill was so astronomical that we had a visit from the water company, to check whether we had any leaks.

The reward was to be actually swimming in our own front garden! It gave a whole new perspective to the fruit trees, to the vines beyond our fence, to our house in the distance. You saw them from a completely different angle, as if you were suddenly levitated a few feet. It was a fantastic feeling, and we used the pool almost every day when it had heated up to the required temperature, which was from twenty-five degrees plus for John. I refused to dip a toe in the water until it reached a balmy twenty-nine degrees, and then it was sheer bliss.

Our other outdoor water feature was the *fosse septique*, or septic tank. If you're ever thinking about buying a house with a septic tank, then don't. Please, just don't. Septic tanks are truly gross, being large containers full of human excrement. They are not things to be added to any of your wish lists. They belong on caravan sites or other temporary accommodation where there is absolutely no viable alternative. If you live in a neighbourhood with a properly functioning waste disposal system, your own waste is dealt with almost imperceptibly, without your personal participation. If you live in a house with a septic tank then all this messy activity takes place on your own property. In houses they are an abomination. People have *drowned* in septic tanks. Like the ancient Greek and Roman gods, they are living beings who need to be placated, cosseted, pampered, worshipped and regularly serviced. I may be a little biased in my opinion, and I'm sure there are plenty of people out there getting on famously with their own septic tanks, but we were not paid up members of that happy band.

When we bought the house, Monsieur Damery had warned us in an intensely irritating, finger wagging sort of way, against Javel.

It really has to be said that I didn't like this man. I had taken against him almost from the start, thinking him overbearing and pompous. The removal of the kitchen and the theft of the pot plants had cemented my opinion. I honestly thought he was talking about a particular brand name. Maybe he had once bought from this Javel company and not been satisfied. So perversely, I decided that Javel would be my all-time favourite brand from now on and I would use it everywhere I could, just to spite him. As a telling act of spite it was fairly useless as he wouldn't know about it, but the effect on me was cathartic. I found it, eventually, in the supermarket, it was in an aisle with the disinfectants and I triumphantly added it to my trolley. Hah, got you! I thought. I knew what it was now, it was obviously a type of cleaner, it would be fantastic for the kitchen, the bathroom, even the floors.

I used it copiously, sloshing it around like one demented and it was great, especially when used down the toilet to get rid of nasty brown marks. It had that distinctive smell that I had always associated with Domestos.

A few days later we began to notice a faint smell. We took no notice, putting it down to the hot weather and assuming that it would fade away. But it didn't. It got stronger with every passing day and the neighbours were starting to notice. It was especially strong just outside the front door and seemed to emanate from a kind of manhole cover.

It was John who valiantly prised the cover off. Then he put it back again very hurriedly. The stench was unbearable. At that moment Monsieur Bellini appeared from next door.

'There is a big problem down there,' he remarked, poking his face dangerously close to the manhole cover. 'Your *fosse septique*, she is blocked. She is dying.'

'Dying?' I asked incredulously. I hadn't even realised that the manhole cover was part of the tank, and it had certainly never occurred to me that it was alive, as was evidently the case. Monsieur Bellini shook his head sorrowfully. 'She will need very much treatment,' he said. 'Come with me, I will show you the correct product.'

I dutifully followed him along the track to his own house, where he invited me to sit in the kitchen until he had found what he was looking for. Madame was nowhere to be seen. He returned presently with a red packet, indicating the title with a bony finger. 'This is the '*Eparcyl*,' he said. 'You need to put one sachet into your tank every week. Here, I give you three of mine, we will go and you will see.' He led us back to our own house.

'Where is your toilet?' he asked, and marching in, he opened the door of our WC, poured the contents of the sachet down the basin and flushed it.

'So, this is needed, every week,' he said. 'She will keep your tank clean and she will work for you. But your tank now, she is not working for you. She will need to be pumped out.' He fished around in his back pocket and brought out a crumpled piece of paper and handed it to me. 'See, this company, they will pump out your tank. It is the only way to treat this problem. Once she is pumped out, then you can use the product. It is payable, but you have to do this every year. You can also buy yoghurt and wait until it is no longer fit to eat, and then you pour it down the toilet. This is what many people do here.'

We thought we would try the official product first, and poured a packet of the *Eparcyl* powder down the toilet before flushing it hopefully.

The effect was non-existent. Evidently our *fosse septique* was far beyond the sticking plaster stage and would need to be urgently operated upon by the specialists. We reluctantly called the number that Monsieur Bellini had given us.

There was a lot of sad shaking of heads and solemn peering down holes when they arrived. We felt like negligent parents who had abandoned their offspring. Finally, after some initial consultation, the two men had the massive hoses properly installed and the purging began. We went inside to wait until the operation was over.

The bill was in the hundreds of euros, which convinced us, if we needed any more convincing, that our *fosse septique* was to be hitherto treated like a delicate newborn infant. Every week after that John religiously saw to its every need, and it continued to serve us well for many years.

Chapter 16
Sightseeing

The absolute necessity of carrying documents around with you in France has been documented many, many times. Nothing was any different for us. Suffice it to say that unless you have an electricity bill on you, your official existence will be denied. You will not be allowed to register for anything, buy anything, go anywhere or have anything installed. The miserable, pathetic excuse that you haven't yet received an electricity bill because they are issued every three months and this is your first week in France will not be accepted. Nor will a *notaire's* deed of sale. Nor will a bank statement proving that you have just this week paid x amount for the property. Officials will laugh at you. It's an electricity bill or nothing. Consider yourself warned.

We lived here, but in the first few years we were tourists like the rest, getting to know our surroundings, with the smug satisfaction that we were not merely here for a visit. We actually lived here. The enormity of it hadn't quite hit home yet, but it would.

One of our first visits was to Minerve, the capital of the Minervois department. To go to Minerve today is sometimes said to transport people back into the middle ages. It is that sort of village. To begin with, there are two routes to the village; one along a reasonably straightforward *départementale* road, the other a twisting narrow road which takes you past the rocky landscape intersected by patches of wild *garrigue* with its low-growing thyme, rosemary bushes, straggly lavender, fronds of dark green artemisia and papery pink rock roses with pale yellow centres. All this is interspersed with terrifyingly high craggy rock faces and the ubiquitous vineyards.

As soon as you reach Minerve, a straight road bridge over the river Cesse leads you over an incredibly deep rocky ravine into the village itself. Today the village functions as a tourist attraction, with small cafes and boutiques selling leather goods, jewellery and pottery. One particular favourite of ours was a small shop on a corner. As soon as you entered, the smell of leather enveloped you. The owner made, or bought in, leather hair barrettes, book covers, sandals and handbags. His particular speciality was the making of mirrors, sculpted all around the edge with a deep wooden border into which he carved all kinds of strange creatures; snakes and gnomes with popping eyes, all manner of fantastic gargoyle-like creatures created out of his own vivid imagination.

But that is today's Minerve. Centuries ago it was home to the Cathar sect; a group of people who rejected the teachings of the Catholic church on the basis that the church was fundamentally a materialistic, rather than a spiritual organisation and that they themselves were the only true Christians. In the thirteenth century these things mattered. They mattered a lot. To everyone. The Catholic church was determined to wipe them out and they besieged the town of Beziers, killing indiscriminately. Any Cathars who escaped this outrage found refuge in the village of Minerve, which didn't save them, as Simon de Montford and his army hunted them down.

Retreat proved to be futile. Simon de Montfort was a name to strike terror into any Cathars in Minerve. He attacked the village's well, their only source of water, and later captured 140 *'parfaits,'* as they were known, condemning them to what must surely be the most horrific death known to man, that of burning them at the stake.

There is one place in Minerve, a kind of ledge with no barrier, perched above a rocky precipice. Some of the Cathars were said to have thrown themselves off this ledge to a certain death, to avoid capture.

John and I stood at this spot, trying to imagine what it must have been like, to be forced to choose between hurling yourself off a precipice, or risk being captured and burnt alive. It was impossible to imagine. As twenty-first century tourists, coming from your own safe part of this world (depending on where you live of course), it is impossible to really imagine yourself in a totally different society. You can know about it, you can look at the place, you can ponder, you can speculate all you like, but you can not even begin to conceive of the mental torture it must surely have been for those poor people. I did think about it as far as I was able, and I concluded that I too would have jumped.

Another of our excursions took us to Lagrasse. Then, as now, dubbed 'one of the most beautiful villages in France.' Our favourite place was down by the shallows of the river Orbieu where on a hot day, we took off our shoes and cooled off by bathing our feet in the deliciously silky water. Straight ahead of us was the ancient rough stone bridge, with a row of houses built from the same stone, as if they were an extension of the bridge itself. A stretch of scrubby greenery grew in front, which petered out into a rocky beach area. On the other bank was low rocky plateau, where daring teens were showing off by jumping in themselves and being pushed in by their friends. We went to the famous abbey and strolled around the cloisters and gardens, but for us, the interest lay behind and above the village where a straight path led beside a row of allotments, with pink and red roses growing in a rambling tangle beside hollyhocks and the inevitable lettuces. John was completely engrossed in the planting, remarking sagely on the success or otherwise of the tomatoes. Beyond and above the village the tall straight cypresses of the region stood proudly pointed, their dark green foliage in stark contrast to the deep blue sky. Lagrasse was firmly on our list of places to take our visitors, who loved it as much as we did.

Andorra was not in our local area, being almost three hours' drive to the south west of us, but we decided to get up early for once and spend the day there.

'It *will* be an early start,' John warned me the night before. 'We shouldn't be setting off much later than five o'clock if we want to get there and back in a day.'

'Can't we simply find a B&B?' I pleaded, early rising not being amongst my accomplishments, even though John was quite cheerfully up and about regularly by seven whilst I was completing my rapid eye movement phases and didn't like them interrupted. Not even for Andorra.

'We *could,*' he admitted. 'But there'll be all the hassle of booking it, then finding it when we get there. And if you look at some of the prices, they charge a fortune. Would it be worth it, do you think?'

I did a rapid internet search and, much as I disliked the idea of getting up early, I disliked the B&B prices even more. I resolved to go to bed early, and get up refreshed and ready for the great trip.

As ever when you try to have an early night before an appointment, sleep knows all about it and evades you with huge success. It must have been nearly one o'clock in the morning before I finally dozed off, with John's heavy snoring not helping matters and increasing my irritation. The alarm rang just before five and I was ready to call the whole thing off. I was still in torpid night mode, my eyes were heavy and all I wanted was to sink my head back onto my pillow and spend the day quietly reading.

But John was already showered, dressed and outside looking the car over, prodding at the tyres and measuring the oil gauge. Very reluctantly I swung my legs out of bed and tried to prepare my body for the day.

In the end, it was around seven o'clock when the sky was lightening and the snowy peaks of the Pyrenees, which were a distant but beautiful backdrop from home, were looming larger and more imposing every moment. The scenery grew ever more spectacular the closer we got to our destination, and I later reflected that it had been the best thing about the whole trip.

Andorra, for us, was disappointing. To be sure, it was ringed by the massing mountains, with picturesque chalet type properties on its flanks, but the centre of the town was a line of shops, catering for those who came in search of cheap tobacco, alcohol, straw baskets and strangest of all, butter. At the back of almost every shop we visited was a waist high stack of the cheapest packets of butter we had ever seen. We wondered about its origins, and concluded that Andorra must have been one of the dumping grounds for the surplus butter mountain caused by various governments' efforts at controlling the economy. As we were there, and as the butter was there, we bought some, and as a souvenir of the visit it was of far more use than a plastic trinket would have been.

The return journey took us once more through the most wonderful scenery, but we were both relieved to see the normal vistas of sunflowers and vineyards which meant that we were home. I put most of the butter into the freezer and went to catch up on my sleep.

The city of Carcassonne is very well known to an enormous number of people, and I suspect to most of the people reading this book. A little superfluous, then, to talk about the many towers, all built to a slightly different design, or the narrow cobbled streets flanked by boutique shops, many of which sell the same type of merchandise. As in every other tourist town in the world, the vast majority of it will surely have been made somewhere in the Far East by people who never have, and never will, visit the towns whose local souvenirs they spend their working lives producing.

In the case of Carcassonne, those far flung machinists are embroidering tea towels, painting lurid-coloured cicadas and small trays to carry olives, salt and pepper and filling up small linen bags with lavender which may or may not have originated from the fields around Grasse. A walk up the main street brings you past shops selling, amongst other items, postcards, keyrings, perfumed soaps, wooden toy swords, sundials, exquisitely dressed dolls, jewellery, and embroidered bags and purses. One shop has a window full of authentic swords, daggers and other lethal weapons that everyone admires and practically no-one buys on the correct assumption that they will never get them past airport security, and that they would in all likelihood get themselves arrested for possession.

If you are sitting on the correct side of Ryanair flight 72 from Stansted to Carcassonne then the walled city is clearly visible from the sky as the plane makes its descent to the airport, and it is truly a splendid sight with the snowy Pyrenees as its distant backdrop. If you are one of the few people who haven't visited, then please put it on your destination list, preferably avoiding the period from June to September when the crowds are at their most concentrated. Other months will also be crowded but manageably so.

As we lived nearby accommodation was no problem, but for those who don't the town is well endowed with hotels, apartments and B&Bs ranging from the budget-friendly to the expensive, or if you feel in the mood to remortgage your house, the Hotel de la Cité will always have a huge welcome for you and cater for your every whim. We never stayed there ourselves, but our friend Odette had clients who had and she regaled us with their various caprices. One guest, she told us, rejected the hotel's coat hangers on the basis that they were too large or too small, I forget which, and other demanded a certain brand of whisky at three in the morning as she couldn't sleep. The hotel rang around the local hotels until they found one that stocked that particular brand and promptly dispatched a minion to collect it.

If you drive then you may just get a parking spot in the car parks at the top of the hill opposite the château. We always parked at the side of the Aude, approaching from under the railway bridge where there was usually a space. From there it is a walk under the road bridge and along a dark and somewhat dilapidated street until a sharp left turn brings you to the Pont Vieux over the rushing River Aude and into Rue de Trivalle. Towards the end of this little street with its dragon-headed drainpipes is a steep road leading up to the château. The emphasis here is on the word 'steep,' and I am not talking a slight incline. When you get to the top there is a small park with benches so that you can fortify yourself before you cross over the massive drawbridge into the city itself. The drawbridge itself with its massive chains is authentically solid, straddling a deep dry moat and is only very slightly spoilt by the incongruous traffic lights just beyond.

We became almost as familiar with the nearby tax office on Place Gaston-Jourdanne, where we spent frustrating hours being advised on our tax returns by clerks who were almost as confused as we were. French income tax forms comprise four pages of small rectangles, each one designated by a number followed by two initials. This is French bureaucracy at its spectacular incomprehensible peak, as the meaning of each set of initials is explained in a separate accompanying booklet, which, depending on your tax obligations and the number of forms to be filled in, can run to thirty-six pages. The forms arrive each year, together with a guaranteed rise in blood pressure. John, with his more logical thought processes and ability to be calm under pressure, was far better at filling them in than I was, but we usually finished up at the tax office anyway, just to make sure.

Chapter 17
Shopping

Shopping in the Languedoc, and very probably the rest of France, takes on a form of logistical challenges. Where you shop, and when you shop, is largely dependent on how far away the shops might be, and on their confusing opening hours. We had a local '*Huit à Huit*', which as its name suggests, really ought to be open from eight in the morning until eight at night. Our own franchise opened at eight, closed at twelve for lunch, opened again at two and closed at seven.

Deciding on your setting off time is essential. In the mornings you need to allow sufficient time to arrive and shop before all the shutters go down for a two or three-hour lunchtime. If shopping in the afternoon, it is useless to set off much before one-thirty unless you are prepared to wait in the car for the shutters to go back up again. Once they do, then you are fine until at least six-thirty. Be wary of trying to drive back home at lunchtime, as all the local employees will be making their own way home at the same time and you will be caught up in tailbacks stretching for kilometres.

It took us thirty minutes by car to reach a shopping centre of any respectable size. Our local *'zone commerciale'* was the one at Salvaza, close to Carcassonne airport.

It improved drastically during our time in France, but at that time it comprised a large supermarket called *La Galerie*, an electrical store named *Darty*, a specialist lighting shop called *Lumi 11,* and *Cultura*, which sold stationery, toys, craft materials and electronic games. Now abandoned, there used to be a little cafe next to the supermarket where you could serve yourself a variety of plainly cooked food and delicious, *patisserie* standard desserts.

Darty was our only option for electrical and electronic goods. One November day our printer's brain had caught electronic obsessive compulsion disorder and was gushing out copies by the score when it was asked in a polite tone of voice to give us one copy. We gave it endless chances but it refused to comply, even when we threatened it with the local tip, so in the end we decided we needed a new one. I seem to remember that there was an urgent need. An official letter to the *notaire,* which would have looked unprofessional when handwritten.

Darty had a shelf of likely looking candidates, and we chose one at the end of a row. We indicated our choice to the pimply teenage assistant, who eyed us very doubtfully and shook his head slightly.

'I will see if we have it in stock,' he told us, striding over to his personal computer. He tapped out a staccato of numbers, then sucked in his cheeks and shook his head. 'Not this one,' he said. 'Unfortunately she is not available.'

We sighed and went back to the shelf of printers, muttering quietly that this wouldn't be tolerated in the UK. 'If they have them on display, surely they need to have them in stock,' John said.

Our second choice was a more expensive model, but we needed a printer immediately, so approached the young man again, to let him know.

Another short, sharp encounter with his stocklist brought the same response. He was desolate, he told us, but that model was not in stock.

'I can order it for you,' he beamed, 'and we can send you an email as soon as it comes into our warehouse, then you can collect it the next day.' I was encouraged by this. Our urgent letter could wait a couple of days, I reasoned.

'Great,' I agreed. 'We'll order it then. When will it be in stock again?' His eyes flicked along a column of figures, and he looked up. 'We will have some more in February,' he announced brightly.

Glumly, we tried the shelf again and made another choice, with each model costing more than its predecessor. By this time, my already limited patience was reaching its end. There was one printer left on the list, and when this was regretfully declined, I saw red. I marched the pimply youth over to the shelf of printers. I spoke very slowly, very deliberately. 'You do have them in stock,' I declared. 'There they are, on your shelf. I would like to buy one of your printers.'

'But, Madame,' he stuttered, 'you cannot buy one of these. They have no boxes, these are not for sale.'

Still speaking in a tone more suited to a stubborn six-year-old, I said, 'Listen to me. I do not want to buy a box. I want to buy a printer.' I pointed to it and spaced my words out. 'I-want-to-buy-that-printer. That one, up there, on that shelf.'

He was becoming confused but I wasn't in the mood to cater to what I saw as blatant incompetence.

'I don't need the box, I just want the printer. And I want it today, not next February.'

'But, without a box, I cannot give you a guarantee...' His sad voice trailed off as he anticipated my reply. Before I could voice it, he capitulated with a shrug and we went home with a printer. One without a box.

Narbonne was another shopping destination. At over an hour, it was further away, but with the added advantage of a splendidly beautiful situation on the banks of the Canal de la Robine, a tributary of the Canal du Midi, and a series of cafes in the deep shade of the plane trees which line the banks. The impressively named *Via Domitia* gave its visitors a glimpse of a section of original Roman paving, and on a hot day, a visit to the stunning architecture of the gothic *Cathédrale St. Juste* provided an ideal break. In its gardens were carefully pruned conical trees and a large stone sundial. We went later with our daughter Janice, when we pointed out the difficulty it must have been, constructing a building of such an immense height.

She cast a brief nonchalant glance towards the hundred and thirty foot ceiling. 'They were probably taller in those days,' she murmured.

I loved our visits to the market. We used to park at the theatre and walk to the it along the banks of the Canal. At the top was an old fashioned traditional gaudy roundabout with its stiff glittering horses carrying shrill, excited youngsters who were rising and falling smoothly in time with the synthetic melody.

The colourful, flower-filled outdoor market had a varied selection of stalls, one of which displayed every possible colour of spices in square, cotton-lined boxes. Another sold pure white crockery, and there were fabric stalls with their heavy rolls of Provençal oilcloths, patterned cottons and heavy upholstery fabrics.

The indoor market, Les Halles, was a dazzling, sensuous array of the freshest fish, meat, poultry, fruits and vegetables anywhere in France. The market was always teeming with people and the air resounded with screeching voices tempting the visitor to their stall; a gastronomic paradise redolent with pungent aromas of spices, brimming barrels of glistening olives stuffed with all manner of peppers, gleaming dark red cherries, cling-wrapped slices of watermelon, shelves loaded with honey of every shade from palest gold to deep umber, gigantic fish on beds of chopped ice, their unblinking dead eyes staring vacantly. There was the heady doughy smell of freshly baked baguettes, cheese-filled pastries and home-baked pizzas, floury topped artisan loaves, piles of freshly picked mud-spotted lettuces vying for space with bunches of vivid orange carrots and tied up bunches of fresh parsley, thyme and rosemary. The twisted bunches of fat garlic bulbs and shining onions hanging in massive plaits from iron bars almost touched the heaped up potatoes and hairy green beans. It was always a huge pleasure to shop there and be secure in the knowledge that the food we had bought was of the highest possible quality. Mamy would have been delighted.

En route to Narbonne was a gaunt, stooped lady who paced up and down endlessly by the side of a parking bay for lorries. She was faultlessly, if somewhat formally dressed in a dark coloured suit, with a ravaged, haggard face that may once have been beautiful. We had the impression that she was as well known to the gendarmerie as she was to the local lorry drivers.

Chapter 18
Elodie

I had never forgotten Elodie, although I had not heard from her for several years, not since a short text had told me of her parents' divorce. From the tone of it I had the distinct impression that the news was not a surprise to her, and nor was she particularly interested.

I was unprepared for the text that arrived as we were in the orchard, picking the ripe figs in mid-September. I always carried my mobile with me in case one of the girls rang, and I felt it vibrate as I was on the second rung of the ladder and leaning towards a particularly plump specimen. Of our three fig trees, this one was the most productive, although the figs never resembled the plastic-packaged sort on offer in supermarkets. Most of them were blackened, shrivelled tear-drop shapes, mostly with tell-tale holes where the insects had got to them first. But not all. The tree had been planted when the house was first built over thirty years ago, and still bore plenty of plump, whole fruits which we loved picking and eating when they were in season.

I gently tugged at the fig, noting with pleasure the slightly ribbed tight purple skin, knowing that the inside would be moist and oozing with grainy seeds. I climbed down with it and laid it alongside several other choice pickings, before I turned my attention to the incessant vibrations.

Hi Stephanie, she wrote. *It has been a long time, I am sorry I have not kept in touch more often. Anyway, here is the latest news but I am afraid it is not good. My mother has had a stroke! She did not go to her work for two days, and one of her colleagues called to her house to find out why. She was lying on the floor, and unable to move or to speak properly. She was in a very poor case when the colleague discovered her. She has been many weeks in the hospital as she was very poorly although the doctors say that she will recover much of her functionality in time if she has good care. The hospital is in St. Tropez as there is not a hospital nearer which specialises in strokes. But, she keeps on ringing me, and she says that she wants us to move to Bormes-les-Mimosas to be near her. She says she has not many friends who can support her. She has not told my father. I do not think he would be interested in her now, since their divorce was very bitter. I do not know what to do. It does not matter for Lucie because she lives now with her boyfriend, but Antoine has his job here in Marseille. My mother says she has no one except for me. I do not want to move but I know that my mother wants me near her. Tell me, what can I do? I am very sad about this.*

Love, Elodie

In my mind I was back in Bormes-les-Mimosas all those years ago. I remembered Véronique's manner towards Elodie; her snappy replies every time Elodie opened her mouth, her quite obvious preference for her beautiful salon than for her daughter. She could have sent for the girl to live with her at any time, and she hadn't. In my eyes, she had completely failed as a mother and I saw no reason for Elodie to uproot herself and her family to be near a woman who had shown her no affection during her childhood.

Even though I felt like that, I didn't feel that it was my place to say so. Elodie would have to make the decision on her own. I only knew that in her place, I wouldn't be rushing to change my whole life for a woman who showed no feelings for me.

I thought of my own mother in my childhood: a touch snobbish maybe but heavily involved in my education; looking over my homework, creating havoc because I had lost the expensive pen she had bought me the previous week, frustrated and annoyed that my gym clothes were still on the ironing pile when they ought to have been in my schoolbag ready for the next day. Making sure in her own way that I had 'the best' as far as it was in her power to provide it. But always there, always an unacknowledged loving presence. The love was so all pervasive that I failed to notice it. It was so much a part of my life, like the sunrise in the morning, that it was an intrinsic part of my existence. I tried to imagine what it would be like if my mother hadn't loved me. I failed. How could a mother not love her child? The idea seemed totally impossible. In my world mothers loved their children, it couldn't be otherwise.

Yet here was a mother who didn't, and my heart was sore for Elodie. Gaudy necklaces were not an adequate substitute for a loving mother, even though Elodie had tried so desperately to convince herself that they were.

Suddenly the figs seemed less important, although I left John to finish off stripping the tree and walked slowly back to the house. My feelings were mixed. Why should Elodie contact me only when she had a problem in her life? Was she really, as others seemed to think, using me as a kind of permanent prop for when life was awkward, or was this a genuine friendship? I couldn't help coming to the conclusion that I was being used as a kind of substitute mother figure. But then, I reasoned, wasn't Elodie in desperate need of one? Just possibly I was the next best thing but I knew that I could never even approach the kind of love and security that she was craving. I decided to answer as soon as possible. I grabbed my phone and threw myself into the soft conservatory armchair.

Hi Elodie,

What an awful thing to happen! Honestly, I don't know what is best. It really has to be your decision. What does Antoine think? Will he be able to get a job in Bormes-les-Mimosas? It's a dreadful situation for you all. And you are so busy yourself, teaching full time. Would you even have the time to look after your mother? Do you really want to? Isn't there any other solution?

Speak soon xxx

Her answer came much sooner than I expected, and the flurry of emails went back and forth.

Hi Stephanie,

My mother does not want me to look after her exactly, she will have someone to care for her every day when she leaves the hospital, until she is able to take care of herself. But the care will not last for a long time. My mother says she will have a few weeks with help, and after that there will be no-one. The care is provided from the state, and with her health insurance, she will pay only a very small sum. She says she will not be able to work. When my parents divorced she stopped working in the perfume shop and she found a job in an office but she will no longer be able to do this as she will not have enough functionality. She says she will not be able to go out and see her friends and that I am her daughter and I should be near to her. I do not know what I should do. xx

Hi Elodie,

I can only tell you that must do as you think best. You said that your mother will get better in time. If that's the case, then this is awful at the moment but it is temporary. Instead of moving, have you thought about renting somewhere on your own for a few weeks, and leaving Antoine in Marseille? That way, your mother will know that you have made the effort to see her, and when she is in a better state of health you can go back to Marseille. And are you sure that she will still want you near her once she has recovered and can meet her friends again? I can remember that you were not happy when you went to live with your parents, so do you think it will be different now? Do the doctors say how long it will take for her to recover? But really, I don't want to influence you. Please think carefully before you decide what to do.

Take care,
Love from Stephanie

Hi Stephanie,

Thank you for keeping in touch with me. I look forward to your emails, you are so strong for me! I still cannot decide what to do about my mother. Yes, as you say, it might be possible to rent in Bormes-les-Mimosas but then I would lose my job. I ask myself all the time, would she move house to be near to me if I was incapacitated with an illness? I tell myself, no, I am certain she would not do this for me. I do not think I will do this for her but I feel very guilty. Antoine says I should be near to her and he advises that I find a flat close to my mother.

Love, Elodie xx

'So, Antoine's quite happy for her to move,' I told John that evening. 'Well, I expect he can cope with his own cooking and housework if she does decide to go.'

He looked up from his book after carefully creasing the top corner of the page to mark his place. 'Not really his decision though, is it?' he said thoughtfully. 'If she moves, she'll need to find a job as well as taking on her mother. And has it occurred to you, it might be very convenient for him to have Elodie out of the way....?'

At the time I was concentrating heavily on my cross stitch; a detailed image of a purple and pink fairy, but I laid it down and looked at him, astonished. 'So, are you saying he's got someone else? What on earth makes you think that?'

'I know what you've told me,' he retorted. 'Didn't you say that he once got one of your classmates into trouble when you first went to France? That doesn't make him one of the most upright beings on the planet, does it?'

'Oh, nonsense!' I said sturdily. 'That's all in your mind. She's never said anything about their marriage not working. Of course he won't be having an affair. Anyway,' I reflected. 'I won't reply just yet, I'll give it a rest for a week. She has to make up her own mind.'

'Sounds to me as if she's half way there already. I can't blame her, from what you've told me about her mother. Why should she expect Elodie to drop everything and go and live in a new place just because her mother whistles for her? I could understand it if they'd been close, but they never were, were they? And I really think it's about time she stopped consulting you on every last detail of her life. Hasn't she got any friends of her own?'

'She must have friends, surely, although, now I think about it I've never heard her mention any of them. She doesn't consult me on everything, either. It's just that – well, I think she wants someone to kind of – guide her...And she *is* Véronique's only child. She'll always feel guilty if she doesn't go, won't she?'

'You're putting yourself in her place,' he said shrewdly, 'and imagining what you would do if it were *your* mother.'

'But my mother's...'

'Yes, yes,' he interrupted a little tersely. 'Of *course* I know it can't happen now, I'm just saying how you would have reacted, that's all. But Elodie's case is different, she never felt loved as a child, I'm just pointing out that she won't be feeling the same as you would in the same circumstances.'

I sighed. I knew only too well how true that was. I wished that I could help her in some way but I knew at heart that there wasn't a single thing I could do.

A few weeks later she emailed again.

Hi Stephanie,

I have been to see my mother. She is still in the hospital. It was expensive for me to visit her as I stayed nearby in a bed and breakfast, and then, there was the railway ticket. She looks much older than she did when I last saw her and she cannot yet eat food which is solid, she has only the liquids that the hospital give her. She still has some pain and for this she takes much medicine and it makes her sleepy. I think that sometimes she does not know that I am here, but other times she speaks. She has spoken to me of the time when she was first with my father. I listened to her but I think she did not know that I was there. What she told me made me very sad. Now, I wish that I had stayed in Marseille. Please email to me soon.

Love, Elodie

'It was in 1952, the year before you were born,' *Veronique began.* 'We were in the park, on our way to our favourite bench – you know the one? Behind all those bushes? I remember it was a hot evening, we went past the children's swings. I wanted a drink but Pierre said the pavilion would be closed.'

She turned her head towards me as if she thought I would know exactly where she meant. She was lifting her head up off the pillow and trying to look straight at me but I could see that she did not have enough strength left to do that and she fell back again. I think she thought I knew what she was talking about, Steph, but I had no idea. I could not decide whether she was awake properly or not, but she carried on talking – it was as if she was talking to someone behind me all the time...'

'That bench was where we always sat, when I could get away from her. I was so sick of it all – sick of her bossing me about. She never stopped. Fetch this, go and get that. Clean this, dust that. I was scared though. I didn't know who to tell first, Pierre or her. I thought if we could go to the bench I'd tell him, and then he could come back with me and we'd tell her together. She couldn't kill me if he was there, he wouldn't let her. Nurse! I want some water!'

I tried to tell her that the nurse was in the other room but I'll swear she never heard me, she just kept on talking, so I pressed the bell.

'He said it couldn't happen the first time, his friend Jules had told him it had to be lots of times and with us, it was only the once, you see. And he had said he would take care of everything. Where's that bloody nurse!'

A nurse came in then with a tray. But she didn't have any water with her, it was only her medicine.

'No, not you. I want to see a proper nurse, I don't want any darkies around me. Why don't you go back to where you came from? This is France, it's not your country. There's no need to bang it. Can't you put it down quietly? My head's splitting as it is.'

Really, Stephanie, I had no idea she was like this! The nurse was so angry, I could see, and I was really embarrassed. She did not speak, but then she gave my mother an injection.

'You clumsy bitch! That hurt!'

I almost laughed. My mother kept rubbing at the plaster the nurse had put on. Then she lay down again and said, 'I was going to tell him as soon as we got to the bench but he said he wanted to talk to me first. Well, I hardly listened to him, he was babbling on about going our own ways or something, but I shut him up and told him how scared I was, how I'd never been as late before.

All he could do was stare at me. You should have seen his face, it was all stretched and his mouth was hanging open like an imbecile.

He said it couldn't possibly happen, not from that one time. And it was only the once. Even I thought we'd be safe. It wasn't as it we were at it non-stop.

I told him that Jules was a liar. He was just a kid, even younger than we were. And then he said that Jules had been with lots of girls, and he should know....

I told him that he should never have trusted a single word that Jules said. He was from La Busserine, and everyone knew what sort of people lived there, in those scruffy apartments. Nobody but a load of Arabs would live there. Then I told him that this wasn't about Jules. It was about us, and what did he think we could do about it? I told him he'd have to come with me when I told her. He must have known how scared I was, he had been with me lots of times when she was bullying me, he'd seen it a hundred times. He still didn't say anything, he looked as if I'd punched him.

Then he said he'd marry me. I told him he needn't sound like that about it. I know I was shouting at him but there was no-one around to hear. I said no-one was forcing him to marry me if he didn't want to....I knew though, as soon as I got the words out, that the alternative would be worse. I would never be able to cope with being an unmarried mother. I couldn't bear it if everyone sneered at me and talked about me. I knew people would cross over the road so they didn't have to speak to me.

Then he said he knew no-one was forcing him and that he really did want to marry me. I could see he was trying to sound as if he meant it but I knew him better than that. He was never any good at lying.

I told him he could come with me and we'd do it the next day. Of course she was fuming when we told her. Called me all the names. I was a slut, she said. She'd never be able to hold her head up. Said we couldn't stay in Marseille. He told her we'd go up north, to where his parents lived. So we went up to Allonne, it was before I was showing. And that's where you were born. Trust you, you couldn't even manage to be born normally. Oh, no. There were complications, they said, and they had to cut me open to get you out. You were a scrawny little thing, too. Not a hair on your head. They were all trying to persuade me to breastfeed you, but I wasn't having any of that rubbish. And you cried! I know all babies cry but you beat them all. Day and night you were at it, you never gave me a break. You only stopped when someone put a bottle in your ugly mouth. Nothing but trouble since the day you were born....'

I could not listen to her any longer, Steph. I know she would not have said all that if she hadn't been pumped full of drugs, but I know now, that was what she really thought. All my life I wanted to know if she loved me. Sometimes I thought that she did, but after I heard all that I was sure. She never wanted me in the first place and she has hated me ever since I was born. I went back to my bed and breakfast. I was very sad all the night and I have cried a lot. But now, I have made up my mind, I will stay in Marseille. If my mother did not want me in her life then it will be the same for me. I do not want to have her in my life. I will say to her that it is impossible for us to go to Bormes-les-Mimosas now. Even if I did want to be near her to go it will take a long time to sell this house and she may be better by then and so it will be wasted effort for nothing.

'Not exactly pleasant to hear, that,' John remarked as he finished reading her email. 'She's had a rough time of it, hasn't she? First her mother, then her grandmother. No wonder she's screwed up, poor kid.'

'I wouldn't call her *screwed up*, exactly. I mean, I know she can be selfish, and she's definitely obsessed with her own weight and Lucie's, and probably everyone else's to be honest, but that's only because of Mamy forcing food down her throat every day when she was growing up. With the life she's had I'm surprised she isn't any worse.'

Not for the first time, I was so glad that my own mother had never been so concerned with what I ate. On the other hand, my mother's idea of good food had always been dictated by what she read on the packet it came in, so perhaps the comparison was unfair.

'Well, I think she's doing the right thing,' he said, locating his marked page and settling down to read. 'She doesn't owe her mother a single thing if you ask me.' I sighed and concentrated on my cross stitch until bedtime.

Chapter 19
Pupils

At my former school in the UK I became heartily fed up with the various parents who, on finding out that we were going to live in France, asked curiously, 'But what will you do?' And, 'Aren't you too young to retire?' These questions were all euphemisms for what they really wanted to ask, which was, 'What are you going to live on?'

We had thought long and hard about it and I tried to explain as best I could. Technically we were not planning to retire; we were moving countries and I would continue to teach as I had in the UK. I had no desire to work in a French school, and I wouldn't have had the necessary qualifications even if I had wanted to, but I was confident that I could find plenty of private pupils. Besides teaching, we had the rental income from the apartment and John's perfectly adequate works pension.

On our arrival I set out to find my pupils. It wasn't nearly as easy as I had anticipated. I had mistaken, or rather not known about, the cultural climate of a hamlet deep in rural France. To begin with, almost the entire population of young boys in the region had their destiny mapped out for them from birth. They would take over the vineyards their parents owned. For this they had no need of English at all as the wine exports were handled by the local cooperatives. The vast majority of boys, therefore, had no need of private tuition. Nor could most of their parents afford to pay for it.

The girls, now. They were a different matter entirely and I thought private tuition might appeal to many of them. But once again my knowledge of their culture was way off the mark. Life in remote rural villages in France resembled that of the UK in the nineteen forties and early fifties. The women mostly stayed at home, cooking and keeping house whilst their menfolk toiled in the vineyards. It was a rare woman who ventured into the rough world of paid employment.

It was a world of sexism that today in the UK would incite violent rioting in the streets. I witnessed it at first hand in the Post Office. The place was small, with a few seats for the elderly and infirm.

When I entered clutching my parcel all the seats were occupied; one of them by a deeply wrinkled man apparently in his nineties whose two crutches were on the floor beside him. The minute I entered he struggled to his feet and politely indicated his seat. Why? Because I was a woman and men did not take up seats if a woman needed one. I smiled and shook my head and he sat down again. Of course, it might not have been that at all. Perhaps I looked even more decrepit than he did. I'll never know.

Eventually, after an advertising campaign that would have given McDonald's a run for their money, I found pupils.

One of the first was Yanis, whose parents were reasonably affluent and who wanted something more for their son than a lifetime's toil in the vineyards. He was a polite, hard working lad and we got on well together. He attended regularly and I was quite surprised when one day, he told me he wouldn't be able to come for his lesson the following Wednesday.

He was very proud. 'I've got my first flying lesson,' he announced.

'*Really?* An actual flying lesson? You mean, in a plane?' I asked incredulously. I knew his parents were not poor, but neither did they seem to me to be the types to offer private flying lessons to their offspring.

Yanis enlightened me. He first shot me a look which clearly said, 'No, you fool, I'll be flying a kite.' Well mannered as he was, however, it wasn't long before he told me the truth. His local *collège*, a state school, offered lessons in theoretical aviation, followed by an exam. Those who passed well were rewarded with a series of six flying lessons in light aircraft at Carcassonne airport.

I was astounded that a state school could offer this course to its students. I thought of Yanis's British counterparts; pupils in schools where teachers paid for basic equipment out of their own salaries, where lessons were taught in 'temporary' classrooms erected thirty years ago, schools which were closing on Friday afternoons to save money; those struggling to keep the rainwater out of the classrooms and where budgets were being squeezed tighter every year.

I tried and failed to imagine such courses in the UK.

'Right now, year 11. Put your hands up all those people who'll be flying a light aircraft at Gatwick on Tuesday....'

I was pleased for him of course. He was such a diligent lad who had no doubt worked his socks off for such a treat. Whether he would be equally adept at the practical side was open to question, and John and I got into the habit of taking immediate cover whenever a light aircraft flew over the house. Just in case.

As time passed and the number of my pupils increased, I was further surprised by what their schools seemed able to offer. Every one of them was an accomplished skier, largely due to yearly school skiing trips in the Pyrenees mountains which were a very handy couple of hours away. Pupils stayed in designated hostels, not completely free of charge but at nominal cost to their parents. Skiing equipment was readily on loan to the students, so that all they really needed to provide were the clothes, and since the vast majority of families took winter mountain holidays, most of the pupils already had the appropriate clothing.

Sailing, too, was catered for at the resort of Port de Plaisance de Narbonne Plage, an amateur sailing port only an hour and a half away, where pupils regularly had sailing lessons which frequently led to a lifetime's passion for the sport.

I began to compare the French and English education systems, and concluded that pretty much the only thing they had in common was children.

Another pupil was Sandrine. She answered one of my advertisements in the local paper and asked me if I could help with the thesis she was writing for her Masters degree in English. I agreed to give her weekly lessons at her home in a small town a twenty minute drive away.

The house was a 'maison de maitre', a large crumbling stone edifice complete with an entrance archway, huge windows with peeling wooden shutters and a small front garden with a remarkable collection of assorted weeds.

Sandrine let me into the darkest hall I had ever seen. The fitted wardrobes which I guessed served as cloakrooms almost reached to the ceiling. She was a thin, pale and very serious girl with short brown hair cut in a neat and severe bob. She was home from university for the holidays, she explained. Her thesis was completed, but she would like a native English speaker to read it and check for any anomalies of tone and spelling.

I read through the first part and smiled faintly to myself. She had chosen to write her thesis on Margaret Thatcher, whom she evidently admired as one of the greatest prime ministers the UK had ever elected.

I quite simply couldn't resist it. My job should have entailed reading and editing for spelling and grammar, but I was diametrically opposed to her opinions in almost every respect. Over the course of many months, her thesis took on a new, and in my opinion, a more balanced point of view. I introduced her to the finer points of the hardships caused to the many northern towns where the mines had been closed, and where shipyards had laid off thousands of workers.

I was far exceeding my original brief but I didn't really care. We were slowly revising her thesis, which turned out to be practically a joint effort from the two of us.

Her mother always welcomed me with a kind of serious enthusiasm, staying for the first few minutes of the lesson before disappearing. She was pleased that I was doing my best to help her only daughter. Sandrine told me that she was taking care of her father who was ill with cancer. He was at home, but weak and requiring constant care, which her mother was happy to provide. He had been ill for at least three years, alternating between hospital treatment and periods of remission that he spent at home. The serious girl, the weighty topic of her thesis, the huge and gloomy house that was badly in need of renovation and decoration and the presence of illness always made me glad when the lesson was over and I was back at home, breathing in the fresh country air.

A few years later, after passing a competitive exam which included the ability to swim twenty-five metres within an insane time limit, Sandrine eventually became a teacher in a tiny village school south of Carcassonne. When she asked me if I would like to teach an English lesson to her class I was highly doubtful. At first. After thinking about it for a while I finally persuaded myself not to miss an opportunity that I was certain would never come my way again, and I agreed. I did a ridiculous amount of preparation for the one lesson, which was to be addressed to her class of seven and eight year olds. I went into my familiar panic mode as I walked into her classroom, and as if I wasn't nervous enough already, there was Sandrine, stationed at the back of the room. Back in the UK I had taught thousands of children, but I had never had to do it in French. Would they understand me? Was I about to make an idiot of myself? Why on earth had I agreed to this?

So, I faced the expectant rows of small French boys and girls and began. To my great surprise, they appeared to understand me. At least there was a noticeable absence of the sort of embarrassed tittering and nudging that I might have expected from a similar group of English children faced with a strange teacher, and by the end of the lesson I was quite enjoying myself. Sandrine joined me towards the end, having the children sing a rendition of 'Twinkle Twinkle Little Star' which they did in almost perfect British accents.

Sandrine was one of only two teachers in the school, the other being the headmistress. I was intrigued, both by the fact that her pupils called Sandrine by her first name, and also by the headmistress herself, since no British headmistress I had ever met came to work in a grubby overall. To me, she looked like the educational equivalent of Mamy. When it was all over, John, who had waited patiently outside the school, drove me home. I was relieved, and happy to have had a very brief experience of actually teaching real French children in a real French school.

Our neighbour Nicole's daughter Manon attended the local *collège*. As Nicole didn't drive I was frequently asked to either take her to school if she had missed the bus, or collect her from school on those many, many occasions when she felt unwell. She very rarely had any illness that could be checked, it was always internal and unfailingly on a monthly basis. On the occasions when I took her in the mornings, it was very evident where the school's priorities lay. A huge red neon sign at the entrance displayed important information for parents and visitors. In large letters were details of the three-course lunch menu of the day, with details of the ingredients used and cooking methods, followed underneath in much smaller writing, by the names of the absent teachers.

I always presented myself at reception where an eagle eyed lady behind a glass compartment looked me up and down suspiciously, asking me my name and my business there.

When I gave the girl's name I was directed to a squat, single storey building at the other side of the playground. To my surprise, when I knocked on the door it was opened by a uniformed nurse and I found myself in a room that closely resembled a hospital ward, with neatly made up beds and plastic chairs lining the walls. Manon was sitting on one of four beds looking gloomy and clutching her stomach.

'She has had a lie down,' the nurse told me. 'The doctor has examined her and given her painkillers. There is no elevated temperature, but we think she will be better at home for now.'

She kept up the agonised stomach clutching as I drove her home, only dropping the act with a triumphant grin when we arrived. I was thinking once again of the completely unbridgeable gulf between the French and the UK education systems.

Paulette was another pupil, a likeable, friendly girl who was approaching her baccalaureate. Her ambition was to be an archaeologist, and she duly attended the careers evening at the *Lycée* in Carcassonne.

She looked around for any leaflets that might point her in the direction she wanted to go, but found nothing, so she approached one of the staff.

'Do you have anything on archaeology?' she asked politely.

The lady looked at her, aghast. 'Archaeology!' she exclaimed. 'That's no job for a woman, dear.'

She rifled through the pile of leaflets on her desk, located the ones she needed and presented them to Paulette. 'Now, we have a lot of information on nursing. Or why not teaching? Or have you thought of secretarial work? There are plenty of opportunities for a good secretary in Carcassonne.'

'No, really. I want to do archaeology,' she insisted. 'Haven't you got anything on it?'

'Absolutely nothing, I'm afraid,' she said stiffly. 'You'll have to try the careers office in town.'

A disgruntled Paulette related the incident to her mother, who was livid.

'Small minded mentality!' she said. 'Stuck in the nineteen-thirties, they are at that school. Listen, don't you worry Paulette. There's a careers office in Carcassonne, we'll go there.'

'Come with me,' she begged. 'They'll take more notice if you're there.' Her mother consulted the opening hours. 'We can go next Tuesday evening,' she said.

Tuesday evening saw both of them in the office. Paulette was excited. Finally she would get the information she needed. Which university would be best, the grades to aim for, the funding available.

The lady on the desk was cheerful and middle aged with an air of competence.

'My daughter would like to do archaeology,' her mother stated firmly. 'She's seventeen, does her *bac* next year. What kind of information do you have?'

The lady's smile faded right off her face. 'Archaeology?' she said, amazed. 'But that's no job for a woman, is it? Now, has your daughter thought about nursing? Or maybe a year's secretarial course.....?'

Chapter 20
Visitors

That morning, I had stripped most of the ripe tomatoes from their vines and while I mechanically plucked each plump red fruit, I fell to appreciating the phrase 'sun-ripened tomatoes,' followed swiftly by the rhetorical question of why did we only apply the phrase to tomatoes? Why not 'sun-ripened lettuce' for example, or 'sun-ripened apples?' Weren't they all ripened by the sun anyway? And then taking it to its logical conclusion and pondering idiotically over such phrases as 'rain-watered onions' and 'earth-grown carrots' whilst I carried my basket of fruit to the kitchen and began preparing my annual tomato chutney. Instead of giving it my full attention, I dumped the basket next to the cooker before turning to John and peering at the letter he was skimming through.

'*Three weeks!*' I shrieked, momentarily diverted. 'Who *are* they?'

'Oh, I used to work with Zak years ago, when I was at Menwith Hill,' John replied distantly, still reading. 'He's a real character.'

'*Everyone's* a real character, come to that,' I retorted. 'If they're alive then they have a character. The dogs in the street have characters. That's what it means. It doesn't mean that I want to see them. Here, give me that,' I said, snatching the sheet of paper from him. 'Let me read it properly.'

'*We are doing our Grand Tour of Europe this year,*' I read. '*We've put it off for years but now that all our little guys are off our hands, we think it's the right time to see a bit of the world. Now that I'm retired we can take all the time we need. We weren't considering France until Tony (remember him, John?) happened to mention to us that you guys have a place down there, and we thought what a great opportunity it would be to catch up with you. So, we've altered our original schedule so that we can take in your part of the world. It will be great if you can put us up from 28th August for around three weeks. Cindy says Carcassonne looks great, so we'll be hiring a car at the airport. I expect you guys know all the best restaurants, huh?*

Until we meet up in the summer, then.'

'Great for them, perhaps,' I retorted loudly, putting the letter back in its flimsy envelope before I continued chopping and piling the pieces into the largest pan we had and adding the other ingredients. 'Naturally they think it's great. They won't be paying for a hotel, for a start. That will save them a good few dollars, I'm sure. And what about us? I don't see any mention of them offering to pay for anything. Do they expect us to feed them and entertain them for free, for three whole weeks?'

I turned around to stir my chutney once more, noting an acrid smell that told me that it was burning slightly at the bottom of the pan. I was more than a little put out. In fact, I was livid. The family was one thing, and we adored visits from them, but these cheeky strangers were in a different category altogether. 'Can't we say no?'

'It would look a bit churlish, though, wouldn't it?'

'Who cares what it looks like? I've never even *met* these people,' I retorted, stirring vigorously. 'Why would I want them in my house? Just say no. Say we haven't got room. Say we're busy. Say we're dead.....'

'But we have got room,' he said mildly. 'We can't lie about it. Tony will have given him our address, and it's easy enough to check up on where people live, even down here. You just look on the Internet.'

I sighed. John taking that attitude was making me feel as if it were me being unreasonable and churlish. But really, I fumed inside, he's the one who's met this person whoever he is, and I'll bet my bottom American dollar that I'll be the one doing all the cooking and searching out places for us to take them.

If you ever dream of living a secluded life in the south of France as a couple, then forget it. Your address will act as a powerful magnet and like iron filings, everyone whoever knew you, however slightly, however tenuous the connection, suddenly becomes your very best friend and will be drawn towards you. You may not have recognised them in the UK if you'd tripped over them in a crowded street, but now that you have a French address, they miraculously know you ever so much better than either party had any idea of, and they will descend on you.

Now, you may just possibly be thinking we are the type of miserable people who are utterly unsociable, who dislike having their routines interrupted, who are awkward with strangers and who cannot cope with accommodating the needs of other people. You would be perfectly correct in this assumption. I was far from thrilled to hear from this couple who hadn't so much as sent us a Christmas card in the last ten years but now, it appeared, would become our treasured guests for three weeks in the summer.

'They'll be hiring a car, though,' John said thoughtfully. 'So they'll probably want to explore on their own. We might only see them in the mornings and evenings.' He was wrong. Very wrong. And I was furious. The bottom of the pan was burnt black and three whole kilogrammes of tomatoes ended up in the bin.

The inevitable day arrived; a day so hot that the roads were beginning to showing glistening half melted pools of tarmac that stuck to tyres and left dark traces in their wake. A car purred to a halt outside the house and we valiantly fixed rictus grins on our faces and went out to meet them.

'John! Well, hey, great to see you, buddy!' An enormous monolith of a man was crushing John in his arms, leading me to fear for his lungs. He let out a gasp when he was released, and then it was my turn. I would have given him the traditional pecks on his cheek if I had been about two feet taller, but as it was, I barely came up to his waist and so offered my hand instead, Why, just *why*, is it considered necessary to have some form of physical contact with people when you meet them? A simple *'hi, how are you?'* really ought to be enough for most occasions. I was fully expecting to have several fingers hanging off my hand in bits but he was surprisingly gentle.

A second later showed that he had evidently had much practice with people smaller than himself. His wife was opening the boot, when he skilfully intercepted her and heaved the suitcases out himself. My mother would definitely have approved of the dark purple, thick leather suitcases. Case after case, ever diminishing in size, hit the dusty pavement, until the heap was finished off by a tiny purple leather makeup bag, with gold zips.

She was a diminutive lady with a pink, blonde-haired fluffy prettiness which was a stark contrast to her husband's beefy bulk.

'Hi, I'm Cindy,' she introduced herself. 'It's sure good to arrive. Travelling don't suit me really. I hate flyin' but there ain't no alternative if we want to see Europe. It's great of you to offer to put us up like this. We're surely grateful.'

Pushing the obvious, churlish reply right to the back of my mind where the daylight couldn't get at it, I smiled. 'It's nice to have you.'

Later on, when Zak had effortlessly taken their impressive luggage collection to their room, we were all seated in the shade by the barbecue, I surprised myself by warming to the couple. Zak was polite, and Cindy sweet, chatty and giggly.

They both showed a lot of interest in the region and hoped they could see the main attractions during their stay.

'We did some homework on this place,' Zak said. 'You have a cute little village not so far from here that we'd love to have a look around if it doesn't put you folk out any. A couple o' miles down the road from here. Cornes? You know it?'

John and I exchanged puzzled glances. Cornes? It took John less than a second, although I was slower. 'You mean Caunes Minervois,' he chuckled. 'It's pronounced like the word cone, you know, like a cone on the motorway.'

Maybe American motorways are not half covered in coned-off roadworks, because Zak looked faintly puzzled, and continued to refer to the village as 'Cornes' as long as we knew him.

We took them to Caunes-Minervois, after a trip to the *Le Chinois Gourmand* at *Pont Rouge*, one of our favourite places to eat and where we always took the grandchildren, as they loved the small white paper bags which they could fill with a selection of sweets at the end of a meal. They also loved the animal-themed measuring chart on the wall, where they had to ascertain their height in order to qualify for a child's price.

Zak and Cindy appeared enchanted by the place. I was certain that the enthusiasm was not entirely sincere, and equally certain when I glanced at John, that he was thinking the same. But, even if fake, they were doing their very best to appear interested and polite. Surely there were Chinese restaurants in the States! They examined the gaudy paper placemats, which gave not only details of the other restaurants in the chain, but also, as I translated for them, details concerning expected behaviour, with instructions to only take the amount you could eat, to respect other guests and to clear your plate after a meal.

'Could do with these at home,' Zak laughed. 'Stop all the little kids from racing around the place.'

'French children normally know how to behave when they're out,' John nodded at him sagely, with completely unjustified pride in children he had never met. 'You won't see any running around in restaurants in France.' As if to demonstrate the accuracy of this, we glanced round at several families whose children were behaving impeccably.

It was a real change for John to have someone to talk to who spoke English. He was actually becoming animated, and laughing far more than he did at home.

Caunes-Minervois proved to exceed their expectations. The 12th century abbey with its original foundations fascinated both of them. We peeped into all the rooms, one of which was currently housing an exhibition of local artists and two more where Zak and Cindy were bewildered by the 'Smurfs' exhibition. Leaving the blue cartoon creatures behind, we continued our tour, seeing the American couple entranced by the original Roman paving in the basement of the Abbey.

'Jeez, a real Roman road and we're walking right on it,' Cindy breathed. 'Can't hardly believe it. We sure don't have anythin' this age in Washington.'

They walked in a respectful silence around the church, mesmerised by the variety of richly decorated red and cream-veined marble chapels. Cindy lit a candle and watched it burn for several moments. We ascended the steps which led us into the shady coolness of the cloisters, finishing off at the tourist office which sold mementos of the abbey and the village, where they bought some postcards and a child's book on the Cathars for one of their grandchildren.

On the way back we were held up by a grape-picking machine, which in early September was not a surprise, as the harvest would begin shortly. Zak was stunned.

'Say, what's that thing? It's as big as a house....'

John explained.

'Wish I could see one of them up close.'

'He's mad keen on all machinery,' Cindy laughed. 'I bought him a tractor for his last birthday, just so that he could tear it down to see how it works.'

After John and I exchanged puzzled glances at the thought of a tractor as a birthday gift, John said, 'If you like, we can arrange that for you. We can take you over to Trausse Minervois to see a friend of ours who works on a wine domaine, I'm sure she wouldn't mind...'

'They've got one of these things? Jeez, this is crazy, Cindy. Never seen one of these before in my life!'

Odette was busy, as usual in the office, surrounded by thick grey files, no doubt filled with past orders from many countries, but she cheerfully closed the papers she was working on and led us outside to a square of bare hard-packed earth where a dark, wiry man was vigorously swabbing out his *pressoir* in preparation for the imminent harvest. A thin film of sticky juice seeped out from its base, and we trod carefully, avoiding it as much as we could. He looked up as we approached, and we saw that it was Patrice whom we had met on previous visits. Zak was as excited as a five year old. He nudged Cindy. 'Will you look at that! Jeez, it's huge! Wonder what it's for...'

After I explained that the machine was used for squeezing the juice out of grapes I introduced them to Patrice and as I had expected, he was happy to give Zak and Cindy a tour around the domaine, and he even provided some hastily washed glasses and poured them some of the previous year's wine. Zak drank appreciatively, casting his eyes around the gloomy interior of the wine cave, and up towards the huge stainless steel vats. Patrice then led them up a metal staircase onto a grilled platform from where they could see the shiny steel lids of the vats, and at the far end, a bank of screens where humidity and temperature were controlled. After examining them closely they clattered their way down the stairs again and followed him out into the blinding glare of sunlight. Turning a corner, they were suddenly right in front of the enormous royal and pale blue painted machine with the company name Braud outlined in stark white. Zak examined it closely, peering at the mud-spattered wheels with their deep treads and then directing his awed gaze upwards towards the enclosed driver compartment which could only be reached by way of several steps. His eyes took in the shaking rods, which detached the grapes before depositing them in the large Noria baskets at each side of the machine. Patrice explained how the baskets sent the grapes to the top of the machine for cleaning, and about the destemmer, which made sure that only the grapes and not their stems finished up in the baskets. I translated all this as best I could, and if I was not entirely accurate in my descriptions for want of the technical vocabulary, I could see that Zak was sagely nodding his head as he inspected each part of a machine which was quite new to him.

'Would he like to sit in it?' Patrice asked me quietly and I translated for Zak. His face stretched into a broad grin and after a nod of assent he was heaving his huge frame up the steep steps. He plonked himself onto the black leather seat and beamed down at us all. 'Get your camera out, Cindy!' he yelled down. 'They're not going to believe this back home!'

'He's in his element,' she laughed as she took the photos. 'He'll trot this out at dinner parties for ever. We'll never hear the last of it.'

For Zak it was one of the highlights of their whole European tour. They had visited the Greek Isles, they had 'done' Venice, Rome and Paris, and for Zak, all their glories paled into insignificance against the experience of sitting in a grape picking machine. They left a few days later and although I had quite enjoyed their stay, I was relieved when it was over. Visitors, even the considerate kind, make it impossible to be totally relaxed, and I was looking forward to having the house to ourselves once more. I went to strip their bed. Tugging off their pillowcase, I saw an envelope. Puzzled, but thinking it might be a note of thanks, I ripped it open. It was a short letter, with words such as 'appreciate' and 'brilliant stay' in it, and it was accompanied by notes to the value of a thousand euros, and a warm invitation to visit them the following year.

John was amazed. 'I didn't know they were wealthy,' he said. 'Although now I come to think of it, I can remember Tony saying they had a fantastic place in Washington. Obviously a tractor as a present is no hardship. I think he said Spring Valley, if I remember correctly.'

Later that evening, we did an internet search for Spring Valley. It was a neighbourhood with property prices in the millions.

'And they wanted to come *here?*' I wondered.

'Ah, but it's the *experience,*' John laughed. 'That's what they came for. He's never been near a grape picking machine in his life. I bet he thought it was well worth a paltry thousand euros.'

We didn't go to America. I would have loved it, I was sure, but John was practical as ever when I insisted that we could afford it.

'We'd be staying with them,' I said. 'We wouldn't need to pay for a hotel. So why not? We could easily save up...'

'It's not just the hotel, though, is it?' he said reasonably. 'There'd be the flight to pay for, and then, we'd have to contribute. Like they did when they were here. They paid for the meals almost every time we went to a restaurant. It wouldn't be fair if we didn't do the same for them. We'd finish up spending a small fortune, and we really can't afford it, Steph.'

Very reluctantly, I conceded that he might have a point.

Chapter 21
Accents

I have always been fascinated by language. I had worked hard at my French in order to be ready for our new life, although my skills were far from perfect, as was demonstrated by a conversation with Monsieur Bellini, who told me a cautionary tale about some polecats he had seen recently in the woods.

I nodded sagely, telling him that I had seen a group of them at the bottom of our garden. It was just a little unfortunate that the French words for polecat and prostitute are remarkably similar.

If it wasn't the words that were wrong, it was the pronunciation. *Pulle*, meaning pullover or jumper, sounds (to me at any rate) almost identical to *poule*. Which left many of our neighbours wondering why I felt the need to pull a warm chicken over my head in winter.

Almost every week I would go over to the farm. It was a walk of around a kilometre by way of a stony path bordered by vineyards and so contributed to exercise at the same time as giving a view of the far distant wooded hills and on the horizon, the undulating peaks of the Pyrenees mountains. Fennel grew waist high, with their thick central stalks and wispy fronds gently waving in the breeze, giving off a pungent scent as I passed. At ground level the sides of the path were sown with clumps of rosemary, thyme and bushes of rock roses with their fragile, paper-like pink petals momentarily obscured by tiny pale blue butterflies alighting on them with stilled wings. It was a delightful walk, and I loved the solitude in the midst of such wonderful countryside.

There was always a warm welcome when I arrived, and usually some snippet of local gossip to pick up. This time, there was something new. On a couch in the salon lay a wizened old woman lightly covered by a threadbare blanket, even though the temperature outside was a sweltering thirty degrees.

Her deeply wrinkled face was mottled with age and there was a huge lump just above one eye. She was not asleep, but staring at me with rheumy eyes. There was a slight dribble of spittle on her chin.

'*Marie-Bernadette,*' whispered Dominique by way of introduction. '*Une cousine. Elle parle bien l'anglais.*'

I had long become very sceptical of the phrase *he/she speaks English*. Generally it meant the ability to say 'hello' in a confident tone of voice, followed by a look of blank incomprehension when I started to speak, so I was completely unprepared when Marie-Bernadette struggled to a sitting position and propped up her frail body on one elbow. The fact that she was a cousin was unsurprising, since both Dominique and Gustave came from very large families and there were cousins scattered all over France and beyond.

'Howdy there,' she said jovially, 'how y'all doin' today?'

Had I heard correctly? Was this living corpse speaking to me in an accent more deep south than Scarlett O'Hara's? Was it for real or had I just imagined it? Her next phrase convinced me I was not dreaming.

'Kinda hot out there ain't it?' she said brightly.

'Er, yes, it is,' I responded, still bewildered.

'I'm from the U.S,' she went on chattily. 'Can't y'all tell?'

'Er, yes, I thought so, from your accent.'

She poked a bony head towards me and nodded eagerly for emphasis as she spoke.

'Did y'all see the moon landings?' she asked eagerly. 'Y'know, Buzz Aldrin an all?'

If today was turning out to be surreal, this just took it to an unprecedented level. What on earth was the old girl talking about? I didn't have long to wait before I found out.

'Betcha didn't know this,' she continued confidentially, leaning towards me, 'but I was one of the guys who helped to put him up there. Yes maam,' she droned. 'I surely was. I was right up there with m'all. Took a heap o' work to do it, but we got 'em up there in the end. We surely did.' Her voice tailed off, as if she was reminiscing of the old days, the days now long gone which would never return.

'Really?' was all I could manage. I was totally bemused by all this. She looked like one of the Macbeth witches. I could happily envisage her huddled over a simmering cauldron, but working on the moon landings? Was she crazy?

'Used to work for NASA, on the space programme. Apollo 11, 1969. Me an' a whole bunch of others,' she told me. 'Boy, but it was some hard work – never a day without some problem croppin' up.

Course I was a mite younger in those days. Better lookin' too,' she cackled. 'Long time ago now.'

The effort of the conversation had evidently wearied her, and Dominique fussily arranged her blanket afresh and patted the pillow invitingly. 'Lie down now, Marie-Bernadette,' she said gently, and the old lady rested her head, closed her eyes and was soon snoring gently, doubtless reliving the days when she was a youthful worker on the USA space programme.

Being well over the age of sixty, I can remember watching the historic moon landing. No-one who witnessed it will ever forget the iconic event itself or where they were at the time. Neil Armstrong took his first step on the moon at around four o'clock in the morning UK time. and I was sixteen at the time, it was a few weeks after my Marseille trip. I had been sent to bed as usual, with promises from the excited parents that they would wake me up 'when it was time.' I know that it was very important to them that I witnessed this staggering event and I believe I was woken around one thirty in the morning to watch with the rest of the world as Armstrong took that memorable, historic step and uttered the immortal words, 'It's one small step for man, one giant leap for mankind.' As an adult I am far more emotional when I see the scene replayed than I ever was as a child, and I contemplated the now sleeping Marie-Bernadette with genuine puzzlement.

Had she truly been a part of all this? I had no reliable way of checking. Certainly she was American and maybe she was right. I guessed her age to be mid eighties, which would have made her in her thirties at the time. All NASA employees had to end up *somewhere,* I just hadn't expected to find one of them on an isolated farm in the French countryside. Since some four hundred thousand people worked for NASA at the time of the Moon landing, I didn't imagine that she had pressed the launch button or was manning a computer in the control room. That was not even possible as the control room was staffed by men only, but maybe she had worked in a secretarial role somewhere and her statement of 'helping to put Buzz Aldrin on the moon' was pure hyperbole, but in any case it was evident that she was coming to the end of her life secure in the knowledge that one day in the distant past, she had been important. She had held down a prestigious job and taken some part in a historic world event. I thought it a touching story, and it couldn't have happened anywhere else but on this extraordinary farm with its superb cast of inhabitants. Would you live anywhere else? I thought.

A few months later the inevitable had happened when I visited, and Marie-Bernadette was dead.

The family at the farm was numerous. There were nine children, all born in quick succession, and Dominique was eager in looking out for anyone, anywhere, who would take care of them. At the time when I lived nearby there were only three at home. The rest were either married, at Catholic boarding school or being cared for by a relative.

One of the boys still at home was called Pierre-Marie. I thought his name bizarre at first until I remembered just how devoutly religious the family was. He was a lanky, gangly fifteen-year-old with a shock of black hair falling over his face, and a look of mischievous innocence. He was a bit of a tearaway in so far as his existence on an isolated farm allowed. His favourite pastime was shooting rats in a nearby barn. It was ever so slightly unnerving to arrive at the farm and be greeted by a rifle toting fifteen-year-old, although I was assured that he only ever shot at rats, never at people. Whilst I was grateful for that, I wasn't quite convinced as I had seen him point his gun at his sister only a few days before.

Dominique decided that he was not paying enough attention to his schoolwork and was falling behind his peers, especially in English where his marks were quite abysmal. I had tried tutoring him for a while, but he only attended spasmodically when it suited him – presumably when the local rat population was in decline, and he made very little progress. The solution was to send him far away to a boarding school in the Loire Valley. An English boarding school, to be exact. How did a family who existed on the bare minimum ever find the funds for a boarding school? The answer was, they didn't. This particular school had some connection to the château where Dominique had grown up and would be well known to the family. It was entirely possible that the school proprietors had been persuaded to take him without payment. Who knew?

He was most reluctant to go of course. The school was run by a group of Catholic priests on quite bizarre lines, with the boys expected to help with the domestic arrangements such as cleaning the dormitories and washing up after meals. The fees were relatively low and it was easy to see why. The school catered for Catholic boys who wanted an English education and whose parents were happy for their boy to help with the day to day running of the place. The standard of education was high, and therefore attracted many students from both France and England. Many of them made excellent progress and went on to university. Not so Pierre-Marie. I saw him during his holidays and it was evident that he was miserable there. The main problem was the language. Lessons were given in English, homework was to be completed in English and poor Pierre-Marie never stood a chance. He showed me his report, in which one particular remark incensed me.

'It is time that Pierre-Marie stopped making the excuse that he cannot speak English,' one of the masters had written. *'His work in history is of a low standard and he needs to make more effort.'*

I was furious. He had had some English lessons with me but as I like my students to have at least some semblance of motivation, we were never going to make much progress. He only came under duress from his parents and totally refused to do any extra work. Besides which I believe he was of quite limited academic ability. Such children do not take easily to being transplanted into a world where everyone speaks a foreign language. How many English lads of fifteen would survive and thrive on being uprooted from their family and friends and sent to a school where they couldn't understand the lessons? Dominique had sent him there, quite confident in the belief that he would 'pick up' English in no time, but that was never going to happen. Whilst they are still very young, children have an innate ability to speak the language they hear around them and the basics of grammatical structure are hardwired into their brains, ready to be adapted to the language of their native country, but as they grow older that ability is lost for ever. No-one 'picks up' a language simply by hearing it. If I listen to a radio programme in Chinese, for example, I am not going to understand it after listening to it ten times. It just doesn't happen. Pierre-Marie fell further and further behind at the school. Eventually he gave up even trying to make any effort, until the day came when his parents were asked, with professions of regret and many fervent prayers for his future, not to return him. He continued his education at a local school for a while and lived at home, happily surrounded by dead rats.

Later on he found his way in the world and completed an apprenticeship in woodwork in the village of Revel, high up in the Haute-Garonne department. Revel is famed for its production of a mint flavoured liqueur with the unlikely name of Get27, and for its *Lycée*, which takes pupils on a weekly boarding basis and offers tuition in cabinet making. He now works for a highly prestigious furniture maker in Paris.

On one occasion we were invited to a barbecue at the farm. John declined the invitation so I went on my own. I didn't go with any expectations of great food. They didn't do great food up at the farm. Basically, they survived on what they could grow, so there was an abundance of figs, which Dominique made into fig jam in huge metal vats and sold at the various markets in the region, and walnuts. There were grapes of course, as everywhere else, and there was a kind of half tended little vegetable plot where they grew lettuces, carrots, onions and potatoes. I expected fairly basic fare which turned out to be the case, but a barbecue always offered the possibility of meeting new people and this one was no exception. There were several people there whom I had never met, including a couple accompanied by their son who appeared to be around eleven or twelve.

The couple themselves said nothing at all to each other, but addressed any remarks to their son who was sitting between them. He turned from one parent to the other, speaking to each in a different language, one of which was definitely English and the other I didn't recognise at all.

Wanting to know more, I picked up a plate of figs and passed them to him. 'Do you like figs?' I asked.

'Yeah, thanks, love 'em, I could eat 'em all day,' was his reply in perfect cockney English.

'Whereabouts are you from?' I was most interested in this youngster who seemed to have at least three languages in his repertoire.

It was immediately apparent that he was slightly confused, probably by the word 'whereabouts,' and so I put the question more simply. 'Where are you from?'

After biting into his fig, he swallowed hurriedly and said, 'I live in Narbonne now but I was born in Hackney. I don't really remember it much though, we moved to France when I was four.'

So that explained his near fluency in English but I was still curious about his parents. Presently when the meal had finished and everyone was standing about in small groups chatting, I collared the boy again and questioned him.

'And your parents?' I glanced towards them but they were far enough away not to overhear, the mother speaking animatedly to another English couple and the father standing by silently, an expression of genial intelligence on his face. 'What nationality are they?'

He sighed. 'Everyone asks me that. Mum's English and Dad is Russian. They don't speak French. At least, Mum's having lessons but she's not very good at it yet.'

'So....you translate for them?' My eyebrows shot up. This sounded incredulous.

He grinned impishly. 'I have to. They can't talk to each other.'

Briefly I wondered how in the world these two adults had ever managed to produce a son without speaking to each other, until it occurred to me that some activities, naturally, don't involve language. It was an intriguing concept.

The child's name was Paul, I discovered, and he was trilingual, speaking French because he lived here and attended a French school, English with his mother and Russian with his father. Interestingly I found out from Dominique that he was also dyslexic which was perfectly comprehensible given the circumstances.

I would have loved to know more about their linguistically challenged lives, but it was not to be. Paul will be an adult now and I never met him again, except to see the three of them once in Narbonne market. I waved across at him but he was chatting animatedly with his father and didn't see me.

Chapter 22
Bodies

I do not do dead bodies. They don't fascinate me and up until now I had never seen one. That is, until Sandrine's father passed away. He had been ill for many years so his death was expected. I was hesitant about going over there to teach Sandrine but she insisted that she still wanted her lesson. I agreed to go ahead but at that point I had no idea that her father was still in the house.

I found out when her mother entered the room. Unexpectedly she embraced me; she was not crying but her plump face was creased and she was evidently upset.

'Would you like to see him?' she asked quietly. At first I had no idea whom she thought I would like to see, until Sandrine murmured, '*Papa.*'

I was startled. He had just died, hadn't he? Why would I go and see him?

In French culture you are either a relative or good friend of the deceased if you are invited to view the corpse. I fell into neither of these categories and I had no desire whatsoever to view the body. I had only ever spoken to Sandrine's father when we said a brief '*bonjour*' to each other before I began my lesson, on the rare occasions when he had been present. Even that, I thought, would be rather a one-sided conversation given his now permanent lack of conversational skills. I emphatically, categorically, did not want to go.

'Yes, of course,' I muttered, lying through my teeth so as not to upset anybody. She led the way into the next gloomy and stuffy room where the open coffin was supported on a long oak table.

I have read descriptions of dead bodies, where the writer insists that the person looked 'at peace,' or 'serene,' or as if 'all earthly cares had flown away,' and so I mentally prepared myself for a surreal experience. It never happened. I gazed at his face. He looked grey, very, very still and well, just dead really.

'Would you like to touch him one last time?' she asked calmly.

One last time! God, no! I had never touched him when he was alive so why would I want to do it when he was dead?

Politeness dictated that I do as she asked but I'm afraid my good manners gave out at that point and I shook my head. Whether she was disappointed or not I couldn't tell, as I left the room as quickly as I decently could.

We started the lesson but I found it hard to concentrate on Margaret Thatcher knowing that a corpse lay in the next room.

The second dead body was that of my neighbour Madame Bellini. Four years had passed since she lost her husband and she had found life tough after he died, although her pride dictated that she tried her best to receive her visitors in the customary polite way. She developed itchiness all over her body, she was on daily tranquillisers and her hair started to fall out. Eventually she fell in the shower and lay there all night before one of her sons found her the following morning. She was alive but frail and she was taken into Carcassonne hospital where she spent several months.

It was decided that she was unable to live alone and preparations were set in motion for her to be placed in the local 'Maison de Retraite' in Caunes.

She did not want to go. She would rather die than go into a retirement home, she said. But it was no use. She really was quite unable to care for herself and she went into the home. From the moment she entered it she seemed to shrivel. When I went to see her, she was unable to raise her head from the pillow, although she made a valiant effort to greet me in the usual way.

True to her word, she was there for a total of six days, refusing all food and taking only occasional sips of water, before she passed away and her body was removed to her home.

Unlike Sandrine's father, I had been genuinely fond of the old lady; we had passed many hours together and I was greatly saddened by her death. I was invited to view her body and I walked the few yards that separated our two houses.

She way lying in her bed as I gazed tearfully down at her body. As a token mark of respect I gently kissed her forehead, to the evident approval of her sons and other mourners who were there.

The hamlet had very few visitors. Occasionally Sophie's sister and two young nephews stayed for a few days in the summer. They were no trouble at all; they rode their bikes up and down the main street, said a pleasant 'bonjour' on the rare occasions when our paths crossed but nothing more.

So I was intrigued at the sight of a thin, tall stranger loping his way down the stony path from the woods towards our house. The only people who could choose that path were the family at the farm, since it petered out into woodland at the end of it.

I looked more closely as he approached. His top half was covered by a faded green tee-shirt, he wore brown shorts which covered his knees and his face resembled a wrinkled walnut in both texture and colour. I judged his age to be around sixty. Seeing me, he stopped by the back gate and beckoned to me.

'Didier Carré,' he said abruptly, holding out his hand. 'I've just noticed your ladders. I'm from Calais and I've bought the little *cabane* near the woods for a holiday home. Can I borrow them?'

Looking at him closer, he appeared to be nearer seventy than sixty. He had deep lines around his eyes and his teeth were a dentist's nightmare. There was no preamble. No, *'Please,'* no, *'How are you?'* Not even a *'Bonjour, isn't it windy today?'*

I was taken aback and confused. Torn between a straight refusal and an almost pathological fear of upsetting anyone in the local community, I fell back on my usual strategy when in a tight social spot. I changed the subject.

'Do you think it will rain later on?' I asked hopefully. He didn't take the bait.

'Your ladders,' he repeated doggedly, nodding towards them. 'Those long ones. Can I borrow them? I'll bring them back when I've finished with them.' There was no deflecting him from his object. I couldn't see any way of getting rid of him except to part with the ladders. I briefly nodded assent and he grinned before heaving them onto his shoulder and struggling through the gate.

That's the last I'll see of them, I thought grimly.

John straightened up from his weeding and was massaging his right leg when I told him.

'You mean you just let him take them?' he said, appalled.

'Well, what else could I say? I couldn't say no, could I?'

'Yes you could,' he insisted. 'They're ours. Technically he's just stolen our property!'

'He said he would bring them back,' I muttered weakly. 'I'm sure he will.'

'If they're not back here within a week I'm going up there,' he said.

That was just the beginning. Stories started to trickle their way into local gossip like a leaky water pipe.

'D'y know, he came into the vineyard when I was pruning and he actually offered to help! Said he knew a different way of doing it. What does he know about vines, he's from Calais? The last I heard they don't have any vines in Calais.'

'He saw our Monique on her way home from school and told her she shouldn't be carrying such a heavy bag! The cheek of the man. How else is she supposed to get her books home from school?'

'They say he's going to live here all summer....'

'Have you seen that great huge dog he's got up there? Massive brute, it is. It barked at me for ages after I went past his gate. Good thing he's got it fenced in....'

'Nicole says she saw him dumping his rubbish at the side of the bin instead of putting it inside....'

This man had not made a great first impression, and from my perspective he was always *there*. When I took my almost daily walk up to the woods I had to pass his gate, and somehow there he would be, waiting to accost me with some trite and idiotic comment. Even worse, he wanted to come with me, on the pretence that his dog needed the exercise. My dislike of him grew greater every time I went for a walk.

My woodland walks were private to me. I adored the solitude, the wind in the trees, the rough ground strewn with twigs and boughs, the wild mushrooms in autumn, even the self seeded tiny tomatoes I once found.

The walks were not simply for the country air and the wonder of the natural landscape. I was desperate to lose a bit of weight, obsessively cross with the bathroom scales when I stood on them and they lied to me every blessed day. I had actually managed to lose a couple of kilogrammes, which didn't go unnoticed.

'You don't want to be going on diets, you know,' Didier told me seriously. 'You're fine as you are. I *like* big women with a good bit of flesh on them.....'

I didn't actually kill him, but it was a close call....

Chapter 23
Crime

It is not only in large cities that crime occurs. We had our share of it in rural France too, although nothing to trouble the TV channels about. It was mostly petty thieving, which was always blamed on the gypsies who lived on a permanent camp just outside the village. Our house had been burgled in the past, when the Damerys owned it. The thieves had forced the kitchen window shutters off their hinges, and made off with the microwave. Unfortunately the Damerys' Sunday lunch had still been inside. We heard the story repeated over and over again for years afterwards. It was a cause of much merriment in a place where little but the changing seasons ever happened.

The crime wave affected us personally on a few occasions. The first was shortly after we had moved in.

It was winter; as bitter a cold as the Languedoc can offer. In a frost competition between Yorkshire and the South of France, Languedoc would have won that year. By miles. Late at night when the frost had hardened into a shining yellow glitter in the light of the street lamp, there was an insistent knocking at the front door. John and I looked at each other. No-one in their right mind would be out in this weather. I decided it must be an emergency. One of the Bellinis, maybe, and so I cautiously opened the door a fraction.

For maybe a second I thought no-one was there. Until I looked down. There, huddled in a pathetic grey heap on the ground was a young man. He had no shoes on. He stood up. He was tall. Much taller than I was, and he scared me. For a few seconds we stared at each before he spoke.

'Let me in. Please. I need to come in. I'm so cold. Please let me in.'

I was completely baffled. My first thought was that he was a decoy, and that there would be several of his burly mates hiding somewhere close by, ready to storm into the house and overpower us. Rob us, kill us.... I didn't consciously think of anything before I slammed the door in his face.

The knocking went on. Louder. More insistent. I went to find John.

John was far more decisive. 'Call the gendarmerie,' he yelled, and I scuttled back to the phone in the hallway. The minute I turned the corner I froze. He was inside. I hadn't locked the door against him and he was there, standing right in front of me.

The right words came immediately. Words that I had heard over the years, foul swear words that people use when they are filled with hatred, or fear. Words that people never use in daily conversation. I hurled all the words I knew at him and to my immense relief, he backed off outside. This time I slammed the door and locked it. I could hear his moaning over John tapping out the gendarmerie's number, and he passed the receiver over to me as soon as someone answered. I was incoherent, but bit by bit, I told my story.

'Keep your door locked,' said the stern voice on the other end. 'Where are you?'

'I'm at home!' I bleated. 'He's still outside, I can hear him....'

I was *so* glad that I wasn't in the police station to witness the eye rolls. 'Madame, your address....?'

'Oh. Yes. Yes, of course.' As soon as I gave our address, the voice told me that someone would be with us shortly, repeating the instruction to keep the door locked.

It was literally only a couple of minutes later that we heard the siren. Out of the kitchen window we saw two policemen get out of the car. There was no scuffle, they simply took a firm hold of the man and guided him to the back of their car. The light in the kitchen came in intermittent flashes from their rotating police lamp. The cupboards turned from black to bright blue every few seconds.

They were obviously interviewing the man, as they had their heads turned to face him. It went on for some minutes, until the car door opened and one of the policemen rapped on the door.

'He's been in a car accident,' he explained tersely. 'About a kilometre down the road. He's left someone injured in the car and yours was the first house he came to...'

'What about his shoes? Why wasn't he wearing any?'

The policeman was unable to answer that. 'We've got a car on the way to the accident now,' he told me.

There are mysteries in life, and that was one of them. I found out later that the injured person was his girlfriend, and that she had been taken to hospital. I believe the man was charged with whatever was the French equivalent of dangerous driving, but we never found out where he had left his shoes.

Our second experience of crime was the disappearance of our cherries. They were taken from our tree, at night, by person or persons unknown. As it was hardly a matter for the European Court of Justice, we accepted it and moved on.

The third was more serious. Our small blue Citroën C3 was normally parked just out of sight of our kitchen window. We parked it one evening and thought no more about it until there was a knock at the door and two burly uniformed gendarmes stood there, asking me to confirm our ownership of a Citroën C3 with a number plate which we recognised as ours.

'We have found your car,' they told me.

I was greatly surprised by this, not having being aware of misplacing it.

'She is in a vineyard near to Trausse Minervois,' one of the gendarmes stated. 'It is very unfortunate but she has been burned out. There is nothing left of her.'

My panic mode took over, and I waved the gendarmes aside as I went to check. It was true. Where the car had been was now an empty parking space.

'John!' I yelled. 'Come here!'

He appeared with his coffee in hand.

'The car! it's gone!'

'What? What are you talking about? Whose car is gone?' He eyed the patiently waiting gendarmes with suspicion, as if the whole scenario might be a practical joke.

'Our car!' I shouted at him. 'It's been stolen. They're saying it's been burnt out in a vineyard somewhere.'

His coffee slopped over onto the tiles as he went outside to look. He came back with a blank expression. 'They're right, it's not there. Unbelievable,' he murmured. 'Have they any idea who might have taken it?'

When I asked, the answer was negative. There were suspicions of a group of young boys from neighbouring Trausse Minervois and they would investigate thoroughly but couldn't promise anything.

'Joy riders probably,' John said after the police left. 'Or possibly gypsies.'

Rather unfairly, I thought, the local gypsy camp was the first port of suspicion when anything untoward happened in the village, although personally we had no reason to suspect them. Their camper vans were partially hidden behind a waist high white wall on the Caunes road and the camp appeared to be well kept, with laundry facilities and electricity provided by the council. Nevertheless, they were almost universally accused of any petty thieving.

If we had only had one car, the theft would have been incredibly inconvenient. Online shopping was still a heady dream for supermarkets, and when it did arrive in France it was only available in the large cities. Our local Géant at Salvaza did offer a light version, whereby customers could order online, but then had to drive to the shop where their bags would be waiting for them.

What Géant *did* introduce were birthday presents. In the year before we left France, I received a letter from the supermarket inviting me to go to reception where my present would be waiting. Intrigued, I presented myself as instructed, where a plainly bored assistant handed me a plastic carrier bag. It contained a birthday card from the shop, as well as two packets of pasta, a can of tomato paste, a bar of chocolate, a packet of mixed nuts and a selection of savoury crackers. Even though the food was approaching its sell by date, I was delighted, as I had been expecting some kind of prize draw. An ingenious way of not only offloading still edible food, but pleasing customers at the same time, I thought.

But, that was in the days when we still had two cars. There were no shops within walking distance and without a back up vehicle we would have had to rely on Sophie. Fortunately we still had my small Toyota Yaris, which was parked on the gravelled drive at the back of the house where it was out of sight of passers-by. Later that day I drove it to Peyriac, a couple of kilometres down the straight road, to fill in a crime report. The police station was located next to *Les Bains de Minerve*, a fabulous swimming pool where I used to do an aquatonic session. Its most amazing feature was a sliding roof over the whole pool, transforming it from indoor to outdoor in the hot summer months.

That was the beginning of one of our encounters with the local gendarmerie. They were very helpful, and for me it was an interested glimpse into the inside of their station, where there were three extremely solid blue metal doors with very secure locks on the outside. At a desk, I filled out the report which we would need for the insurance claim.

It was a straightforward procedure, and as insurance claims go, fairly quickly dealt with. There was no dispute, and about six weeks later we were awarded a sum of money which enabled us to buy a purple Toyota Verso, on the basis that it would be very useful to have a six-seater when the family came to stay. We had learned a valuable lesson, and the new car was never parked at the front of the house.

Our other, and final, encounter with the police was not as pleasant. The Tour de France was finishing a stage on a blisteringly hot day in Narbonne in June 2008, but we were not aware of it. There were no signs posted when we found a rare empty spot in the theatre car park. After a leisurely stroll around Narbonne, with lunch at one of the waterside cafes, we returned, hot and weary, along the canal path at around four in the afternoon. There was a red and white tape closing off the car park, and not a single car in sight. We were stunned, and totally confused. There was no indication at all of where all the cars had gone. I briefly conjured up an image of a possible Dr. Who episode and then dismissed it.

The only possible course of action was to ring the police and report the car as stolen. They arrived to a cacophony of wailing sirens and flashing blue lights, to find a disconsolate, hot, hungry and irritable couple waiting by the entrance to the car park.

Our car, together with those of all the other unwitting unfortunates who had parked there had been impounded, as the car park was needed for the Tour de France.

'But there was no notice!' I fumed. 'There was absolutely nothing to tell us that we couldn't park here. If we had known, we'd have found somewhere else.'

The gendarme seemed unimpressed. 'Your car,' he stated laconically, 'she has been towed away to the pound. You can go and take her away but you will have to pay for her.'

'The pound! But we don't know where it is! And how can we get there if we have no car?' I was almost in tears by now. We didn't use the local buses in Narbonne so we would have had no idea of which bus to catch, if indeed there was a bus to take us there. I had a little money in my purse, but possibly not enough for a taxi. I was distraught. 'So where is it?' I asked.

The gendarme was showing a little more sympathy now. Quite possibly they had dealt with more than one case like ours that afternoon.

'We can take you to the pound,' he offered, and we barely had to look at each other before we gratefully accepted and slid into the back seat of the police car. It was the first time in either of our lives that we had been in one. A young couple on the pavement turned to look as the car started off, and they both put their fists up to their eyes and wiped away mock tears as we drove off. We both laughed ruefully as the car sped off.

It cost us over a hundred euros to get the car out of the pound, but we were just so relieved to get it back that the price barely warranted a few swear words before we forgot about it.

Chapter 24
Divorce

The next time I heard from Elodie, there was no need for letters as the ubiquitous mobile phones were the most favoured method of communication.

Our daughter Pamela, her husband Len and their two children Harry and Gillian were making their annual summer visit, and I was helping Gillian to pick the ripest strawberries which we would have for tea when John came out to join us, handing me my mobile.

'I can't be certain, but it sounds like Elodie,' he said. I was puzzled by this, as he knew her voice well enough, but when she tried to speak I understood. She was sobbing so much that the words were choked off before she could voice them.

'Elodie, try to calm yourself. Please. 'What's wrong?'

'I'm at the end, Stephanie, I just can't take any more of this,' she sobbed. 'I've put up with it for years and it's just unbearable now. I don't know what to do any more....'

I was completely bewildered. Was it her mother? Lucie? Problems at work? Could it be that John was far more intuitive than I was, and the problem was Antoine?

'Take any more of what, Elodie? Listen, I can't hear you properly when you're crying like that. Tell me what's happened.'

'It's Antoine, what else would it be? He's been seeing someone. I've suspected it for a long time. For years, and he always denied it. He tries to turn it round as if it's all my fault, he says I'm poking into his private life, that I don't trust him. He says I should know that he'd never cheat on me. But I can't help it, Steph. He goes out nearly every night, he never says where he's going or who he's seeing, and if I ask he just tells me it's none of my business. So last night when he was in the shower I looked at his phone. He's been ringing the same number nearly every day, and when I looked for who the number belonged to, it's someone called Liliane, and I *know* her Stephanie. She was at the *Lycée* with me, but she's a few years younger.'

'You looked at his phone?' I said, startled. By this time I had left John to supervise the strawberry picking and I made my way into the lounge, where I sat down. This wasn't something I wanted to discuss in front of Pamela. Len had gone down to the *boulangerie* to pick up a baguette for the tea.

'How else would I have found out? What would you do if John started ringing the same woman every day? You'd want to know who it was, wouldn't you?'

I couldn't even envisage the possibility of John behaving like that, but to say so would not be helpful, I thought, so I waited for her to speak again.

When she did, she sounded a little calmer and the sobs had diminished but I could hear the anguish in her voice.

'This is only the latest thing,' she went on. 'We have not been getting on well together for years. I have more or less brought Lucie up on my own. He was never interested in her. He never helped her with any of her schoolwork. He did not even want to know when she went on one of her diets and couldn't stop. I know I never wanted her to be as fat as I was, but she became obsessed with her weight. You should have seen her, Steph, she was as thin as a rake, I was demented over it. He was no help at all, he just kept telling her to eat more.'

'And is she better now?'

'She got over it eventually but she was in hospital for a while. I had no help from anyone. You know how it is. It was no use telling my mother, she has no more time for Lucie than she had for me.' She was sounding very bitter. 'In the end she saw a counsellor and that helped. She eats properly now, thank goodness.'

'Does she know about Antoine and ...er... Liliane?'

'I have tried to keep it from her but I'm sure she knows really, although she does not say anything. I do not want to burden her with it. Besides, she does not really need us now, she is at the university. It will not matter to her if I get divorced.'

I disagreed with her about that, but I didn't want to upset her by saying so. My mind flew back to the time when she found out that she was pregnant with Lucie, and I had waded in with my crass suggestion of an abortion. This time I decided to be more circumspect. A sudden memory came to me, of Lucie's first visit to us after we had moved in. At that time, it was Elodie, I remembered, who had been the obsessive one, endlessly directing Lucie to choose this low calorie option, or that low fat dish. How many of Lucie's problems with food had their roots in her childhood, I wondered, just as Elodie's may have begun in her own, when she was a chubby child with Mamy practically forcing food down her? Not for the first time, I was thankful for my own laid back parents, who viewed food as a fuel for the body rather than a lifestyle choice.

'So what happens now?' I asked. 'Have you definitely decided? Where will you live?'

She sounded stronger now. 'I will live right here,' she said angrily. 'He is the one who will be leaving. He can go and live with her for all I care. I just want him out of my life for good.'

'Elodie, I'm so sorry this is happening to you. Is there anything we can do? Would you like to come and stay for a while?' As soon as the words were out of my mouth I regretted them. I really couldn't cope at the moment with Elodie. Pamela was not due to go back to the UK for another two weeks, there wouldn't even have been room for her. Thankfully, she gulped and said, 'No, Steph, thank you. It is good of you but I have many things to sort out here. I will make an appointment with a solicitor in the morning and I will tell him tonight. Antoine, I mean, not the solicitor.' At that point I heard a rather sour laugh. 'I have already packed three suitcases of his clothes....'

'Well, ring me whenever you want,' I told her. 'If you want to chat, I'm always here. You know that.'

'It is *so* good to talk to you, Steph. I feel a bit better already, just knowing that you are there. You have always been my best friend, ever since we were young. I will let you know what happens.' With that, she hung up and I went back into the garden to hear shrieks of, 'Granny, there's a bug on my strawberries. Come and get it off for me!' Gillian was delighted with her crop and I kissed her before we all went back inside for tea.

'It's taken her a long time to realise,' John remarked laconically after I related most of her conversation. I stared at him.

'A long time?' I repeated, amazed. 'How would you know anything about it? Has he been confiding in you or something?'

'He doesn't need to confide in me. I saw how he was looking at Elodie when they came here, that time when we first moved in. He has no respect for her at all. *And* I walked in on them both once when you were watering the veg. I don't know what it was all about exactly, but he was telling her she was useless. *'A useless idiot,'* was what he said. He shut up the minute he saw me, but I always knew there'd be trouble between them.' He smiled at my outraged expression.

'So, why didn't you say anything? I'm sure I'd have said something – to Elodie, at least...'

'No, you wouldn't,' he retorted. 'You might have thought about it but in the end you'd have kept quiet. What was I supposed to say? And who to?' he said with a slight shrug. 'You can't interfere with someone else's marriage. Unless you're a parent, perhaps, and even then it's usually wiser to keep out of it. People always resent interference in their private lives. I really don't know why she keeps on asking *you* for advice. You're not her mother.'

It came back to me, in a rush of memories, how my own mother had voiced much the same opinion, and for a moment I felt as if I was the only person unable to see into people's minds and analyse their motives. Perhaps it was possible that Elodie *did* look upon me as a kind of mother-figure. If she did, then I felt that she was making a huge mistake. There was no doubt about it; John was far more perceptive than I was.

A few months later I received an email.

Hi Stephanie,

It has happened at last! I am officially divorced and I cannot tell you how good it is for me! It has taken so many months and I have been in and out of solicitors' offices, which was not easy because I needed to be sure that Antoine will pay me enough money each month for Lucie. He wanted to pay the very least amount but my solicitor has forced him to pay the standard money for a dependant, so this is better. I have not seen him for a long time, since I threw out his suitcases, but my friend Pauline has told me that he lives with Liliane and his parents have paid for him an apartment close to their home. For me, it is good, but for Liliane I do not know. I hope he will treat her the same as he treated me,' she added viciously. 'For the money, the situation is not very good for me, as I still have to pay for the apartment, the payments are not yet finished, but I hope that I will be able to earn more money besides my salary. I have started painting again. Do you remember, this was always my ambition but Mamy was against this. I have made an exhibition last month, and at this I have sold three paintings. So, I will continue this. In addition, I have two people who ask me for a painting of their dog, so this I can do in my next holidays, and I ask for five hundred euros for each one. This will help me. I hope you will email me soon.

Love, Elodie

Chapter 25
Wildlife

I have heard that flying ants have been found in the south of England recently. We had them in the south of France too although we were unaware of their presence when we first moved there. The first indication we had was when a few crawled out from a crevice in one of the roughly hewn stone steps leading from the conservatory to the garden. They were joined by some more whilst the first ones to emerge found their wings and flew off.

Not being either a Durrell or an Attenborough, I find it hard to get excited about ants. I am sure they have their uses and I can't say I actually mind them, except when they are on my patch. I hurried indoors looking for the can of insect spray that we always kept in the kitchen cupboard and by the time I got back outside armed with my can of destruction the air was black with them. Wildly, I sprayed in any direction at all, not being in the least particular where I was aiming for, and thankfully the spray was taking effect. Several of them were in spasms before they stopped moving and I was able to concentrate my efforts on the hole where they were emerging.

After a few years it became apparent that early June was hatching time, so we got into the habit of dousing the steps with insect killer before they could emerge. I make no apologies to anyone frantically clutching their pearls or striking their foreheads in horror on reading this. For the last few years we were there we had conquered them and never saw a flying ant again.

Not so for the cicadas. You didn't exactly see cicadas as they were extremely well camouflaged against the rough bark of the tree trunks in the orchard; you simply heard them. They were one of the harbingers of summer as they remained silent until the temperature was in the mid-thirties or above. When they started up you could barely hear yourself speak for the racket they made. The only way to silence them was to approach the tree from where you thought the noise was coming, which was difficult as their noise seemed to be surrounding you. At a distance of a few feet they apparently became aware of your presence and stopped their screeching. They fell gradually silent as dusk approached. That was when the bats came out of wherever they had been hiding during the scorching heat of the summer day.

The bats were pipistrelles and unlike the cicadas, they swooped and swirled swiftly and silently, no doubt gorging themselves on any remaining flying ants and other troublesome small creatures. Only one of them had an unusual habit of flying during the day, being quite possibly blind as a bat and failing to realise that the dusk had not yet arrived. The main flock of them was a nightly pleasure in a way that the flying ants were definitely not.

The sheer multitude of creatures previously unknown to us was staggering. Inner city Leeds where I grew up had its share of birds, mice and no doubt rats, but neither lizards nor snakes nor hoopoes ever troubled or fascinated us as they did in France.

The mice were not much trouble since they mostly lived in the vineyards. If they'd have *kept* to the vineyards there'd have been no problem. But when harvest time came and the monstrous grape picking machines obliterated their homes, they scurried indoors looking for shelter and somewhere cosy to bring up their young. One of them decided that the top drawer in my kitchen cabinet looked a likely residence, until my shrill scream when I opened it made her think again. She shot across the floor to wriggle herself underneath the facia of the cupboard and I never saw her again.

When John's sister Elizabeth arrived for a week's visit, I knew we had to be careful since she detested all animal life. It was after eleven o' clock at night and she had gone to bed when we heard the scream and a door slam. As soon as we arrived outside the door, the cause of it was lying on the floor; a massive black beetle which had found its way inside and was now on its back, helplessly wriggling all its hairy legs in the air.

'I'm trapped!' she yelled from inside. 'I need to go to the toilet! Get rid of it!'

John arrived with a square of kitchen paper and gently removed the beast and set it down the right way up just outside the front door, where it crawled away until it was out of sight in a bush.

'You can come out now,' he called. She gingerly poked her heard around the door, checking that the way was devoid of nasties before she took herself off to the toilet. We heaved a sigh of relief. That was a close one.

We were all in bed an hour later when the second scream rang out. That one was enough to rouse the village and we both sat up in bed, shaken to the core.

Elizabeth appeared in our room, completely oblivious to the fact that we may not have wanted interruption. 'It was in my hair!' she yelled. She was incoherent, red in the face and actually shaking. 'A mouse!' she screamed. 'A bloody mouse and it was in my hair!'

Neither of us laughed. It wasn't funny. It really wasn't. Well, actually it was. It was hilarious but we didn't laugh, I promise. We sucked in our cheeks and tightened our lips and did our best to look serious. It wasn't easy. The tiniest little smirks might have swept over our faces but we didn't guffaw out loud or anything.

We all trooped into her room but there was nothing to see. The screams would have given any self-respecting mouse a coronary. We didn't expect to see it alive again. Elizabeth retreated to her room, but she swore the next morning that she hadn't closed her eyes all night. To be fair, I wouldn't have done either.

In contrast to the mice which were a total nuisance, the small lizards were cute, friendly little creatures. They were so affectionate that they often wanted to make close contact by hiding in the toe of your empty shoe or wriggling themselves from the back of a chair and running down your arm. It was not the greatest fun but it didn't faze us particularly. No, the worst of the lizards was the mess they left behind them. Lizards seem to have an urgent need to defecate constantly, and they do it well. Small white elongated pellets which they deposited all over the furniture. I was forever hoovering them up. When I think back I am *so* glad that I live in the UK now.

Many of them lived on the roof and in the gutters, which frequently proved to be their undoing, as the gutters fed into a huge green rainwater vat. The sensible ones, when they fell in, simply wriggled onto their backs and placidly floated until a human came along to fish them out with a net. The panicky ones, of which there were many, struggled and tried swimming which they were not physiologically equipped to do. They drowned.

Wild boar are plentiful in the woods of the Languedoc but it is a rare occasion when they are spotted. They are shy creatures who do most of their foraging in the inky blackness of the deep countryside night, although they sometimes appear during the day. I was driving home at dusk, along a lonely, narrow country road which wended its way through the woods. There was a much faster route along the main road, but this woodland track road saved at least a couple of kilometres. Suddenly I braked sharply. Two adult wild boar and their family of four youngsters emerged from the dusky undergrowth and lumbered across the lane directly in front of me. Not wanting to advertise my presence I switched off the engine, and watched them, totally fascinated. There was a crashing rustle of dry leaves and they were out of sight as quickly as they had come.

No one in our immediate vicinity rhapsodized about the romance of wild boar. Quite simply, they are shooting targets and every afternoon during the August to February season, men in camouflage outfits used to take their dogs, their guns, equip themselves with copious quantities of whisky in hip flasks to patrol the woods and fields around our house. It was unnerving, as they often passed close to our windows, pacing silently up and down and we got used to the sound of gunshots punctuating our afternoons. During the shooting season I suspended my daily walks. Hunters can get excited and shoot at anything that moves, and a gently bobbing head can be mistaken for an animal. It was not unknown for the hunters to accidentally shoot their friends, especially during the partial light of dusk when sensible people are indoors and the only humans around are their fellow hunters.

Hoopoes were another unexpected fascination, with their exotic orange plumed heads and vividly striped black and white wings. In the air they are ungainly, rising and falling with a ponderous flapping of fat wings, and on the ground they give the impression of being slightly deranged as they nod and peck at the ground for insects.

One hoopoe delicacy was the processional caterpillar, which is famous for its insect version of the hokey-cokey. We had seen their nests; great balls of fluffy cotton wool in the tops of the nearby trees, without ever once associating them with the marching caterpillars on the ground. Later on we learned that they leave their tree in order to search for soft soil in which to bury themselves before forming cocoons.

When we first saw them we took great pains to avoid driving over their wriggling column, until Monsieur Bellini warned us of how dangerous they are, with their venomous tiny hairs which can cause skin reactions and allergies in humans.

Dogs and cats need to keep their distance from them too, in case they step on them either by accident or out of curiosity. Any caterpillar hairs touching their mouth or tongue will cause itching and swelling. They can damage the eyes too, to the point of causing total blindness if left untreated. Small wonder, then, that their nests are destroyed by professionals wherever they are found.

Our own cat was never disturbed by them, stepping over them with a haughty disdain on the rare occasions when she encountered them. We had adopted her at a local barbecue, when a young girl had carried her hopefully around the participants, searching for a home for her. At that time we had had no intention of housing a pet, but this tiny bundle of black and white fur was far too irresistible to be denied. As soon as I held her in my arms and stroked her, I fell in love. Once we got her home we showered her with every attention a cat could possibly have. We fed her on large prawns which she adored, on the most delicious commercial cat food available, we bought her a bed and a scratch mat, we lavished attention on her and she rewarded us by killing our mice. Then she grew up. Eventually she was the most enormous cat we had ever seen, with fur that tangled and a tail which lashed viciously at any intruders into her space. She began, slowly at first, to reject the food we offered her and began to source her own, mainly at night, when she would come back home with dead rats or mice which she would eat in the kitchen.

When she was outside, she had a habit of hiding in the large stone barbecue we had built shortly after moving in. She would track pigeons with a relentless, vigilant eye until they were in her range, and then hurl herself in a screeching fury, clawing at them until she brought her dead victims back to the barbecue where she would devour them whole.

One hot August night we made the mistake of sleeping with the window open. It must have been around three o'clock in the morning when we were awoken by a crash. The cat flew through the open window into our room with a live rabbit in her claws. They both landed with an almighty thud on the floor, the rabbit thrashing its body and squealing in agony as our cat proceeded to skin it, shedding blood and fur around the room as she ripped it to pieces and ate it in front of our eyes; every last morsel of flesh was gnawed off in a frenzied attack and gulped down until the bedroom resembled an abattoir.

The live rabbit was only the beginning. Gradually, the cat became entirely self-sufficient, evidently living comfortably on any small mammals she could catch. Days passed without a sign of her, then weeks, and finally she simply disappeared up the lane one afternoon and we never saw her again.

Chapter 26
Preparations

Clothilde from the farm was still living at home, and over the years I had got to know her quite well. She would appear at our back gate on her way to the daily mass at the church of Notre Dame de la Cross, always with further news of the family, and of her woes, which were plentiful. She still had no job despite many interviews. I was sorry for her but saw no practical way of helping, apart from lending a sympathetic ear. John usually hurried into the house whenever he saw her coming.

I was very surprised when she came to see us one day and proudly showed off a very large engagement ring which was studded with diamonds surrounding a huge sparkling emerald. Where had that come from? She had never mentioned a boy. All her sisters had boyfriends but so far she had not found one. It was one of the things she was depressed about.

She had no dowry, I was absolutely sure of that. Her family was extremely poor. She had no evident physical attractions either, and as far as I knew, she never went anywhere to meet boys. Apart from the rare church socials, there was literally nowhere for her to go. But when she told me his name, little light bulbs exploded in my mind and everything suddenly clicked into place.

He was Monsieur Fréderique de Letois. In France that tiny word *'de'* in the surname is not necessarily an indication that the family is aristocratic but sometimes it can be, and Clothilde herself came from a family with that important word 'de' in her name.

In the salon at her home was a coffee table with a heavy glass top, underneath which was a faded family tree demonstrating that they were quite conclusively, with a few sideways moves, descended from the House of Bourbon. So Monsieur Fréderique was getting hitched to an honest to God aristocrat; albeit a poverty-stricken one but an aristocrat nonetheless. Although very poor, the parents had made sure from their earliest years that the children were aware of their noble status. All of them had impeccable, world class manners. Standing up when a visitor entered was the norm for them, as was always ushering a female into a room ahead of a male. They had undoubtedly made the most of this family connection which had been enough, apparently, to attract Monsieur Fredérique. I believe they were the only family in the region who addressed their own parents using the formal *'vous'* form of the verb 'to be.'

The fact that Monsieur Fréderique was also a staunch catholic made it fairly obvious that someone, somewhere, very probably a priest who was part of Clothilde's extended family, had arranged this forthcoming marriage.

However it had come about she was very excited about her wedding, which was to take place in a few months' time. She appeared to have few qualms about the fact that she barely knew this man.

About a week before the ceremony there was a knock at the door and there stood Clothilde clutching a bolt of cloth.

'Could we make some lavender bags?' she asked excitedly. She knew that my hobby was sewing, but as the wedding was scheduled in three days' time, I felt that logistics might be an issue.

She let herself into the lounge and opened out the cloth on the dining table, a pretty cotton in shades of pink and lilac.

'I expect we can make a few,' I said rather doubtfully. 'It depends how many you want. And why lavender bags?'

'I'm going to scatter them on the tables,' she said in excitement. 'They will look very pretty and for the guests, they will be a good memento of my wedding.'

'I'm sure they will. So how many?'

'I was thinking about a hundred and fifty.'

'A hundred and fifty!' I was aghast. 'But that's going to take ages. Is everything else ready? Your dress and everything? Is this the last thing you have to do?'

'I have everything ready,' she promised. And what a blatant lie that turned out to be. 'If we begin now we can make them all.' She looked at me pleadingly and I capitulated.

I sighed. 'I can't promise a hundred and fifty but we'll have a go. You can cut them out and I'll sew them up.'

She looked very relieved as I heaved my sewing machine onto the table and we set to work; Clothilde feverishly cutting out rectangles and pushing them over to me where I was sewing non-stop. I was stressed out, thinking of the short time left before the lavender bags would be needed. A few hours later I had had enough and I took my foot off the machine's footplate.

'How many do we have?' she asked anxiously. A quick count revealed that we had completed thirty-two.

'We're never going to get a hundred and fifty,' I said decisively. 'It's ridiculous. We just haven't got time Clothilde.'

She was disappointed but reluctantly accepted that the job was just too much.

'I will put them only on the most important tables,' she conceded.

Then came the final straw. I looked round for the lavender.

'Clothilde, where's the lavender?' I said urgently. Great suspicion was now dawning.

'Lavender?' she repeated, eyes wide with innocence.

'Yes, lavender.' I repeated impatiently. 'You know, to fill the bags with.' And then it dawned on me. 'You haven't got any, have you?' I asked flatly.

She was just slightly embarrassed. 'But, you have some in your garden, *non*?'

'*Non*' was right. The lavender season hadn't yet begun and in any case we only had a couple of scraggy plants.

'No, we haven't got any right now. We'll have some in a couple of months but that will be too late for you. And in any case, we haven't got nearly enough to fill thirty-odd bags.'

'What do you have? Something with a scent?' She was really pushing it now and my patience was limited to begin with. We had just spent hours on making lavender bags and now there was nothing to fill them with.

She continued hopefully. 'Have you some thyme perhaps, some rosemary? Anything? Can we go and look?'

Resigned now, I followed as she led the way through the French windows and down the stone steps into the garden. She spotted a large clump of rosemary and darted away, feverishly stripping off tiny leaves without so much as asking permission. Although I was still annoyed, I was well aware of the urgency of the situation, so swallowed my ire and helped her to pick. Finally, we had enough leaves of rosemary, thyme and various varieties of mint to fill the bags and we headed inside.

I heaved a sigh of sheer relief as I waved her off, clutching the finished bags and the remnants of the cloth.

The days passed with no further interruptions, until the wedding day itself arrived. I was quite looking forward to it. There weren't many entertainments in this sleepy hamlet and I thought it might be fun.

At around ten in the morning I was half ready, showered, hair done and clothes pressed when there was a knock at the door. It might be the postman possibly, or it could be next door. I was staggered when I opened it and beheld Clothilde, once again clutching a bolt of cloth to her chest.

'Clothilde, what are you doing *here*? You're getting married at three o'clock! You should be getting ready!' I was genuinely appalled to see her. What was she *thinking?*

She wasn't far from tears, with flushed cheeks from her apparent stiff walk from her house.

'It is a problem. A big problem. It is the bridesmaid. The mothers were supposed to make a skirt. They promised they would be ready, but this mother, she tells me today that she has no time, that her daughter's skirt will not be here. I do not know what I can do.' Her face was working uncontrollably and I could see the emotions in her face. Huge anxiety over the knowledge that her wedding was imminent and she was not ready, with even more distress about the as yet unmade skirt.

'Have one less bridesmaid then,' I suggested pragmatically. It seemed to be the only reasonable solution.

'I cannot!' she wailed. 'The little girl, the little Diane, she is my cousin. She will be desolate if she cannot be a bridesmaid. Can you....?'

The sheer effrontery just left me stupefied. I looked at my watch. 'Clothilde, your wedding *starts* in under five hours from now. You must have so much to do. What about your hair? Your makeup? This isn't the time to start making clothes!'

'But if we start this now, right now, we will be able to finish it. It is a simple skirt,' she pleaded. 'It will be easy for you to do.'

Briefly, I contemplated stabbing her with the scissors but decided that that course of action might result in more trouble than it was worth. After a few seconds' thought, I decided. 'Alright,' I said resignedly. 'We'll give it a go.' I looked at her very directly. 'But you'll have to help me, I can't do this all on my own.'

She was grateful. 'Thank you, this is kind. You are like a mother to me.' At heart I was desperately sorry for her, and with this in mind I reluctantly I searched for my sewing machine. The sooner we got started, the quicker Clothilde could get home and hopefully be ready in time. 'Do you have the pattern?' I asked.

She nodded. 'Yes, I have it.'

I couldn't see a pattern anywhere but assumed it was in her handbag. 'So where is it?'

'It is in my head,' she replied.

This was unbelievable. I did know about her mental health problems though and tried my best.

'Listen, it might be in *your* head, Clothilde, but it isn't in mine,' I said patiently. 'How can I make a skirt without a pattern?'

'It is very simple,' she told me. 'Just a skirt.'

'Is it straight? Flared? Gathered, what?'

'It is like this.' And she gestured with her arms, making roughly an A shape.

I could see that this was all going to be down to me now. 'How old is the child?' I asked resignedly.

'She is four.'

'Right then.' I mentally calculated and then reached for my laptop. *Average four year old height,* I typed, and from there I had a rough idea. I cut two sections, allowing enough fabric for an elasticated waistband which would be the quickest and easiest way of making up a skirt. It was basically two seams, a hem and a casing for the elastic. The whole thing was done in half an hour. There were just under three hours to go before the ceremony.

Thinking back to the lavender debacle, I didn't even bother asking Clothilde if she had brought any elastic. She wouldn't have done. I had a stash of haberdashery in a green plastic box and I rummaged through it. Damn! No suitable elastic. I had ribbons, thread, lots of other bits and pieces but no elastic. I told Clothilde and she had an idea.

'Madame Sanet will have some. We can go and buy enough for one skirt.'

Madame Sanet was the proprietor of the only haberdashery shop in Rieux Minervois, which she ran from tiny premises hidden away in a back alleyway. Her customers were all locals as a stranger would never have found the shop by accident. I had lived in France for six years before I discovered her. There was only one problem and I voiced it.

'She closes at twelve, doesn't she?'

Clothilde consulted her watch. 'It is only twelve minus five,' she said. 'If we hurry...'

Rieux was a good five minutes away by car. I doubted if we could make it in time, but we would try. We both raced to the car. I backed it out of the gate and we were speeding down the long straight road leading to Rieux in less than a minute. Would we be on time?

I parked in the nearest spot I could find and we raced to the shop. Madame Sanet was visible, just. She was letting down the shutter after locking the door. Clothilde frantically rapped on the window, startling Madame who raised the shutter slightly.

'Elastic, Madame!' yelled Clothilde. 'Please, it is urgent!'

Thankfully the old lady peered out of her window. Recognising Clothilde, she unlocked the door.

Another five minutes saw us racing back to the house with the precious bag of elastic. I had the casing of the skirt ready and I slotted the elastic through as fast as I could. I held up the finished skirt in a burst of triumph.

'If it's too long you'll have to turn it over at the waist,' I said, but I was speaking to her retreating back.

'Thank you a thousand times!' she yelled over her shoulder and disappeared around the corner.

The next time we saw her was at the church in Trausse Minervois. The couple had already been officially married at the registry office in the *Mairie* in Trausse as French law dictated, and this was to be the church ceremony which some people thought to be unnecessary, but for devout Catholics, it was essential.

The church was packed, and John and I took unobtrusive pews towards the back. Being heretical non-Catholics we had no idea of the correct responses and we didn't attempt making them. Instead we dutifully rose and sat down again many, many times during the mass, which we both found drawn out and boring.

Our reward came as we watched a beaming Clothilde walk slowly back down the aisle and out of the church on her new husband's arm, and then into the strong Mediterranean sunshine where their coach was waiting.

The coach consisted of a kind of padded cart on massive wheels with a high black leather backrest, attached to two black and very restive horses. Clothilde and husband were helped into it by various well-meaning friends and relations who pushed at the two of them until they were finally triumphantly seated, flushed and laughing with their exertion and the heat. The coachman flicked his whip at the horses, who by this time were neighing and stamping their hooves. Quite unexpectedly, the crack of the whip startled them into a sudden bolt, and the crowd yelled as the newly-weds were flung back against the seat, Clothilde's dress flying up to reveal her frilly underwear, and they were off, clinging to each other for dear life as they disappeared in a flurry of hot dust that all but obliterated them.

All that remained was the evening celebratory meal. To be organised by the French Foreign Legion. Now, as an organisation, the French Foreign Legion are renowned for their aggressive fighting skills. They are known for looking pristine in their immaculate uniforms. They are known for accepting recruits from dubious backgrounds. They are known for their disciplined marching ability. They are known for singing. They are not generally the first port of call when it comes to wedding organisation, mainly because they never do it. That's why I was very much surprised to learn that they would be providing the marquee for the event and would be on hand to make sure everything went smoothly for the evening reception.

The most likely explanation was that Clothilde's family had some high-ranking family connection in the Legion to facilitate this unusual event. This particular unit was based in Castelnaudary, some forty kilometres away so the possibility was not out of the question.

When we arrived, the long white marquee was erected and several soldiers in their pristine summer uniforms with white round caps were gathered in a corner by a table which held plates and cutlery. Some were putting finishing touches to the long trestle tables, whisking knives and forks into place with all the aplomb of accomplished waiters and breathing on glasses before polishing them up with muslin cloths. One of their superiors was standing by directing Legionnaires with short, sharp gestures which sent them scuttling off to the kitchen area, from where they emerged carrying heaped piles of white crockery and bundles of napkins. A particularly husky Legionnaire was fussily placing lavender bags in exactly the right spots on the top table.

I was genuinely intrigued by the whole thing but also very pleased for her. All she had ever needed, I felt, was to become a wife and mother to numerous children. At the time of writing, several years on, her mental health has improved enormously, she is still a devout Catholic, still married and the happy couple are shortly expecting number six.

Chapter 27
Blood Pressure

Véronique's own body had evidently begun the process of letting her down, and I had once read that humans can expect, on average, sixty-three years of good health before the body starts creaking and groaning and otherwise protesting that it has been around for a long time and needs a bit more tender loving care than has hitherto been the case. If true, then my sixty-three years were fast approaching.

Nothing specific at first. Things don't normally go dramatically wrong. I mean, bits of your body don't fall off or anything. You don't usually wake up missing a left ear, for instance. No, it's the *inside* that goes first. The bits you can't see so are unable to contradict the doctors when they say you are falling apart. Suddenly everything needs to come down. Your blood pressure needs to come down. Your cholesterol needs to come down. Your waist size needs to come down. Your hips need to come down. Your BMI needs to come down. Your blood sugar needs to come down. Basically, you need to shrink. Or so you are told. Then you are prescribed little pills to make sure that everything is as low as it can be without you disappearing. Your body needs to shrink so that the pharmaceutical companies can grow. The more you need their pills, the greater their profits.

The only thing that doesn't come down is your age, and so far all the doctors I have seen have been unable to treat me for this. I have asked. I have pleaded. I have nearly gone down on my knees and begged, but so far no joy. I don't ask for the moon. Ten years off would be great. Fifteen if they could manage it. I am sure it's just a case of a little extra training, or paying more attention in medical school.

My blood pressure was the first to go. I went to the doctor with something quite unconnected. My big toe was hurting, I think. That turned out to be down to a toenail that needed clipping, but she took my blood pressure in any case, just to make sure that it wasn't affecting my toe nail.

She looked at the numbers and her eyebrows shot up. Maybe they needed to come down too, but she sent me to wait in the crowded waiting room whilst she saw a patient who needed more urgent attention than I did.

She was obviously concerned, as she presently came into the waiting room clutching a blood pressure monitor and handed it to the old man sitting next to me.

'Just take her blood pressure, will you?' she asked him casually.

The man looked at the machine, confused. 'What do I do with it?' he asked.

Patiently she explained. 'You wrap this cuff around her arm and press this button,' she said. 'It's easy. Then tell me the numbers.'

He shrugged. I proffered my arm and he complied. The doctor came out and he told her the numbers. She looked aghast and said, 'Do it again, will you?'

The old man, evidently feeling that he had missed his way in life and should have been a doctor, complied. He had a bright idea. 'Listen, I'll put the results on my phone, shall I?'

She agreed that this would be a great idea, and left.

The old man was getting into his stride now. He assumed an air of professional competence while he wrapped the cuff around my arm as instructed, and pressed the large button on the accompanying monitor.

By this time, the other would-be patients in the room were deeply interested. As the machine beeped they leaned forward, craning every muscle to view the results. From those nearest there came a sharp intake of breath. My numbers were evidently off the scale.

'Don't worry,' the old man said comfortingly. He patted my arm. 'You're in the right place if you have a heart attack.'

This did nothing whatsoever to reassure me.

He was now well on his way to becoming a specialist. He took my blood pressure six more times, assiduously noting the numbers on his phone, each time to the deep interest of those sitting close enough to see.

When I finally saw the doctor again, she reached for her prescription pad. 'You will need to get these tablets, take one a day in the evenings,' she said briskly. 'I'd like you to have a blood test as well.' She slid two prescriptions across to me before turning to her computer, no doubt recording all my highly unsatisfactory data.

I looked at the two prescriptions, both written in the faithfully illegible handwriting of the practised medic that she was. I managed to decipher one of them as instructions for a blood test.

Now, I hate to be the Brit in France who compares everything French unfavourably with its English counterpart, but in this case I really needed some information.

'In the UK,' I began hesitantly, 'we take prescriptions to the chemist. Do I go to the pharmacy for my blood test?'

Still typing and without looking at me, she said nonchalantly, 'No, just call the nurse.'

This statement failed to clarify matters for me. I didn't know any nurses. Was I meant to wander the streets until I found a likely looking candidate and say, 'Excuse me, are you a nurse? Because I need a blood test and if you have time, would you mind.....?'

'But I don't *know* any nurses,' I cried. At this she swung round in her chair and wrote again on her pad. Was this yet another illegible prescription, I wondered. But no. There were two phone numbers.

'You can call either of these nurses,' she explained patiently.

Once home I rang the first of the numbers she had given me and told the nurse of my predicament. Did she do blood tests, and where did I have to go to get one?

'What's your address?' she asked. 'And when do you want me to come?'

I was amazed. There appeared to be no waiting list, no long trek to a chemist.

We agreed the date. She would come the next day.

'What time?' was her next question. Still stupefied, I replied that around ten o'clock would suit me, and I rang off.

The following morning, as promised, she bustled into the lounge with her equipment. After the test she asked brightly, 'And where would you like me to send the blood?'

Several answers came to mind. I considered. Perhaps John's sister might be interested. Or next door maybe. Or Sophie across the road?

Seeing my hesitation and evidently realising that here was someone who was unfamiliar with the French health system, she added helpfully, 'Which laboratory would you like it to go to?'

Once again I was the new girl at big school, not knowing my way around.

'I'm afraid I don't know any laboratories,' I told her timidly.

'Well, we usually use one in Trèbes,' she said patiently. 'But you can specify a named laboratory if you like.'

Being unequipped with a list of the local medical laboratories, I nodded sagely and told her that would be fine.

'Good,' she said briskly. 'You should have the results in the post tomorrow, or by the next day at the latest.'

So this was the efficient French health service I had read about. I was experiencing it in all its glorified action for the first time. True to her word, an envelope dropped onto the doormat the next day. It contained my results. They were horrific. I apparently had several potentially deadly diseases that I was completely unaware of, which were causing me no symptoms whatsoever, but the numbers on the sheet of paper clearly indicated that unless my life included a daily routine of swallowing little white pills then there was no chance. I became deeply suspicious of the numbers.

Chapter 28
Prizegiving

In an effort to save on electricity I was hanging washing out for once instead of using the tumble dryer, when Nicole appeared in a gap through the trees. At first I thought she would be asking for a lift, as she did on many occasions, despite her husband having a car. Madame Bellini had warned me soon after our arrival that I needed to take care or she would use me as a personal chauffeur, but as always, I found it hard to refuse her. I often took her to the local supermarket, usually waiting in the car for her. I wouldn't have minded if she had finished her shopping quickly, but she would come out with a loaded trolley, meet one of her friends and they would have a long chat whilst I was getting increasingly hot and irritated in the car. If it wasn't the supermarket it was the doctor's, and afterwards she always needed to pick up her prescription. The first time this had happened, I knew that there was a chemist on the way home, so I parked just outside.

'This isn't my chemist,' she protested. 'I always go to the one in Peyriac.'

It was my turn to be surprised. 'But, Nicole,' I said. 'Any chemist can fill in a prescription for you, and this is the nearest.' Apparently she hadn't known that this was possible. This was the chemist she had used all her life. They knew her there, she said. I came across this attitude many times during our years in France. Most of the people in the hamlet depended on their local shops and facilities and it never occurred to them to use any which had not served them, their parents and their grandparents before them. Some had never been further than Carcassonne in their lives, and even this was a great experience, to be planned for days in advance.

I was slightly wary, but for once, she wasn't asking for a lift.

'Manon has succeeded her *Brevet*,' she declared proudly. 'There will be a ceremony at the college, for her to receive her certificate. Would you come with me?'

With great difficulty I finished pegging out my sheet, as the Tramontin was strong that day and pushing the billowing white folds around my face.

I knew why she was asking, of course. The *Brevet* was an important examination taken at *collège*, with success ensuring a place at the *Lycée*, the next stage of education. Apart from the local *loto*, or bingo sessions, Nicole was not fond of social occasions, and her husband was a *vigneron* of the most solitary type, much preferring his own company and shunning all attempts at joining in any activities in the area. There was no chance of him attending a school award ceremony.

I agreed to go, unenthusiastically. Being excessively familiar with award ceremonies from my own schooldays and those of my daughters, I knew exactly what to expect. The long rows of seats in a large hall, with a stage at the front and a local dignitary or a dog (Distinguished Old Girl) to present the certificates. There would be an inspirational speech, with congratulations to those who had succeeded so well, all thanks to their dedicated teachers, (who would at this point smile and shake their heads deprecatingly) who had given up their whole lives so that the present company could celebrate today.

Cameras would be pointed, the chosen ones would trip up to the stage, shake hands, bob and run lightly down the steps to take their place with their form.

I dressed carefully for the ceremony, not wanting to let Manon down on what was, naturally, a very important occasion for her. It isn't easy dressing up on a hot day but I did my best with a floral summer dress and the high heeled sandals I had bought in Carcassonne. I decided against a hat.

I was cringing with embarrassment when I saw Nicole. She was wearing her jeans, her hair looked messy and her sandals looked as if she had just come out of a vineyard, which, come to think of it, she may well have done. When we arrived at the school, no-one else was dressed up. There were a few fathers there in their habitual bright blue bibbed dungarees that was traditional attire in the vineyards, and some young children racing around playing 'tag.' I could see that this was going to be totally unlike my usual idea of an award ceremony. But still, I was doing it for Manon and I hoped that she appreciated it. I looked around, craning my neck over the other guests. Where was she?

The room we were in was evidently a classroom, not a hall as I had expected. The tables had been arranged end to end to form the shape of an E without its middle bar, with more of them lining one wall to make a long table which was covered with the inevitable plastic cloths bearing many bottles of wine, plastic wine glass and some flat looking pastries.

In the centre of the tables, a gaggle of teenagers was gathered, loudly chatting to each other. I gathered from Nicole that these were the people in Manon's year who would be presented with their diplomas. I looked around again for the girl but couldn't see her. I assumed that she would appear very soon. Nicole was now looking slightly nervous; whether this was a result of the unaccustomed social gathering, or the fact that Manon was still nowhere in sight, I couldn't tell.

A bearded man dressed in a dark blue suit detached himself from the group of parents and walked to the front of the room. There was an immediate hush, and he cleared his throat somewhat portentously and began his speech. He thanked all the people who had made this evening such a special occasion, and he lauded the teachers, and the pupils whose great academic efforts were now being rewarded. Still there was no sign of Manon. Nor was there any sign of a distinguished old girl to hand out the certificates.

A tall lady with long thin legs encased in black leather trousers now took over, standing in front of a cardboard box which appeared to be full of rolled up papers. She called out a name and one boy loped her side, smirking and casting sideways mocking glances at his mates, evidently deeply embarrassed to be the first. She muttered something to him along the lines of making sure that he had several photocopies of his certificate, as he would need them in the future, and he rummaged inside the open box until he found what he was looking for. He held it aloft triumphantly while the adults clapped and his friends guffawed loudly. There were several flashes from phones and he melted into the crowd again. Student after student followed him, with more rummaging until each owner had been united with the correct, if crumpled piece of paper recording their achievements.

And that was it. That was the award ceremony. The main focus of the evening seemed to be the wine, which everyone, including the students, was drinking freely, and growing increasingly raucous with each passing minute. The teachers had decamped after a hasty glass, and Manon never appeared at all. I later heard from Nicole that she had been out with her boyfriend and had forgotten about the awards. She would pick up her certificate at school. If she remembered.

Chapter 29
Decision

Fifteen years passed. They were years of routine, and visiting our daughters in the UK and staying with them after the births of their children. We were now both in our sixties and visits to the doctor were becoming embedded in our routines. We began to think of going back to the UK. It was a difficult decision. We absolutely loved our lives in France, where we had made good friends and were part of the neighbourhood. We were interested in the lives of our friends and they were interested in ours.

We had plenty of visits from Pamela, Len and their two children. Each time they came to stay the children were fascinated by our massive garden, and by the wildlife which they never saw at home. They adored helping John in the garden, wielding spades that were far too large for them, and watering the plants with their miniature cans. A favourite activity was making 'potions' by stripping petals and leaves from various plants and adding them to jugs of water. They played at 'soldiers' in the garden, using the wooden bows and arrows we had bought them in Carcassonne, aiming at a hand-drawn target pinned to an apricot tree. The pool was a total delight for them and they spent hours in it, happily squirting each other with water pistols. On one visit we very proudly gave each of them an orange picked straight from a tree which we had grown on the terrace. There would be none of this in England. Our younger daughter Janice had recently been delivered of a baby girl, and as both she and her husband worked full time, we were well aware that Janice might need help when the child started school. That was some years away, but it contributed heavily in our several years of thinking, 'shall we go or shall we stay?' And then, one particular event almost made up our minds for us. At least it cemented what had been a very loose strain of thought.

On New Year's Eve, our neighbours across the road, Sophie and Marc, invited us for dinner and to see the New Year in. We looked pleased and we accepted enthusiastically. To me it's quite amazing how far people will go for the mere sake of being polite. Both of us showed huge pleasure and we were both groaning inside. I don't know if it showed. Detection is possible, depending on the acting skills of one party and the discerning capabilities of the other. Even if real feelings are detected, politeness normally demands that the true feelings are hidden and both parties maintain a bright, brittle cheerfulness until they are in the privacy of their own home, when they can give free vent to their displeasure.

'I can't stay up until midnight, Steph,' John complained. 'It's way past my bedtime.' It was early evening and he was already preparing for bed.

'Just for once? She'll be mortified if we don't go. And anyway, we've said yes now, we can't back out.'

'You could go on your own?' he suggested hopefully, but I crushed that idea right away.

'And where will I say you are?' I said acidly. 'If I say you're poorly, she'll be over here in the morning to see how you are. You know what she's like. And I'm not going on my own either. Why should I? If I've got to prop my eyelids open until midnight, then you can do it as well.' I was distinctly cross at his suggestion.

We were an extremely mundane couple. We were far removed from characters on the TV whose lives are filled with huge drama from morning until night, and are forever either screaming with pleasure or sobbing into their coffee at the unfairness of it all. We were normally in bed by ten o'clock and we hadn't seen the New Year in for years, preferring to watch the highlights on TV the following morning, when we could properly appreciate the fireworks over Sydney Harbour bridge and the Houses of Parliament.

The discussion ended as we both knew it would. We would nail smiles onto our faces and go across the road.

Our normal evening meal was at six o'clock, but on the great day we had a light lunch of the previous day's soup, with half a baguette, secure in the certainty that we would be eating at, say, a reasonable eight o'clock which we thought we could cope with.

After the normal pecking at cheeks, we sat down, pretending not to be hungry, and being entertained with tales of the September harvest and how Bernard was getting on with this year's wine. By nine o'clock, our stomachs were rumbling and our smiles were increasingly strained. Inwardly I was panicking. Had I misunderstood Sophie's intentions? Did she think we had already eaten at home, and we were here just to watch the midnight fireworks and kiss each other all over again? By half past nine I was certain that no food would be forthcoming, and I was in an agony of indecision. Should I pretend we had forgotten to feed the cat and needed to go home urgently, when we could grab a sandwich and then come back? As a cunning plan it had its failings – mainly due to the lack of a cat. To be honest, if we'd had a cat I would probably have gone back over the road and eaten it.

Finally, and to our immense relief, Sophie left the room at ten o'clock and reappeared with a tray of plates, each one with an *apèritif* biscuit topped with bits of olives and tomatoes. Politeness dictated that we didn't grab the plate off her and wolf its contents down in one go, but the necessary restraint was almost unbearable. We each took one biscuit and nibbled at it daintily. It seemed that real food might be on the agenda, and we waited expectantly.

Another hour passed, by which time I could see that John was suffering, and I was growing properly, increasingly concerned for him.

With a sweet smile, Sophie beckoned us into the kitchen and we sat down to eat. It was eleven o'clock. We couldn't have held out much longer. We realised now that her intention was to finish the meal just before midnight, when we could toast the new year with the liqueurs that were kept for special occasions.

John had been very quiet, but then, he always was in company. His French was not of a level where he could join in a conversation, although he understood most of what was being discussed. So his silence didn't surprise me.

What did shock me, though, was when he swayed slightly, and said faintly, 'I don't feel very well.'

For John to interrupt like this was unheard of, and everyone stopped eating and looked at him, eyes wide with consternation.

'Bring him into the lounge,' Sophie commanded. Between us, we led the still shaky John into the lounge, where Marc and Bernard gently helped him to the sofa.

We thought he would rally with the water that Sophie brought him. As he began to sip, the glass slid from his hand and he fell back against the sofa, unconscious. The colour had drained from his face, which was a white as a sheet.

Sophie was practical and very decisive. 'Marc, call the *Pompiers*,' she ordered, 'and Bernard, you get Stephanie some water. He's going to be fine,' she reassured me, holding me tight.

The *Pompiers* were officially firefighters, with many of them working on a voluntary basis, and in addition to fighting fires, they were often the first port of call in medical emergencies. They were professional and reliable, with their training incorporating everything needed by paramedics.

Marc, too, was a rock that night. With Bernard's help, he manoeuvred John onto the floor and the two of them laid him in the recovery position. Marc took his pulse. At that moment, John's eyes flickered open and he tried to move.

'Stay still,' Sophie said sternly. The *Pompiers* will be here any minute now.

'I'm fine,' John muttered weakly. 'I'll be alright in a minute. I don't need an ambulance.'

'Yes you do,' Marc insisted. 'You were unconscious, you need to go to the hospital.'

I knelt down to be beside him. 'My love, you're going to be alright,' I said. I was determined not to cry, to be strong for him.

'There's nothing wrong with me,' he insisted, but no-one was listening. We were all straining to hear the sirens of the *Pompiers*. The nearest station was Trausse-Minervois, so we knew it would be at least fifteen minutes. In the event it was twenty minutes, during which time John continued to protest that he had no need to go to a hospital.

When they arrived they were calm and highly efficient. They checked his blood pressure, his blood sugar and asked detailed questions. When they found that he had been unconscious, there was no more arguing. They were taking him to Carcassonne hospital. They placed him gently onto a stretcher and loaded him into the back of the ambulance. As there were four *Pompiers* besides John, there was no room for me to go with him and I watched as the ambulance tore off into the blackness of the night.

There was no more talk of a celebration. I insisted that I wanted to go home, and Sophie came with me across the road. Very shakily, I poured myself a whisky. And then another. I wanted to be with John, to be near him, to find out what was wrong with him, but the hospital was a forty minute drive and I had never driven at night.

Besides, I now had two whiskies inside me. I knew that I couldn't go.

A taxi might be available, I thought, and I phoned Sophie. 'Do you think you can get me a taxi?' I pleaded. 'I need to be with John.'

Evidently they had been discussing the events, and she was immediately reassuring. 'Don't even think of a taxi,' she said firmly. 'Come across the road and I'll drive you.' I was humbled and grateful for her concern. We drove in silence, with Sophie telling me to cry if I wanted. I didn't. I was completely numb. What was I going to find when we arrived? What if he had collapsed again? Would he even be alive? I was unable to take anything in properly, my mind had shut down.

Carcassonne hospital is a very large establishment. I had been there a few times on my own account, for afternoon appointments, but now it was dark. I was in total panic and I couldn't even have found the entrance on my own. Thankfully Sophie remained calm. She found the main doors, asked several pertinent questions and led me to a waiting area. I began to relax a little and look about me. The waiting area was divided into cubicles, to give visitors a modicum of privacy. In the next cubicle a whole family was waiting, with a toddler who was awake long past his bedtime. He was alternating between whining plaintively, and dispiritedly kicking a small red ball into the communal corridor. It was some distraction to watch him, and to wonder what crisis was happening to that family.

Presently a doctor arrived, and let me know that John had been examined, and was now in a ward where he was waiting for the results of the tests that had been performed.

Sophie was so tired. I could see her valiant efforts to stay awake, and as the hours dragged by I was feeling more and more guilty. Her head drooped from time to time, until she awoke with a jolt and smiled at me. My own adrenaline kept me awake for the first couple of hours, but as the clock ticked round to half past two I was feeling the strain. Finally, as it was nearing four o'clock in the morning, a different doctor appeared, with the great news that John could go home. They had not found anything amiss except for his blood pressure, which was extremely high, and he went home with a prescription for tablets.

There were many repercussions to the night's events. One of the first was that we bought Sophie and Marc a bottle of the most expensive Moët and Chandon champagne we could find, along with some handmade Leonidas chocolates. It was an inadequate recompense for all they had done, but we couldn't think of anything better.

A more serious one was that the events had acted as a catalyst, for both of us. This might happen again, and the next time it could be worse. We realised that the right people to have on hand in an emergency had to be our own family, not the neighbours, however delightful they were. However much we loved France, the fact remained that we were not, and never would be, French. Every French person we had ever met had numerous relatives –albeit some of them far away – but their lives revolved around the same reference points, the same culture as well as the same language. We had had many splendid years, but it was time for us to go home.

We made our plans, consulted with local estate agents and after many emotional goodbyes we moved back to the UK.

Epilogue
2017

A few years have passed since we left France, and John and I are now very comfortably installed in the beautiful town of Harrogate. I go to Leeds every so often, usually stopping off for a coffee at either Starbucks or Costa. This time I happened to be nearer to Costa. The shop was crowded and noisy, with background music competing with customers' voices and children's shrill clamours for attention. I claimed my Americano and slid into one of the few remaining seats, opposite a lady of around my own age and a man sitting beside her. He was around forty, I guessed, with tight black curls.

She placed her coffee on the table and stared at me. Her attention was far greater than the casual glance you would expect when sharing a table with strangers and after a while she was making me uncomfortable. I spotted a table with two empty chairs and I was just getting up to leave when she leaned towards me.

'I hope you don't mind my asking,' she began hesitantly. 'But I was sure I recognised you. It *is* Stephanie isn't it?'

I looked at her more closely now. She was tall, with a face that stirred a distant memory. I absolutely knew that I ought to recognise her; there was something about her that was so familiar, but I was still at a loss as to who she was.

'Yes, I'm Stephanie,' I said rather cautiously. 'And you are....?'

'Charlotte,' she said. 'Charlotte Maddox,' and suddenly all the memories flooded back. Of course she was Charlotte. How could I not have recognised her? But the years had passed and she had gone completely out of my memory. She introduced the man with her.

'This is Richard,' she said. 'My son.' He smiled at me politely and I knew at once. He was a little taller, much younger and somewhat tubbier, but otherwise he was the image of Antoine.

'Charlotte! Of course, I *knew* I should have recognised you! Goodness, how many years is it?'

She bore an almost imperceptible resemblance to the girl who had been in Marseille with me all those years ago and in place of the leggy, long-haired blonde with boundless confidence, was a woman with lines on her face, a short crop of hair and heavy makeup. I honestly would never have recognised her if she hadn't told me her name.

'I'm fine,' she said, although her downwards glance into her coffee cup said otherwise. There was an awkward pause, with neither of us quite knowing how to carry on the conversation. And then she said, 'I suppose you know what happened to me, do you? I'm sure it was the talk of the school at the time.'

'Mum,' the man interrupted. 'Look, if you don't mind, I'll meet you at the station when you've finished here. Don't be too long, we've only got half an hour before the train leaves.' He got up and held out a hand politely. 'Good to have met you,' he said with a tight smile, and he left.

Charlotte gave him a wave, saying, 'Yes, I won't be long,' before turning back to me.

I gazed after him, even his rambling walk reminding me of his father. 'Well, no, not actually,' I replied hastily. 'I mean, there were rumours of course, but I didn't believe them, not for a single minute....'

'You should have done,' she said wryly. 'It was all true, everything people said. Richard is Antoine's son. You might as well know now, it's what everyone was saying at the time...'

'Well,' I began, 'I can see the resemblance actually. He's the image of him,' I said before I could stop myself, and she looked astonished.

'How do you know that?' she asked, shocked. 'Do you *know* Antoine? *How* do you know him? It was nearly fifty years ago...!'

'He got married to Elodie, she was my French penfriend,' I said rather sheepishly, wishing that I had stayed silent. 'You probably don't remember her now.'

She took a sip of her coffee, frowning lightly. 'Yes, I think I do, vaguely. Little girl, chubby, red hair?'

'That's the one,' I agreed.

'And you're still in touch with her?' She was incredulous. 'After all this time?'

'Well, only Christmas cards,' I said deprecatingly. 'You know how it is. We were good friends for years and then we just drifted apart. But I've met Antoine a few times.. And Richard, does he know..?'

'Richard has never met him,' she said bitterly. 'Antoine never wanted anything to do with him. He told me that right from the start. He even had the nerve to deny that the baby was his. Everyone supported him. His parents were threatening to sue me for defamation of character. You wouldn't believe the drama of it all. And the whole thing was just so unnecessary. It was stupid, letting me stay for three weeks in his house. We were so young. The French teacher lost her job over it of course. She never checked who else would be in the homes we stayed in. Dad was livid about that. He went up to the school and said he'd complain to the governors if she wasn't fired. I don't know if she ever taught again.'

'Yes, I remember now! It's all coming back! It was Mrs Thomas, wasn't it? I know she left school at the same time as you did, but I hadn't realised she'd lost her job..'

'Yes, she did. Not that it helped me, though. I was still left to bring Richard up as a single parent.'

I was sympathetic, when I thought of our two girls and how John had always been there for me; calm, sorting out problems with his logical, unemotional reasoning. It was impossible for me to comprehend how I would have coped alone.

'It must have been really hard,' I said with concern. 'But your own parents, didn't they help you...?'

'They threw me out,' she said bitterly. 'I think my dad would have supported me but my mum, she was a complete wreck about it all. She cried for days. The only person who helped me was my sister...'

'I didn't realise you had a sister...'

'No, you wouldn't have known. She's a lot older than I am. Mum had me late. Fiona was married and in her thirties when it all kicked off. She took me in and I lived with her until Richard was at school, then I got a job in Littlewoods, on the umbrella counter, would you believe, and I found a flat in Leeds. It was bloody hard work though...' She stopped, as if reliving the hard slog of bringing up her child single-handed.

'But, aren't there tests and everything now? Couldn't you have proved that Richard was Antoine's?'

'Probably, if he'd been English,' she replied. 'But this was France in the sixties, remember. It would have meant solicitors who dealt with French law, we'd have had to pay for it, my mum and dad just couldn't afford it. And then there would have been all the publicity. They couldn't face it. The easiest way out for them was to throw me out and leave me to it. I never forgave them. They're both dead now, anyway...'

There was a slightly awkward pause, until I asked lightly, 'And did *you* keep in touch with anyone from school? I remember there was Lydia, you two were always together...'

She looked up, bewildered, and when she spoke, her voice was high with surprise. 'Yes, we did keep in touch, of course,' she said. 'We even wrote, for a few years, until she died...'

It was my turn to be shocked. 'She *died?*' I exclaimed. 'I never knew that! When? What happened?' I can't believe no-one told me...'

'Not many people knew,' she went on. 'You wouldn't have heard, it was after she emigrated. She got married, not long after she left uni. He was an Australian, and they moved over there a couple of years later...'

'And what happened?'

'It was a car crash,' she said simply. 'I never heard all the details, I only knew about it when I bumped into her dad in town. He was devastated, naturally. And I don't think her mum ever got over it. They got divorced a few years later. Lydia was their only child. Her dad said they'd been planning a visit for July... she died in the April...'

'God, how terrible. And what a shock for you, as well.'

Charlotte shrugged. 'Nothing's ever quite as it seems, is it?' she said. 'You'd think we were the best of friends, but it wasn't like that really. It was habit more than anything. I remember she used to try to get me into trouble at school. She was always wanting me to miss lessons, go into town with her, buy cigarettes....' She stopped, evidently as disturbed by her memories as I had been at her news of Lydia. 'So tell me,' she said now, eager to know. 'You've met Antoine, you said. D'you mean recently? What is he like now?'

'Oh, I haven't seen him for years,' I said hastily. 'The last time was when we were in France...'

'Oh, yes, I remember now. Someone said you lived in France.'

'Actually, the last time I saw him, I didn't take to him at all. He came with Elodie and they had a daughter Lucie, she'd have been about fourteen at the time. They came to see us a few days after we'd moved in – we weren't ready for visitors – we hadn't even unpacked, but they turned up anyway. They didn't have a single positive thing to say about our house, and all Antoine could do was criticize our wiring! Honestly, we were glad to see the back of them. They divorced eventually, after their daughter grew up. Probably the best thing she could have done, and she made a decent living for herself afterwards when she took up painting again, she was always fantastic at art.'

For the first time, she smiled. 'It's funny how things turn out, isn't it? I was always so jealous of you at school. You always had everything you ever wanted. And then, going to live in France....'

I was incredulous. 'Jealous of *me!*' I cried. 'What on earth for? *You* were the brainy one, the good looking one. Everyone in the *school* was jealous of you. What was so special about me?'

'Oh, your clothes and everything. Your mum always being around school organising fairs and stuff. Your parents, they were always there for you. Mine didn't give a toss about me when I was growing up.'

'You've got it wrong, Charlotte,' I insisted. 'It wasn't all that brilliant, living in France. Why d'you think we came back? Anyway, going back to Antoine. He was a total loser the last time I saw him.' Her eyebrows raised at my choice of language. 'He probably hasn't changed much. Honestly, I'm sure you were better off on your own than with him. The last I heard he'd run off with another woman. Elodie was beside herself....'

She drained her coffee cup and laughed. A genuine laugh, and at that moment I had a brief glimpse of the Charlotte of so many years ago. She glanced at her wristwatch, and then stood up, smoothing down her coat.

'It's been great to see you again, Stephanie,' she said, picking up her handbag. 'And I'm sorry I have to rush off like this, but Richard'll be at the station by now. Look, if you can manage it, we must meet up again and you can fill me in on all the details.'

'I'd love that, Charlotte,' I said, and we kissed briefly before she left for the station.

I finished my coffee slowly, with each sip taking me further and further into the past, until the noises of the coffee shop faded around me and I was once more in Marseille.

My journey home took me past an antique jewellers' shop, and as I had contemplated buying John a new watch for his birthday, I stopped briefly to look at the brilliance of the shiny rings, watches and necklaces. A necklace caught my eye. It was expensive; normally I wouldn't have dreamed of paying that kind of money for jewellery. It was a gold chain interspersed with small dark red stones. If the price had not convinced me already, the jeweller assured me that, yes, the chain was 22 carat gold and the stones were indeed small, though perfectly cut rubies. I barely hesitated before I bought it for Elodie.

THE END

Printed in Great Britain
by Amazon